Dungeon

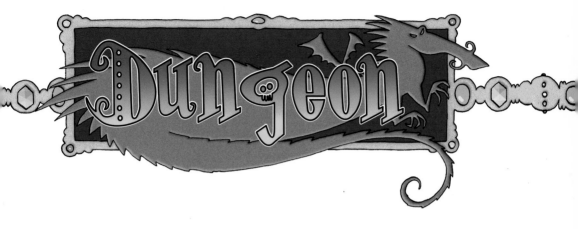

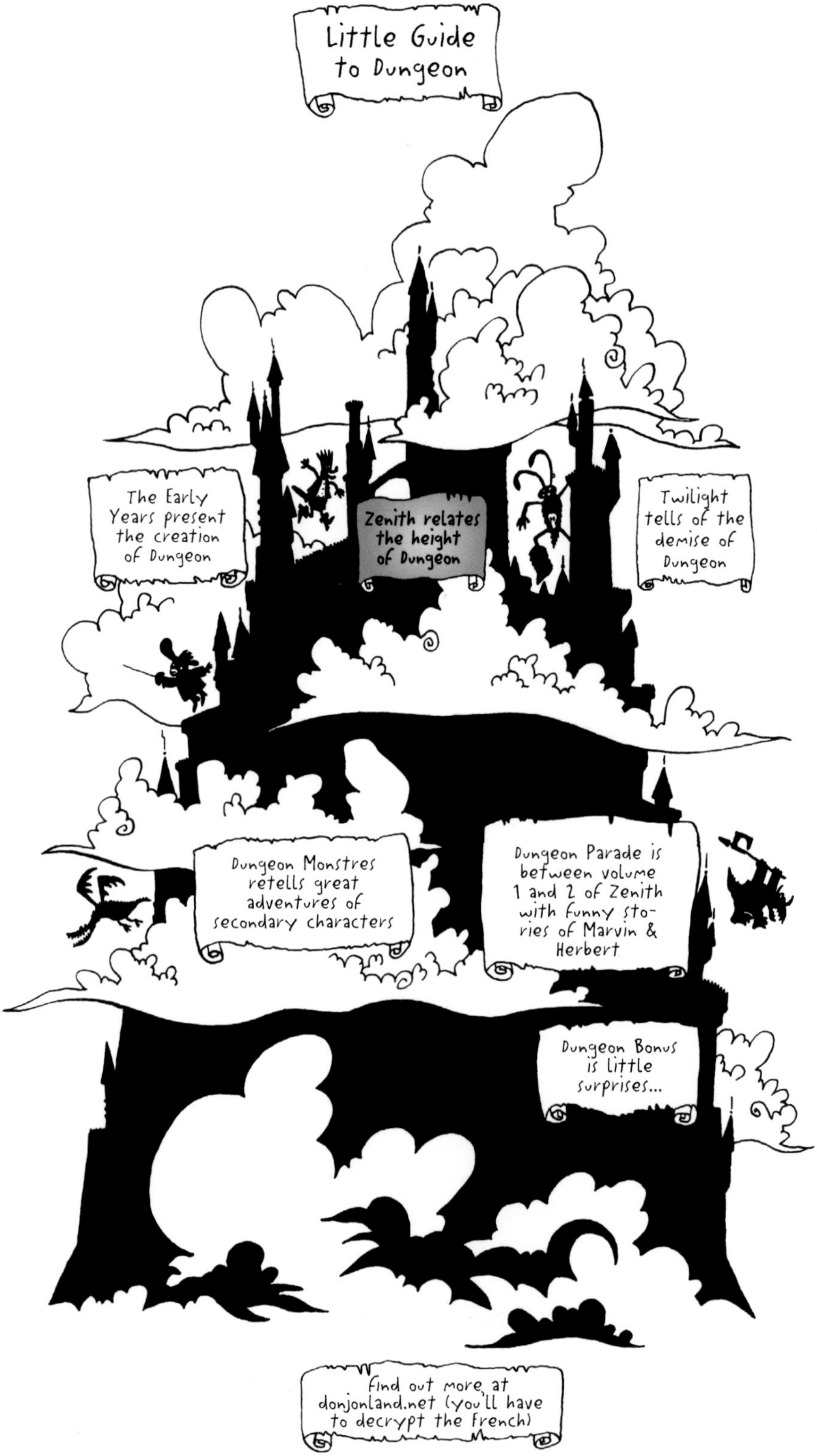
Little Guide to Dungeon
The Early Years present the creation of Dungeon
Zenith relates the height of Dungeon
Twilight tells of the demise of Dungeon
Dungeon Monstres retells great adventures of secondary characters
Dungeon Parade is between volume 1 and 2 of Zenith with funny stories of Marvin & Herbert
Dungeon Bonus is little surprises...
Find out more at donjonland.net (you'll have to decrypt the French)

GN
SFA

Zenith
Vol. 3:
Back In Style

Joann SfAR,
Lewis TRONDHEIM,
BOULET

NANTIER · BEALL · MINOUSTCHINE
Publishing inc.
new york

Also available
Dungeon, Zenith, vols. 1, 2: $14.95 each, 3: $14.99
Dungeon Early Years, vols. 1: $14.99, 2: $12.95
Dungeon, Twilight, vols. 1, $12.95, 2: $14.99, 3: $12.99, 4: $14.99
Dungeon, Parade, vol. 2: $9.95
Dungeon, Monstres, vols. 2: $12.95, 3: $12.99, 4: $14.99
Also by Trondheim:
Little Nothings, vols. 2, 3: $14.95 each
Mr. I, $13.95
with Thierry Robin:
Happy Halloween, $14.95

See previews, get exclusives and order from:
NBMPUB.COM

we have over 200 titles available
Catalog upon request

NBM
160 Broadway, Suite 700, East Wing
New York, NY 10038
If ordering by mail add $4 P&H 1st item,
$1 each addt'l

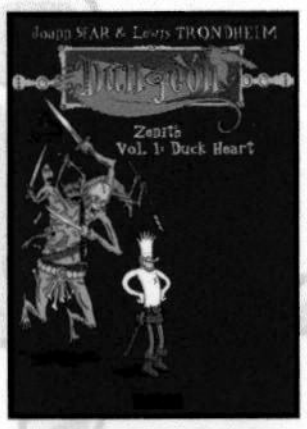
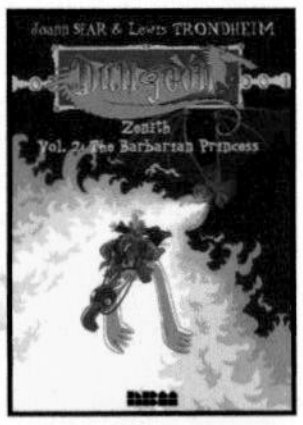
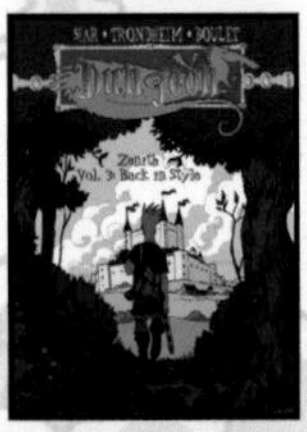
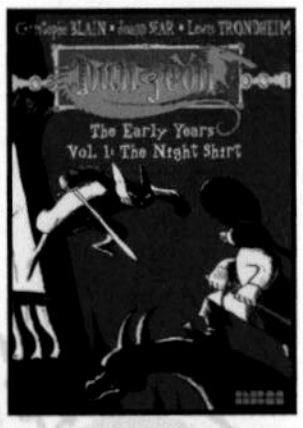
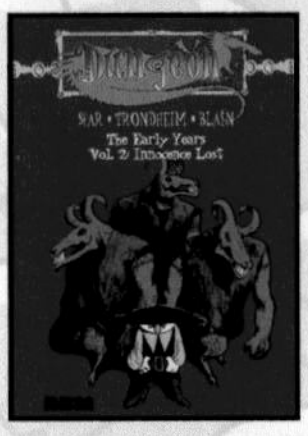
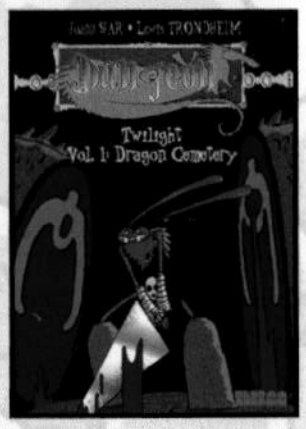
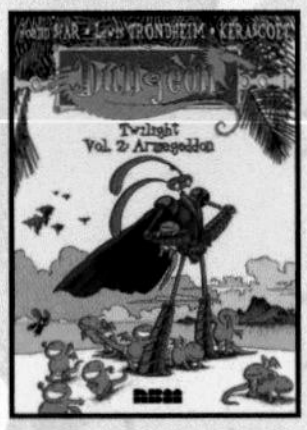
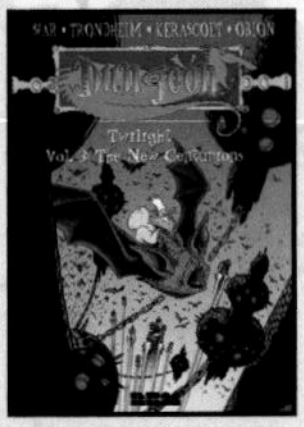
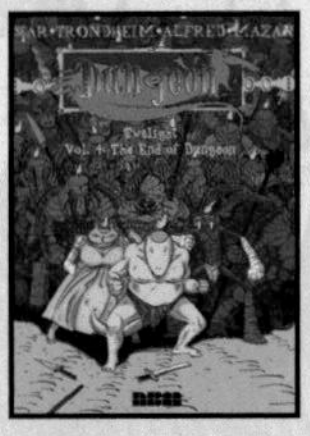
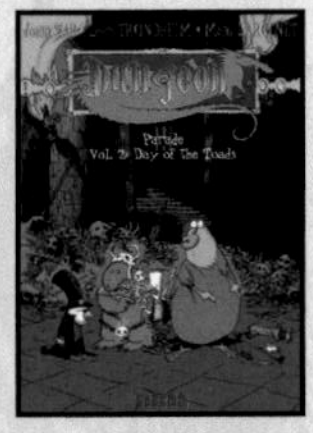
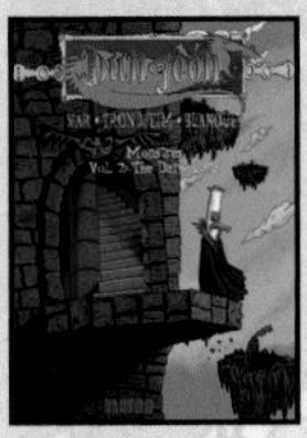
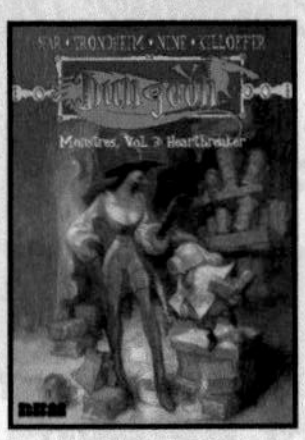
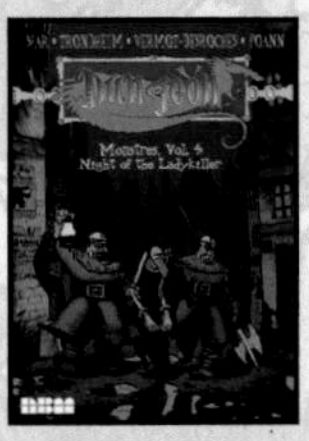

Originally published in French in 2 books:
Un Mariage A Part and *Retour en Fanfare*
ISBN: 978-1-56163-550-4

Translation by Joe Johnson
Lettering by Ortho
Printed in China

2nd Printing December 2014

T 108501

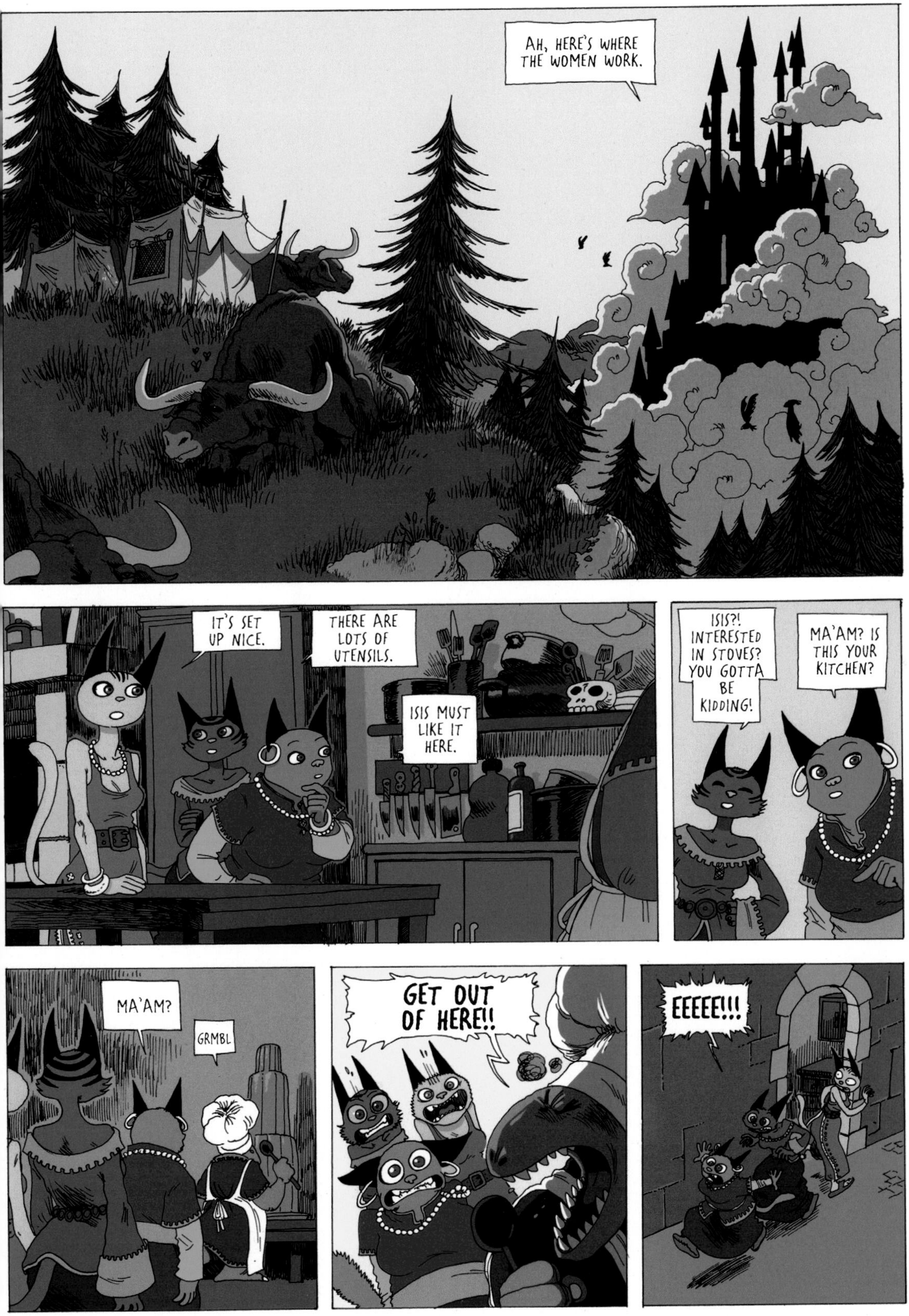
AH, HERE'S WHERE THE WOMEN WORK.
IT'S SET UP NICE.
THERE ARE LOTS OF UTENSILS.
ISIS MUST LIKE IT HERE.
ISIS?! INTERESTED IN STOVES? YOU GOTTA BE KIDDING!
MA'AM? IS THIS YOUR KITCHEN?
MA'AM?
GRMBL
GET OUT OF HERE!!
EEEEE!!!

STUPID OLD WOMEN POKING AROUND IN EVERYTHING.

DRAGONISM SHOULD'VE BEEN THE ONLY RELIGION IN TERRA AMATA.

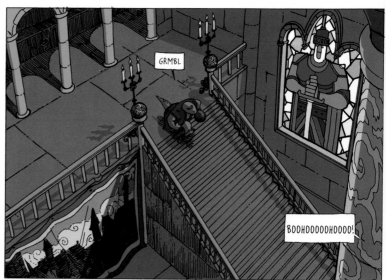

GRMBL

BOOHOOOOOOHOOOO!

AH! MARVIN! IS IT OVER?!!

IS ISIS MARRIED? WILL YOU LET ME LOOSE?

NO, TONIGHT, AFTER THE FESTIVITIES.

I BROUGHT YOU A DRUMSTICK.

YOU KNOW, MARVIN, YOU CAN LET ME GO. I'M NOT GONNA EAT YOUR BIG CAKE.

YOU PROMISED ME THE SAME THING YESTERDAY.

EAT YOUR DRUMSTICK. I'LL BRING YOU ANOTHER ONE IN A BIT.

CAN I SUCK ON IT?

YES.

AND CHEW ON IT?

YES.

AND CAN YOU TELL ME A STORY AT THE SAME TIME?

NO.

A SHORT ONE, PLEASE, MARVIN. A SHORT ONE...SNIFF...

AND DO YOU PROMISE ME TO STOP SNIVELING AFTERWARDS?

YES, YES, YES... PROMISE!!!

SO, HERBERT AND I WENT TO THE HOME OF THE MEAN DRAGON TO GET THE DUNGEON'S TREASURE BACK.

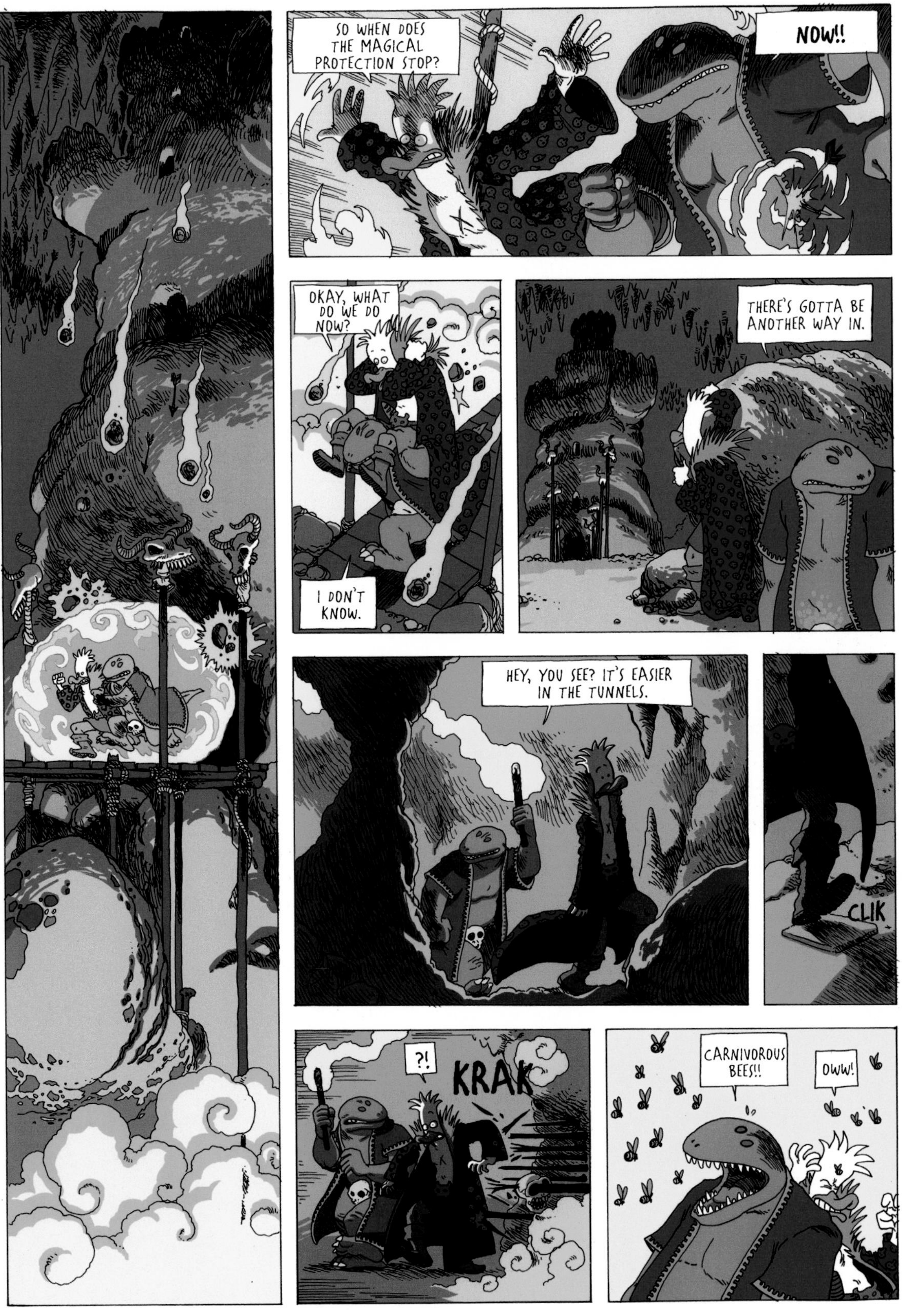
SO WHEN DOES THE MAGICAL PROTECTION STOP?
NOW!!
OKAY, WHAT DO WE DO NOW?
I DON'T KNOW.
THERE'S GOTTA BE ANOTHER WAY IN.
HEY, YOU SEE? IT'S EASIER IN THE TUNNELS.
CLIK
?!
KRAK
CARNIVOROUS BEES!!
OWW!

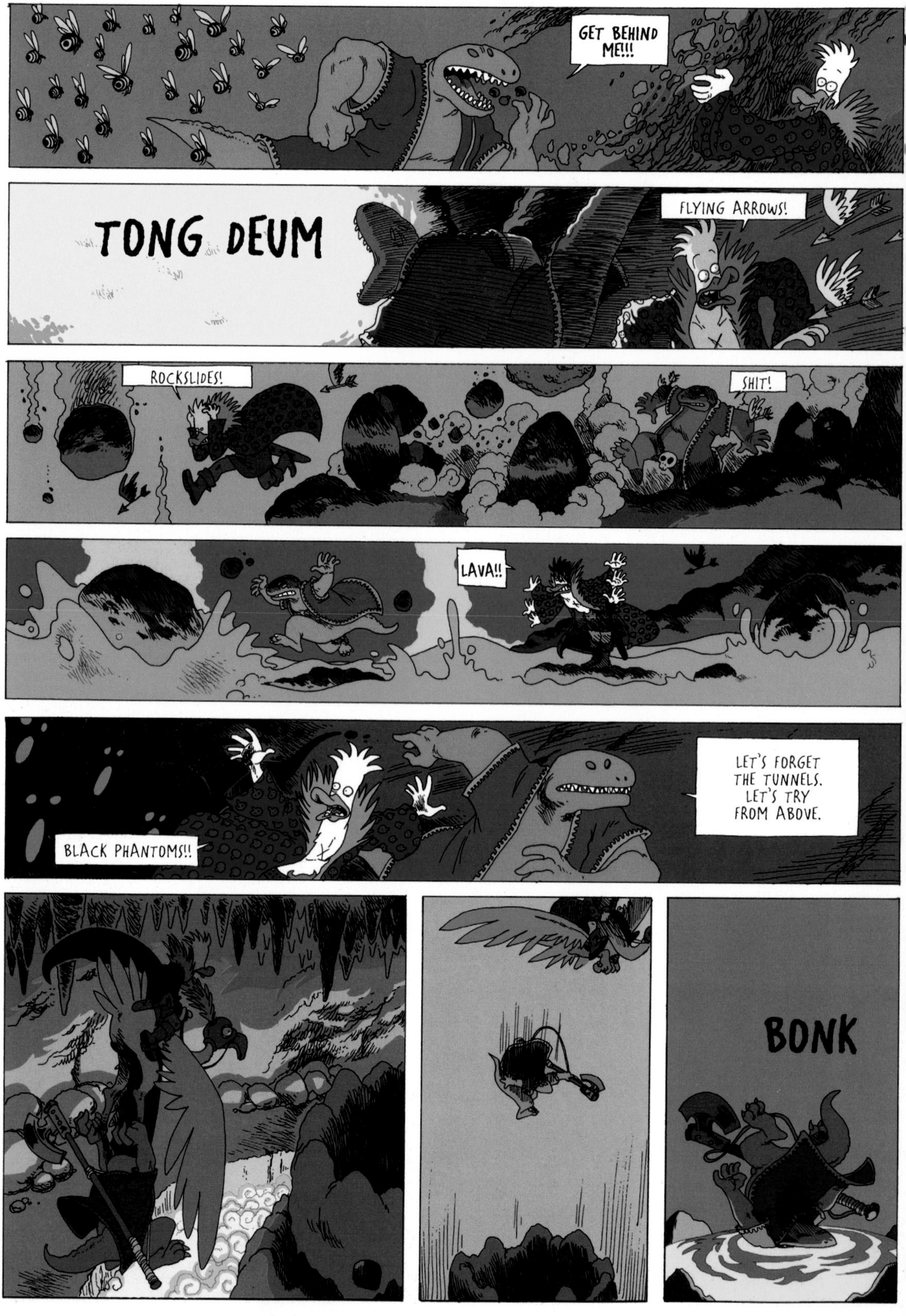
GET BEHIND ME!!!
TONG DEUM
FLYING ARROWS!
ROCKSLIDES!
SHIT!
LAVA!!
LET'S FORGET THE TUNNELS. LET'S TRY FROM ABOVE.
BLACK PHANTOMS!!
BONK

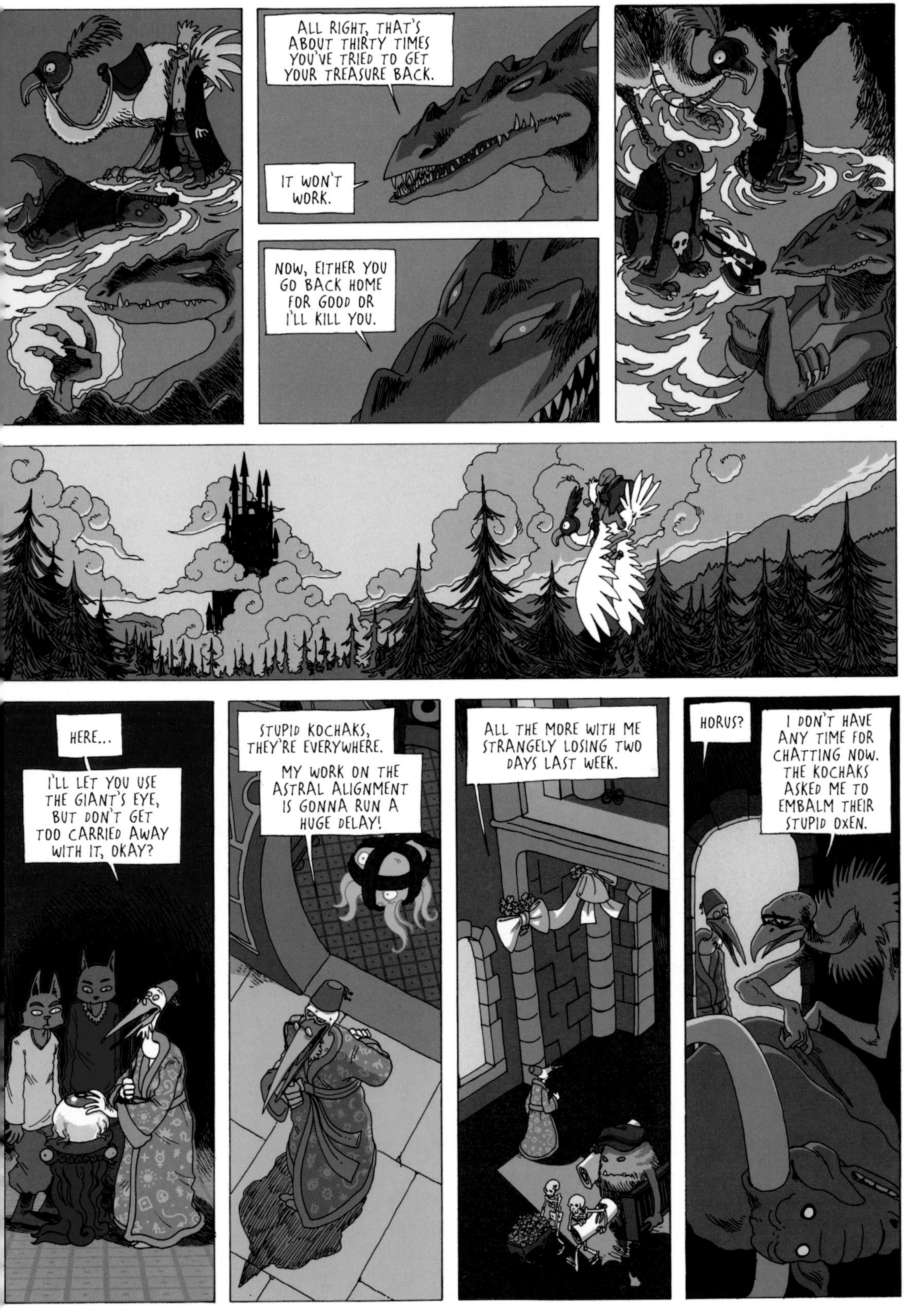
ALL RIGHT, THAT'S ABOUT THIRTY TIMES YOU'VE TRIED TO GET YOUR TREASURE BACK.
IT WON'T WORK.
NOW, EITHER YOU GO BACK HOME FOR GOOD OR I'LL KILL YOU.
HERE...
I'LL LET YOU USE THE GIANT'S EYE, BUT DON'T GET TOO CARRIED AWAY WITH IT, OKAY?
STUPID KOCHAKS, THEY'RE EVERYWHERE.
MY WORK ON THE ASTRAL ALIGNMENT IS GONNA RUN A HUGE DELAY!
ALL THE MORE WITH ME STRANGELY LOSING TWO DAYS LAST WEEK.
HORUS?
I DON'T HAVE ANY TIME FOR CHATTING NOW. THE KOCHAKS ASKED ME TO EMBALM THEIR STUPID OXEN.

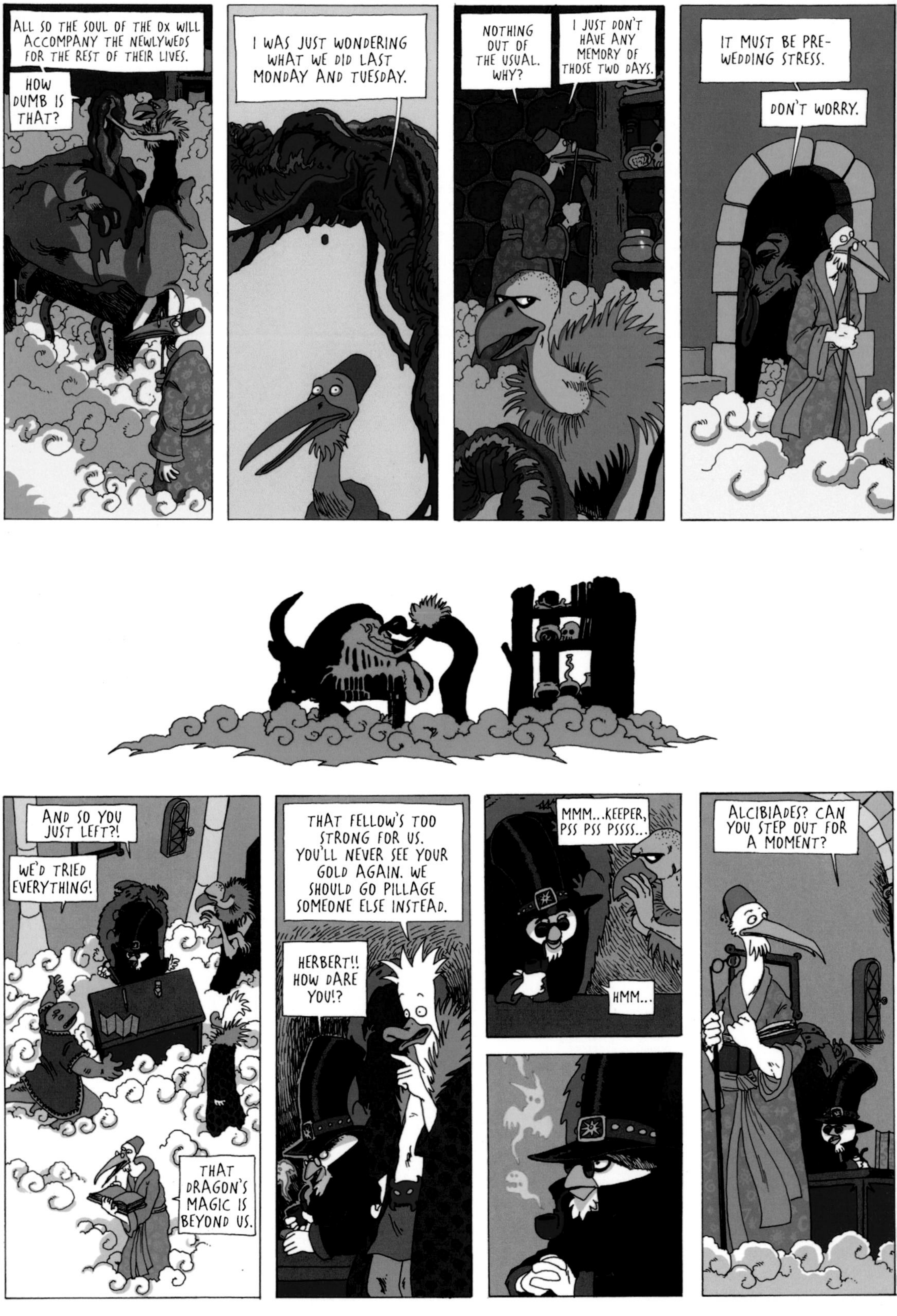
ALL SO THE SOUL OF THE OX WILL ACCOMPANY THE NEWLYWEDS FOR THE REST OF THEIR LIVES.
HOW DUMB IS THAT?
I WAS JUST WONDERING WHAT WE DID LAST MONDAY AND TUESDAY.
NOTHING OUT OF THE USUAL. WHY?
I JUST DON'T HAVE ANY MEMORY OF THOSE TWO DAYS.
IT MUST BE PRE-WEDDING STRESS.
DON'T WORRY.
AND SO YOU JUST LEFT?!
WE'D TRIED EVERYTHING!
THAT DRAGON'S MAGIC IS BEYOND US.
THAT FELLOW'S TOO STRONG FOR US. YOU'LL NEVER SEE YOUR GOLD AGAIN. WE SHOULD GO PILLAGE SOMEONE ELSE INSTEAD.
HERBERT!! HOW DARE YOU!?
MMM...KEEPER, PSS PSS PSSSS...
HMM...
ALCIBIADES? CAN YOU STEP OUT FOR A MOMENT?

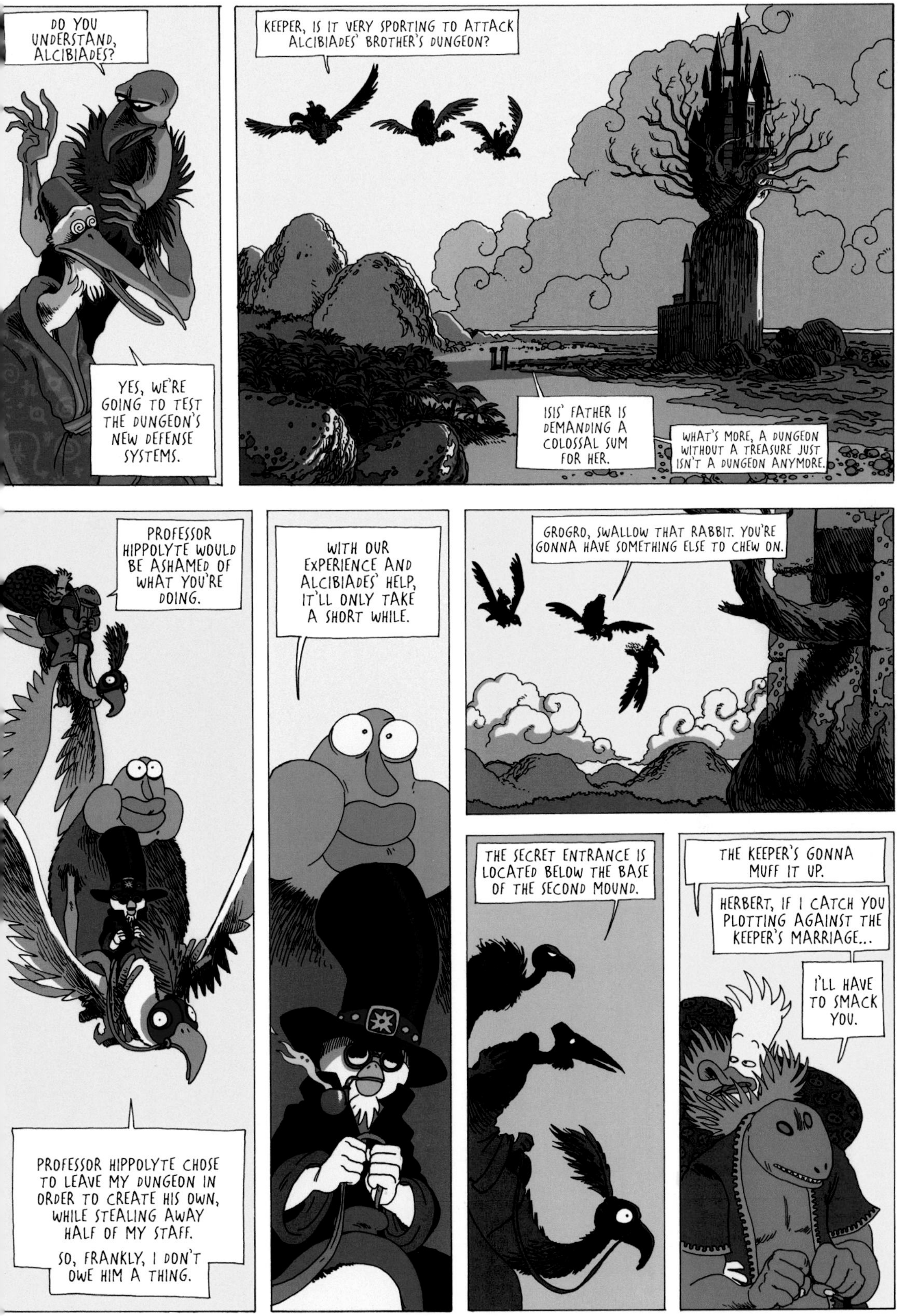
DO YOU UNDERSTAND, ALCIBIADES?
YES, WE'RE GOING TO TEST THE DUNGEON'S NEW DEFENSE SYSTEMS.
KEEPER, IS IT VERY SPORTING TO ATTACK ALCIBIADES' BROTHER'S DUNGEON?
ISIS' FATHER IS DEMANDING A COLOSSAL SUM FOR HER.
WHAT'S MORE, A DUNGEON WITHOUT A TREASURE JUST ISN'T A DUNGEON ANYMORE.
PROFESSOR HIPPOLYTE WOULD BE ASHAMED OF WHAT YOU'RE DOING.
PROFESSOR HIPPOLYTE CHOSE TO LEAVE MY DUNGEON IN ORDER TO CREATE HIS OWN, WHILE STEALING AWAY HALF OF MY STAFF.
SO, FRANKLY, I DON'T OWE HIM A THING.
WITH OUR EXPERIENCE AND ALCIBIADES' HELP, IT'LL ONLY TAKE A SHORT WHILE.
GROGRO, SWALLOW THAT RABBIT. YOU'RE GONNA HAVE SOMETHING ELSE TO CHEW ON.
THE SECRET ENTRANCE IS LOCATED BELOW THE BASE OF THE SECOND MOUND.
THE KEEPER'S GONNA MUFF IT UP.
HERBERT, IF I CATCH YOU PLOTTING AGAINST THE KEEPER'S MARRIAGE...
I'LL HAVE TO SMACK YOU.

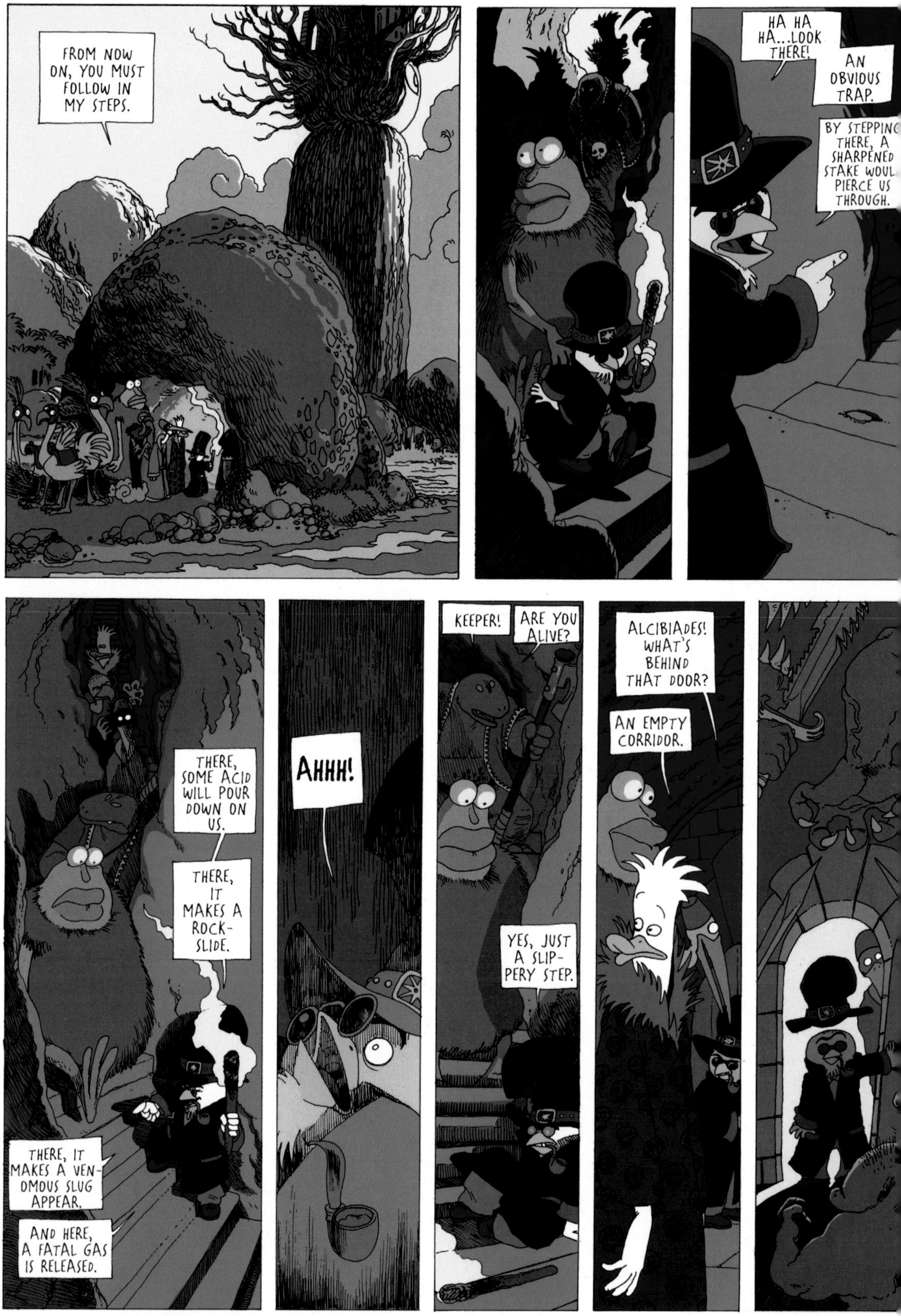
FROM NOW ON, YOU MUST FOLLOW IN MY STEPS.
HA HA HA...LOOK THERE!
AN OBVIOUS TRAP.
BY STEPPING THERE, A SHARPENED STAKE WOUL PIERCE US THROUGH.
THERE, SOME ACID WILL POUR DOWN ON US.
THERE, IT MAKES A ROCK-SLIDE.
THERE, IT MAKES A VEN-OMOUS SLUG APPEAR.
AND HERE, A FATAL GAS IS RELEASED.
AHHH!
KEEPER!
ARE YOU ALIVE?
YES, JUST A SLIP-PERY STEP.
ALCIBIADES! WHAT'S BEHIND THAT DOOR?
AN EMPTY CORRIDOR.

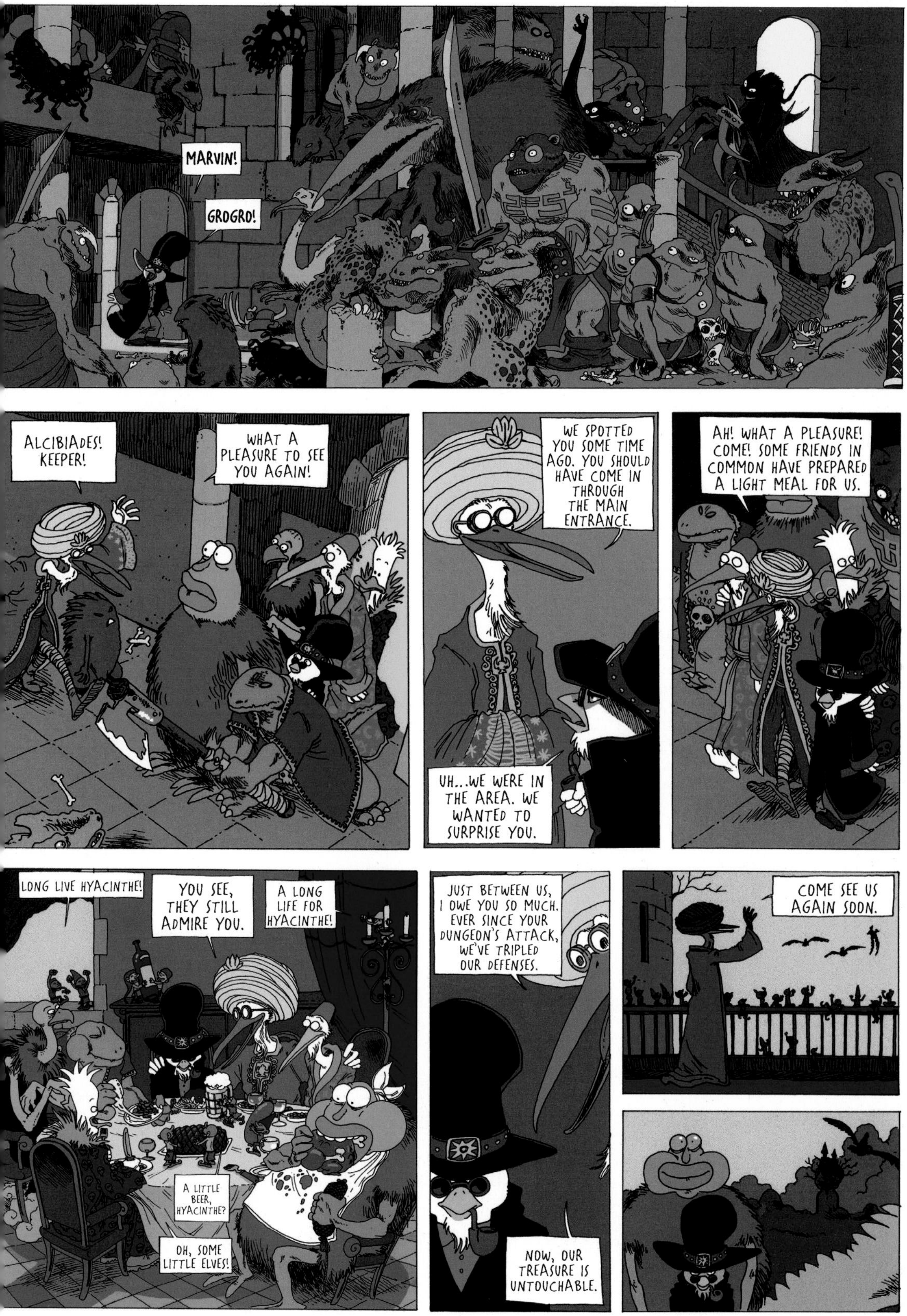
MARVIN!
GROGRO!
ALCIBIADES! KEEPER!
WHAT A PLEASURE TO SEE YOU AGAIN!
WE SPOTTED YOU SOME TIME AGO. YOU SHOULD HAVE COME IN THROUGH THE MAIN ENTRANCE.
UH...WE WERE IN THE AREA. WE WANTED TO SURPRISE YOU.
AH! WHAT A PLEASURE! COME! SOME FRIENDS IN COMMON HAVE PREPARED A LIGHT MEAL FOR US.
LONG LIVE HYACINTHE!
YOU SEE, THEY STILL ADMIRE YOU.
A LONG LIFE FOR HYACINTHE!
A LITTLE BEER, HYACINTHE?
OH, SOME LITTLE ELVES!
JUST BETWEEN US, I OWE YOU SO MUCH. EVER SINCE YOUR DUNGEON'S ATTACK, WE'VE TRIPLED OUR DEFENSES.
NOW, OUR TREASURE IS UNTOUCHABLE.
COME SEE US AGAIN SOON.

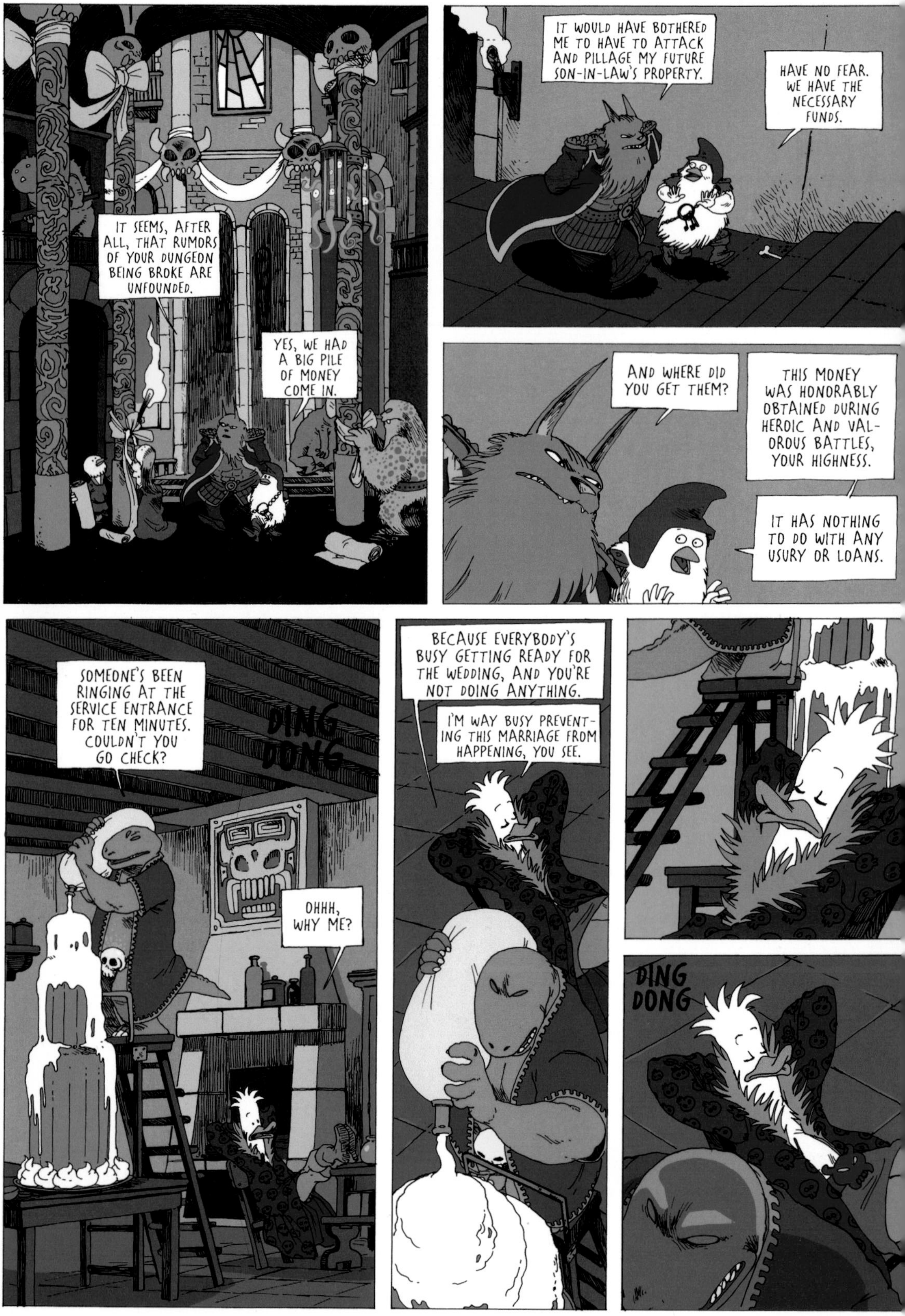
IT SEEMS, AFTER ALL, THAT RUMORS OF YOUR DUNGEON BEING BROKE ARE UNFOUNDED.
YES, WE HAD A BIG PILE OF MONEY COME IN.
IT WOULD HAVE BOTHERED ME TO HAVE TO ATTACK AND PILLAGE MY FUTURE SON-IN-LAW'S PROPERTY.
HAVE NO FEAR. WE HAVE THE NECESSARY FUNDS.
AND WHERE DID YOU GET THEM?
THIS MONEY WAS HONORABLY OBTAINED DURING HEROIC AND VALOROUS BATTLES, YOUR HIGHNESS.
IT HAS NOTHING TO DO WITH ANY USURY OR LOANS.
SOMEONE'S BEEN RINGING AT THE SERVICE ENTRANCE FOR TEN MINUTES. COULDN'T YOU GO CHECK?
DING DONG
OHHH, WHY ME?
BECAUSE EVERYBODY'S BUSY GETTING READY FOR THE WEDDING, AND YOU'RE NOT DOING ANYTHING.
I'M WAY BUSY PREVENTING THIS MARRIAGE FROM HAPPENING, YOU SEE.
DING DONG

OKAY, I WARNED YOU ONCE. I'M NOT GONNA REPEAT MYSELF.

OOOOOH! ALL RIGHT, I'M GOING. IT'S NOT WORTH GETTING ALL WORKED UP OVER A DOOR!

HERBERT! IF I CATCH YOU CONCOCTING SOME TRICK TO SABOTAGE THE KEEPER AND ISIS'S MARRIAGE, YOU'RE GONNA HAVE A VERY BAD DAY!

TSSS

SOMETIMES YOU DON'T UNDERSTAND ANYTHING.

DING DONG

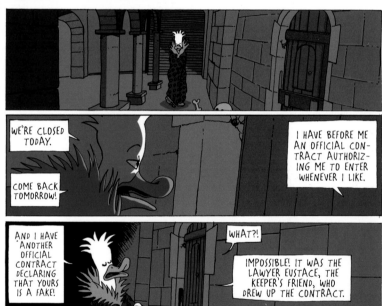

WE'RE CLOSED TODAY.

COME BACK TOMORROW!

I HAVE BEFORE ME AN OFFICIAL CONTRACT AUTHORIZING ME TO ENTER WHENEVER I LIKE.

AND I HAVE ANOTHER OFFICIAL CONTRACT DECLARING THAT YOURS IS A FAKE!

WHAT?!

IMPOSSIBLE! IT WAS THE LAWYER EUSTACE, THE KEEPER'S FRIEND, WHO DREW UP THE CONTRACT.

WELL, I DON'T GIVE A HOOT. THAT'S LIFE.

COUNSELOR CALLISTUS, PLEASE NOTE THAT AT 4:30 P.M. PRECISELY, ACCESS TO THE DUNGEON WAS DENIED ME, BRINGING INTO EFFECT THE ADDENDUM TO CLAUSE 27.

NOTED!

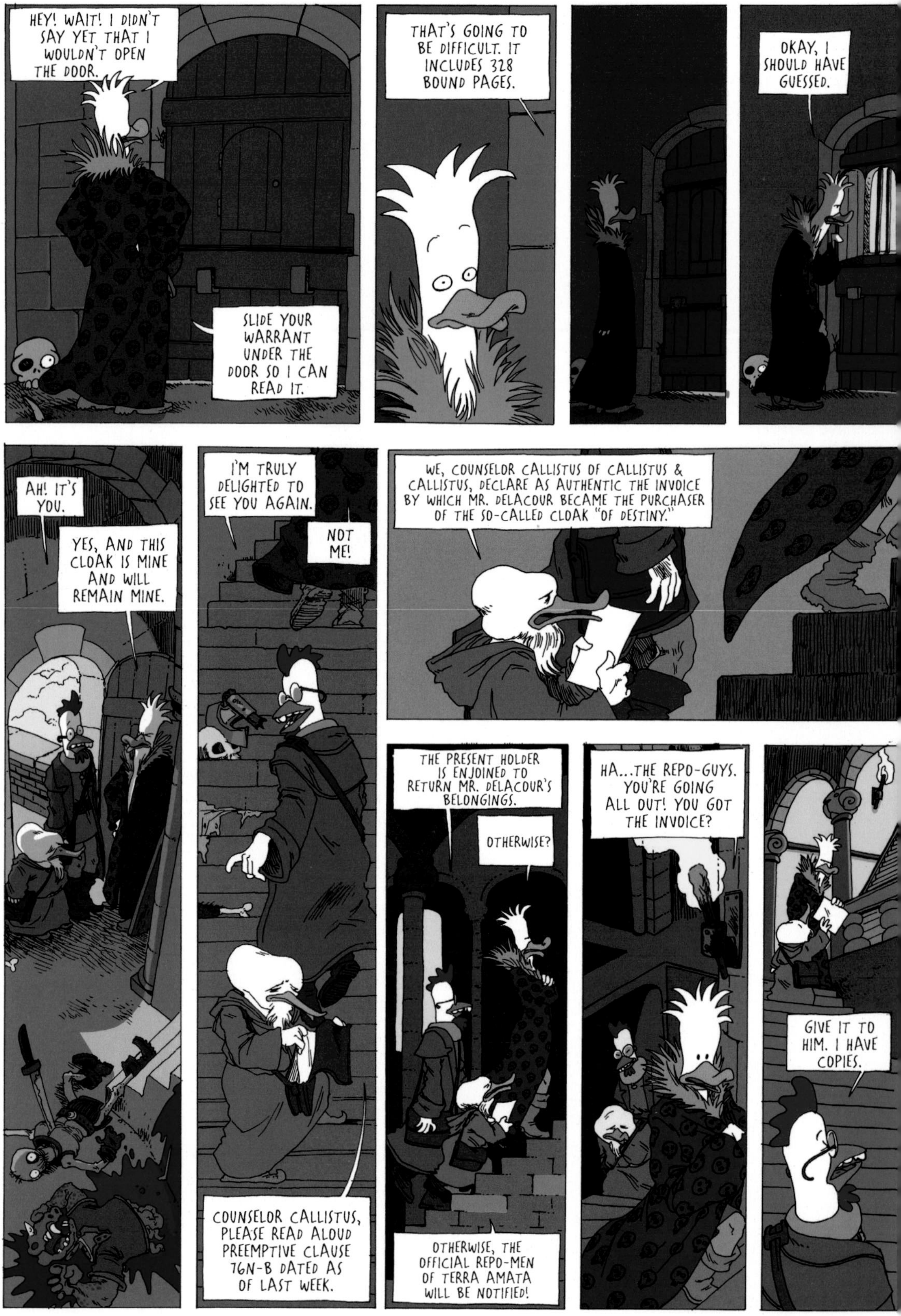
HEY! WAIT! I DIDN'T SAY YET THAT I WOULDN'T OPEN THE DOOR.
SLIDE YOUR WARRANT UNDER THE DOOR SO I CAN READ IT.
THAT'S GOING TO BE DIFFICULT. IT INCLUDES 328 BOUND PAGES.
OKAY, I SHOULD HAVE GUESSED.
AH! IT'S YOU.
YES, AND THIS CLOAK IS MINE AND WILL REMAIN MINE.
I'M TRULY DELIGHTED TO SEE YOU AGAIN.
NOT ME!
COUNSELOR CALLISTUS, PLEASE READ ALOUD PREEMPTIVE CLAUSE 76N-B DATED AS OF LAST WEEK.
WE, COUNSELOR CALLISTUS OF CALLISTUS & CALLISTUS, DECLARE AS AUTHENTIC THE INVOICE BY WHICH MR. DELACOUR BECAME THE PURCHASER OF THE SO-CALLED CLOAK "OF DESTINY."
THE PRESENT HOLDER IS ENJOINED TO RETURN MR. DELACOUR'S BELONGINGS.
OTHERWISE?
OTHERWISE, THE OFFICIAL REPO-MEN OF TERRA AMATA WILL BE NOTIFIED!
HA...THE REPO-GUYS. YOU'RE GOING ALL OUT! YOU GOT THE INVOICE?
GIVE IT TO HIM. I HAVE COPIES.

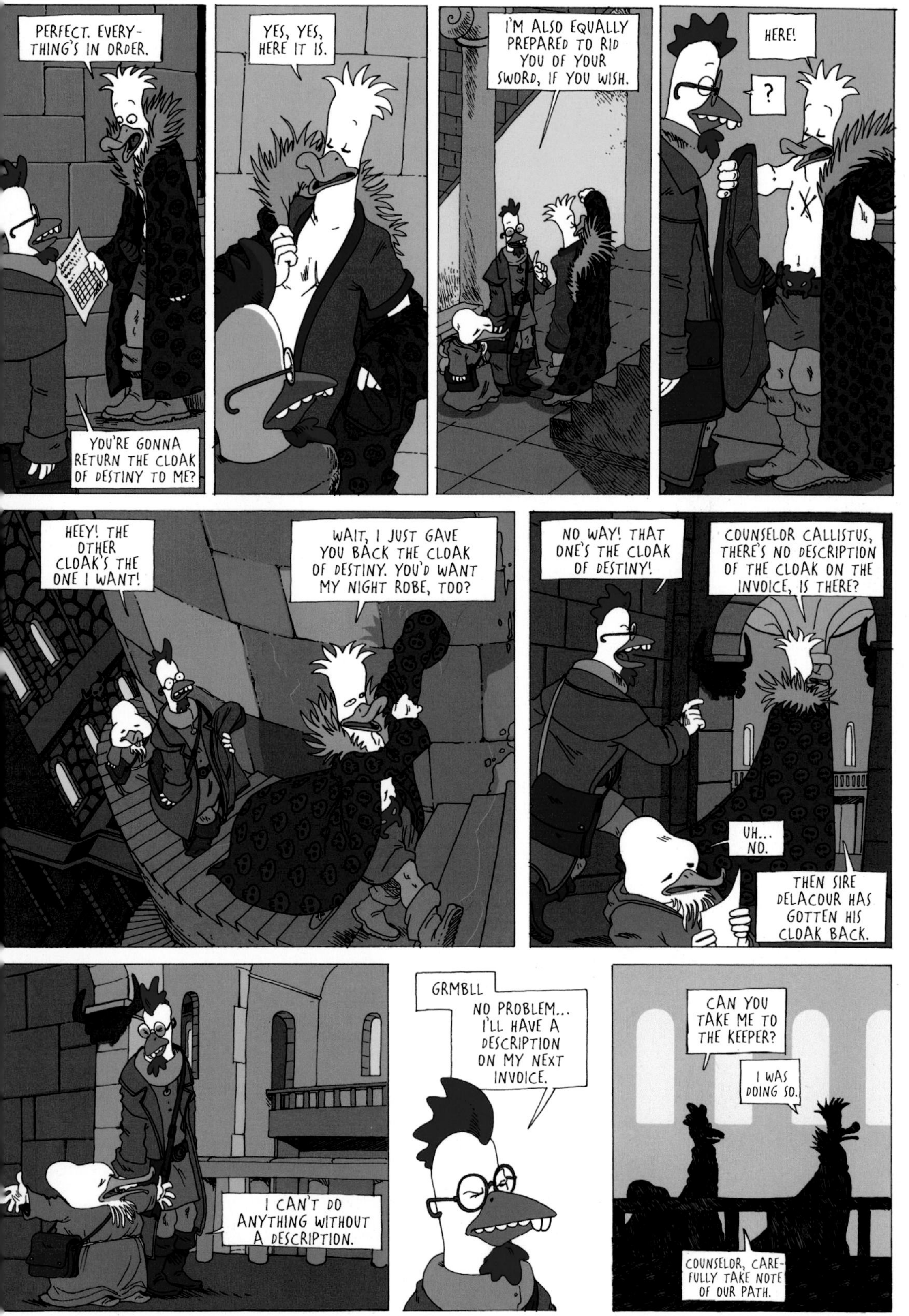
PERFECT. EVERYTHING'S IN ORDER.
YOU'RE GONNA RETURN THE CLOAK OF DESTINY TO ME?
YES, YES, HERE IT IS.
I'M ALSO EQUALLY PREPARED TO RID YOU OF YOUR SWORD, IF YOU WISH.
HERE!
?
HEEY! THE OTHER CLOAK'S THE ONE I WANT!
WAIT, I JUST GAVE YOU BACK THE CLOAK OF DESTINY. YOU'D WANT MY NIGHT ROBE, TOO?
NO WAY! THAT ONE'S THE CLOAK OF DESTINY!
COUNSELOR CALLISTUS, THERE'S NO DESCRIPTION OF THE CLOAK ON THE INVOICE, IS THERE?
UH... NO.
THEN SIRE DELACOUR HAS GOTTEN HIS CLOAK BACK.
I CAN'T DO ANYTHING WITHOUT A DESCRIPTION.
GRMBLL
NO PROBLEM... I'LL HAVE A DESCRIPTION ON MY NEXT INVOICE.
CAN YOU TAKE ME TO THE KEEPER?
I WAS DOING SO.
COUNSELOR, CAREFULLY TAKE NOTE OF OUR PATH.

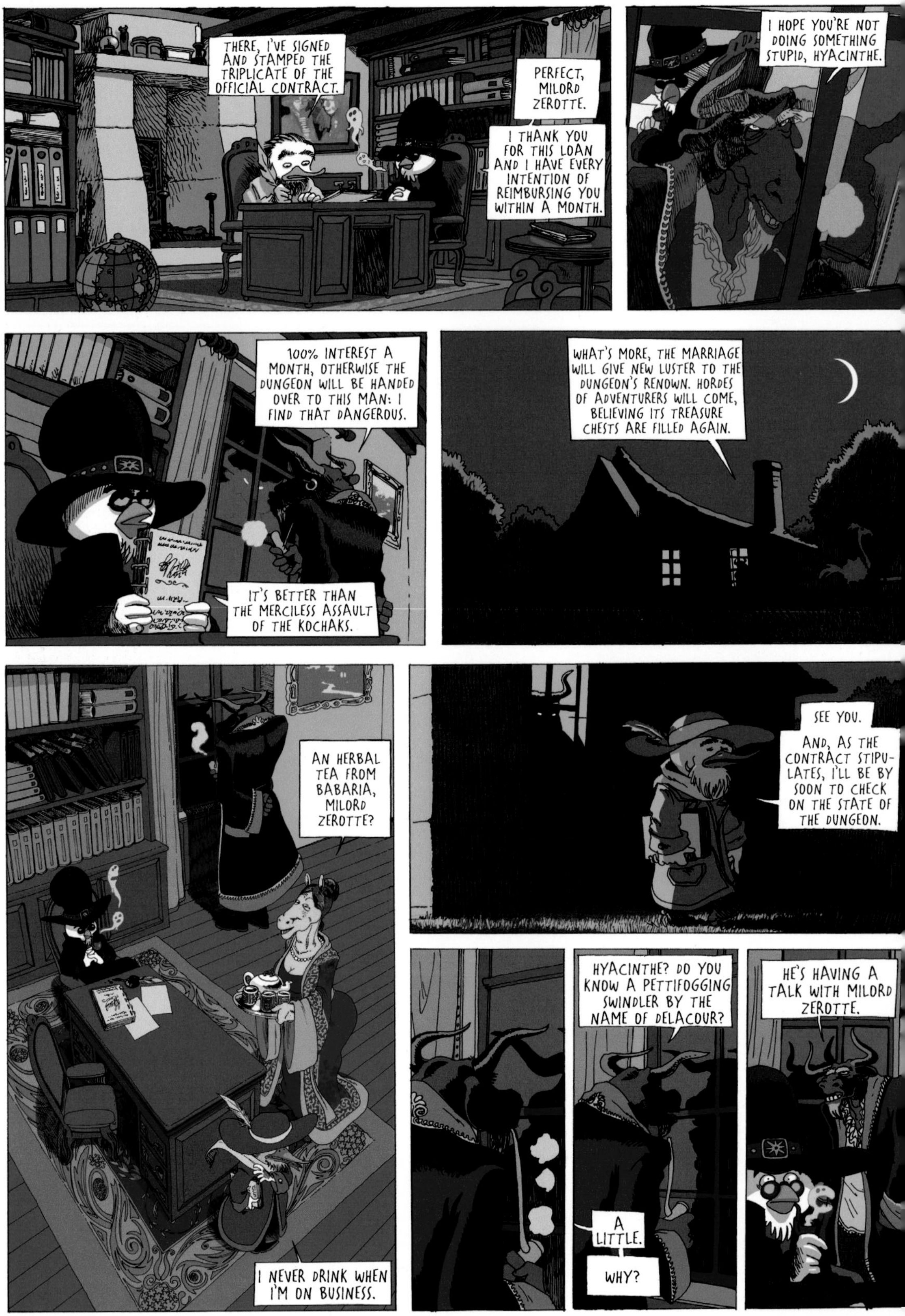
THERE, I'VE SIGNED AND STAMPED THE TRIPLICATE OF THE OFFICIAL CONTRACT.
PERFECT, MILORD ZEROTTE.
I THANK YOU FOR THIS LOAN AND I HAVE EVERY INTENTION OF REIMBURSING YOU WITHIN A MONTH.
I HOPE YOU'RE NOT DOING SOMETHING STUPID, HYACINTHE.
100% INTEREST A MONTH, OTHERWISE THE DUNGEON WILL BE HANDED OVER TO THIS MAN: I FIND THAT DANGEROUS.
IT'S BETTER THAN THE MERCILESS ASSAULT OF THE KOCHAKS.
WHAT'S MORE, THE MARRIAGE WILL GIVE NEW LUSTER TO THE DUNGEON'S RENOWN. HORDES OF ADVENTURERS WILL COME, BELIEVING ITS TREASURE CHESTS ARE FILLED AGAIN.
AN HERBAL TEA FROM BABARIA, MILORD ZEROTTE?
I NEVER DRINK WHEN I'M ON BUSINESS.
SEE YOU.
AND, AS THE CONTRACT STIPULATES, I'LL BE BY SOON TO CHECK ON THE STATE OF THE DUNGEON.
HYACINTHE? DO YOU KNOW A PETTIFOGGING SWINDLER BY THE NAME OF DELACOUR?
A LITTLE.
WHY?
HE'S HAVING A TALK WITH MILORD ZEROTTE.

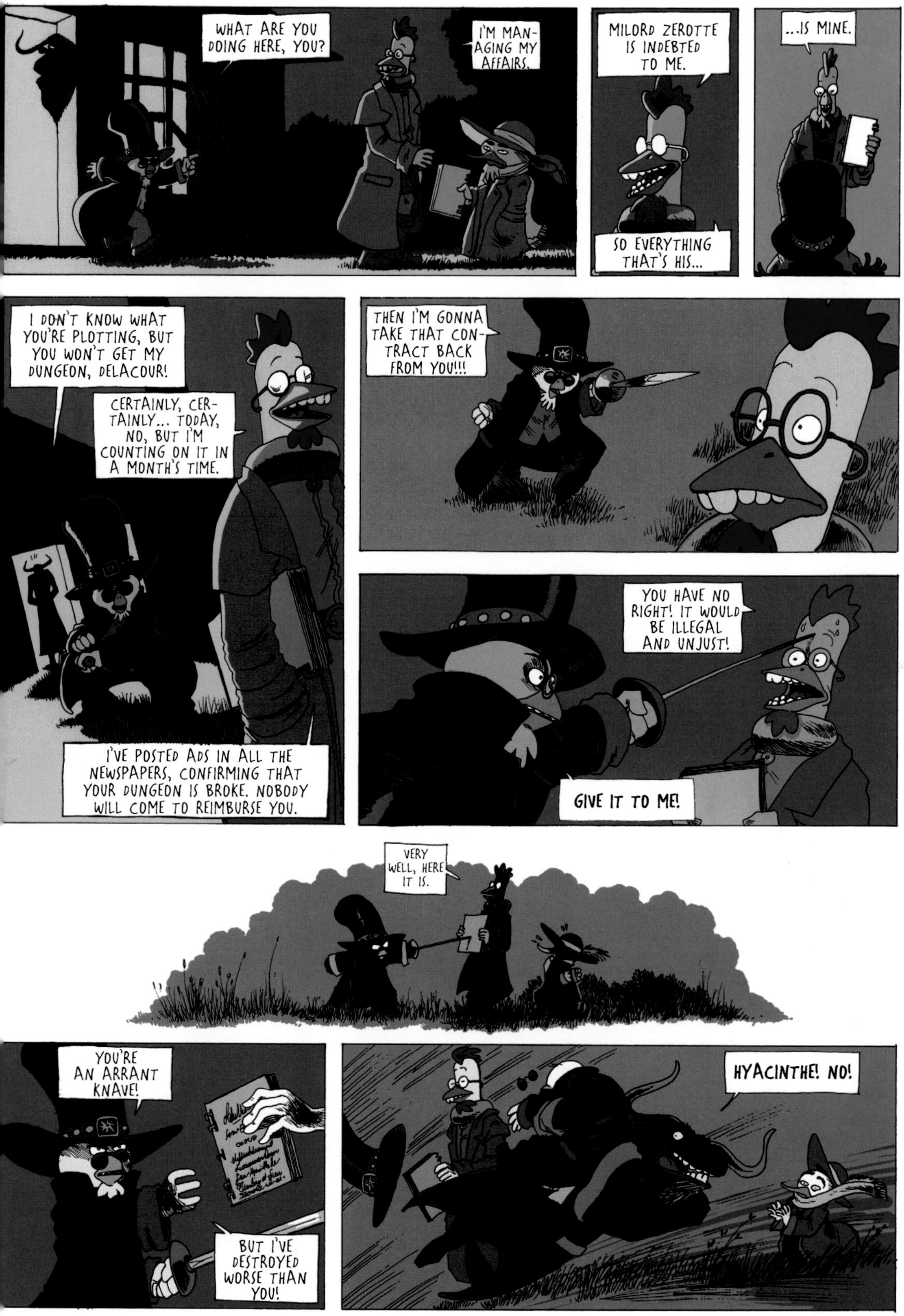
WHAT ARE YOU DOING HERE, YOU?
I'M MAN-AGING MY AFFAIRS.
MILORD ZEROTTE IS INDEBTED TO ME.
SO EVERYTHING THAT'S HIS...
...IS MINE.
I DON'T KNOW WHAT YOU'RE PLOTTING, BUT YOU WON'T GET MY DUNGEON, DELACOUR!
CERTAINLY, CER-TAINLY... TODAY, NO, BUT I'M COUNTING ON IT IN A MONTH'S TIME.
I'VE POSTED ADS IN ALL THE NEWSPAPERS, CONFIRMING THAT YOUR DUNGEON IS BROKE. NOBODY WILL COME TO REIMBURSE YOU.
THEN I'M GONNA TAKE THAT CON-TRACT BACK FROM YOU!!!
YOU HAVE NO RIGHT! IT WOULD BE ILLEGAL AND UNJUST!
GIVE IT TO ME!
VERY WELL, HERE IT IS.
YOU'RE AN ARRANT KNAVE!
BUT I'VE DESTROYED WORSE THAN YOU!
HYACINTHE! NO!

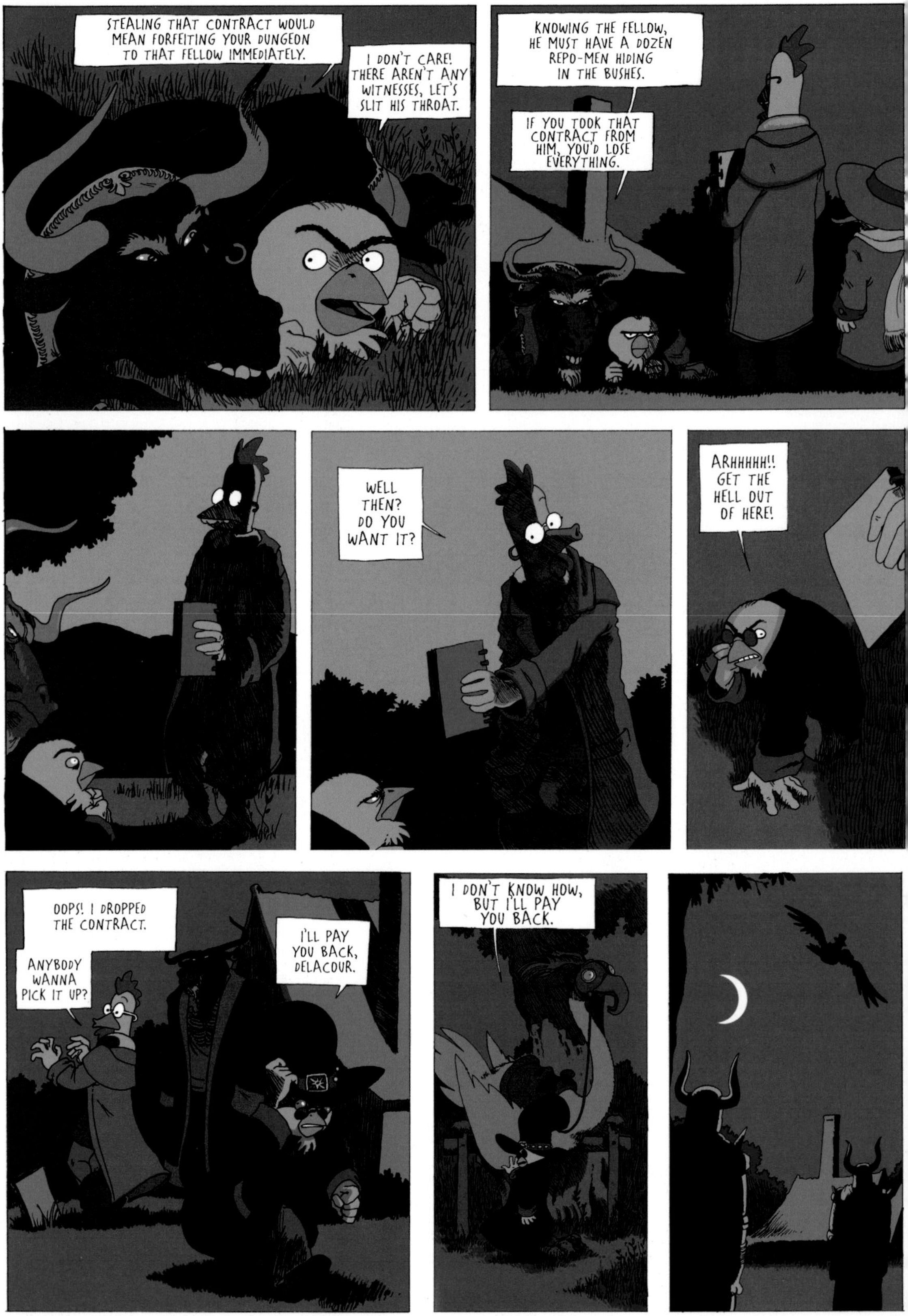

STEALING THAT CONTRACT WOULD MEAN FORFEITING YOUR DUNGEON TO THAT FELLOW IMMEDIATELY.
I DON'T CARE! THERE AREN'T ANY WITNESSES, LET'S SLIT HIS THROAT.
KNOWING THE FELLOW, HE MUST HAVE A DOZEN REPO-MEN HIDING IN THE BUSHES.
IF YOU TOOK THAT CONTRACT FROM HIM, YOU'D LOSE EVERYTHING.
WELL THEN? DO YOU WANT IT?
ARHHHHH!! GET THE HELL OUT OF HERE!
OOPS! I DROPPED THE CONTRACT.
ANYBODY WANNA PICK IT UP?
I'LL PAY YOU BACK, DELACOUR.
I DON'T KNOW HOW, BUT I'LL PAY YOU BACK.

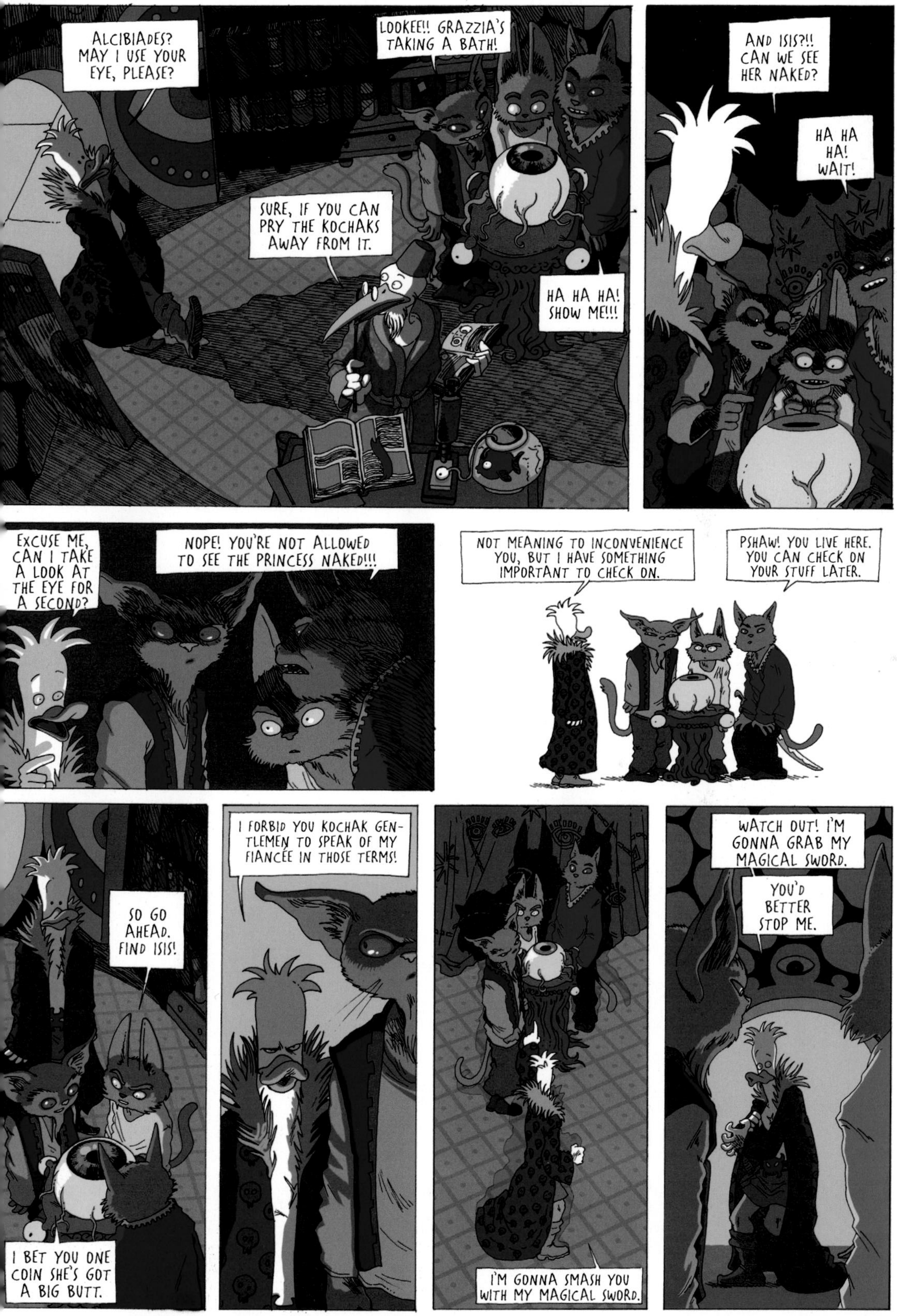
ALCIBIADES? MAY I USE YOUR EYE, PLEASE?
LOOKEE!! GRAZZIA'S TAKING A BATH!
SURE, IF YOU CAN PRY THE KOCHAKS AWAY FROM IT.
HA HA HA! SHOW ME!!!
AND ISIS?!! CAN WE SEE HER NAKED?
HA HA HA! WAIT!
EXCUSE ME, CAN I TAKE A LOOK AT THE EYE FOR A SECOND?
NOPE! YOU'RE NOT ALLOWED TO SEE THE PRINCESS NAKED!!!
NOT MEANING TO INCONVENIENCE YOU, BUT I HAVE SOMETHING IMPORTANT TO CHECK ON.
PSHAW! YOU LIVE HERE. YOU CAN CHECK ON YOUR STUFF LATER.
SO GO AHEAD. FIND ISIS!
I BET YOU ONE COIN SHE'S GOT A BIG BUTT.
I FORBID YOU KOCHAK GENTLEMEN TO SPEAK OF MY FIANCÉE IN THOSE TERMS!
I'M GONNA SMASH YOU WITH MY MAGICAL SWORD.
WATCH OUT! I'M GONNA GRAB MY MAGICAL SWORD.
YOU'D BETTER STOP ME.

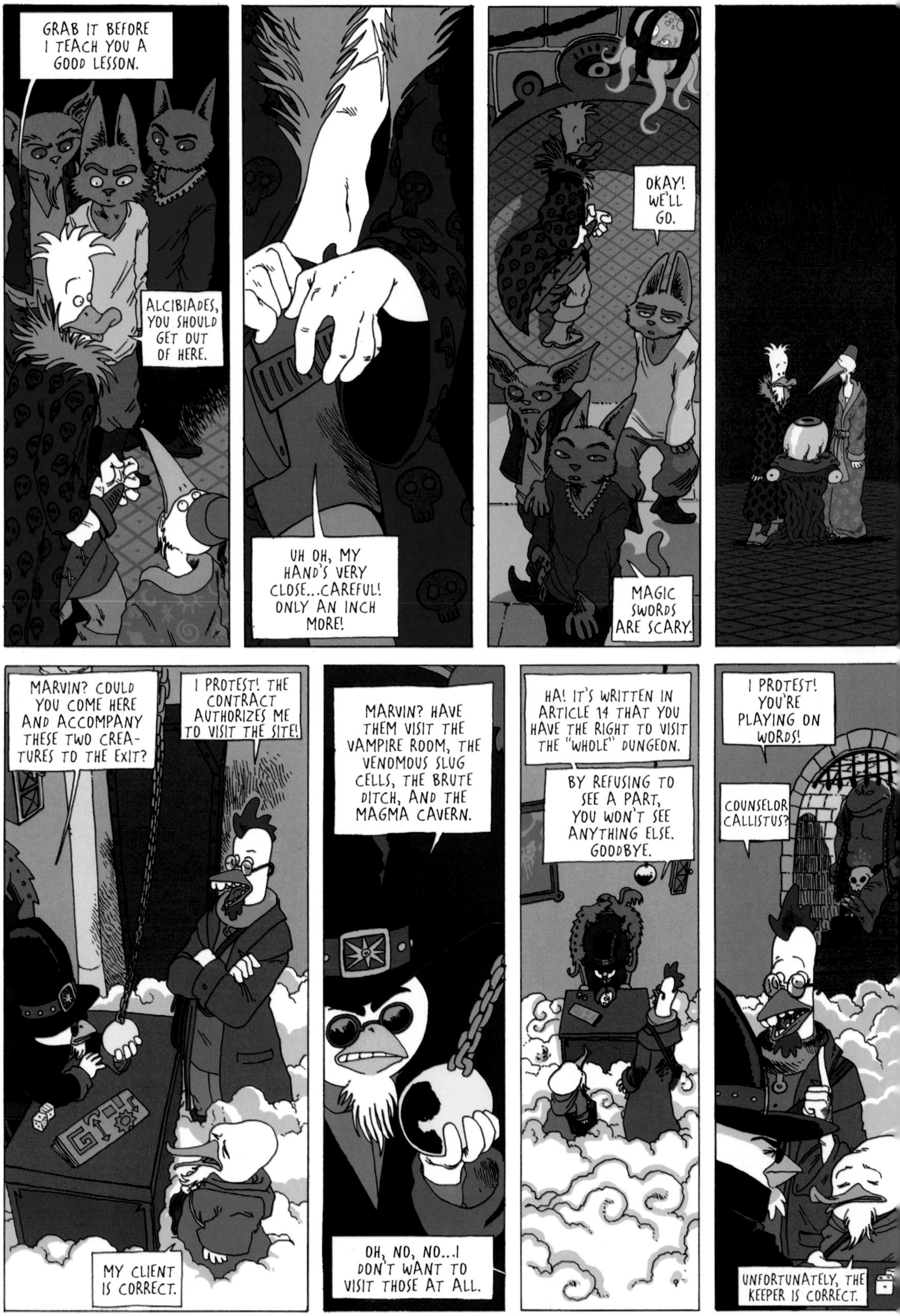
GRAB IT BEFORE I TEACH YOU A GOOD LESSON.
ALCIBIADES, YOU SHOULD GET OUT OF HERE.
UH OH, MY HAND'S VERY CLOSE...CAREFUL! ONLY AN INCH MORE!
OKAY! WE'LL GO.
MAGIC SWORDS ARE SCARY.
MARVIN? COULD YOU COME HERE AND ACCOMPANY THESE TWO CREATURES TO THE EXIT?
I PROTEST! THE CONTRACT AUTHORIZES ME TO VISIT THE SITE!
MY CLIENT IS CORRECT.
MARVIN? HAVE THEM VISIT THE VAMPIRE ROOM, THE VENOMOUS SLUG CELLS, THE BRUTE DITCH, AND THE MAGMA CAVERN.
OH, NO, NO...I DON'T WANT TO VISIT THOSE AT ALL.
HA! IT'S WRITTEN IN ARTICLE 14 THAT YOU HAVE THE RIGHT TO VISIT THE "WHOLE" DUNGEON.
BY REFUSING TO SEE A PART, YOU WON'T SEE ANYTHING ELSE. GOODBYE.
I PROTEST! YOU'RE PLAYING ON WORDS!
COUNSELOR CALLISTUS?
UNFORTUNATELY, THE KEEPER IS CORRECT.

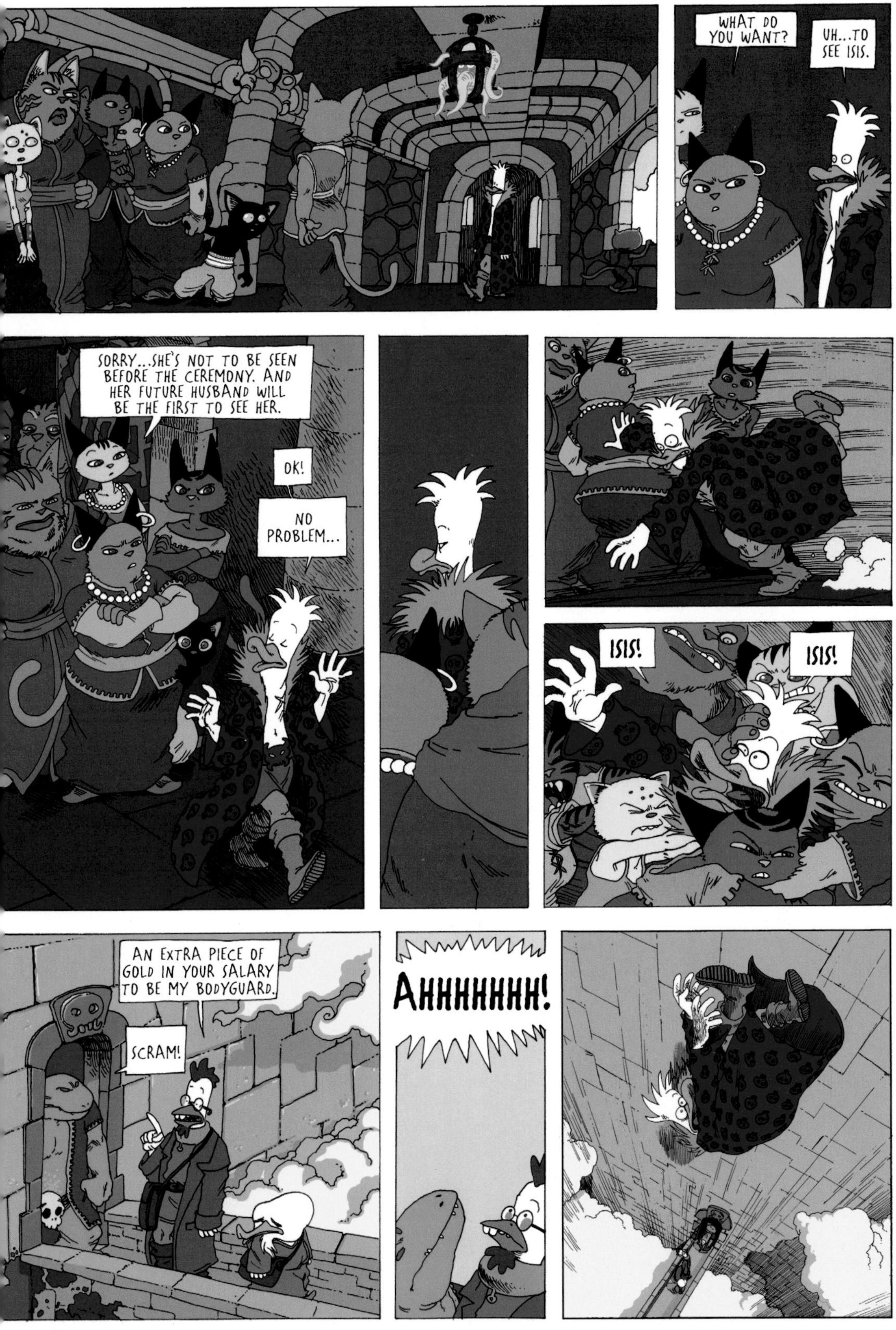
WHAT DO YOU WANT?
UH...TO SEE ISIS.
SORRY...SHE'S NOT TO BE SEEN BEFORE THE CEREMONY. AND HER FUTURE HUSBAND WILL BE THE FIRST TO SEE HER.
OK!
NO PROBLEM...
ISIS!
ISIS!
AN EXTRA PIECE OF GOLD IN YOUR SALARY TO BE MY BODYGUARD.
SCRAM!
AHHHHHHH!

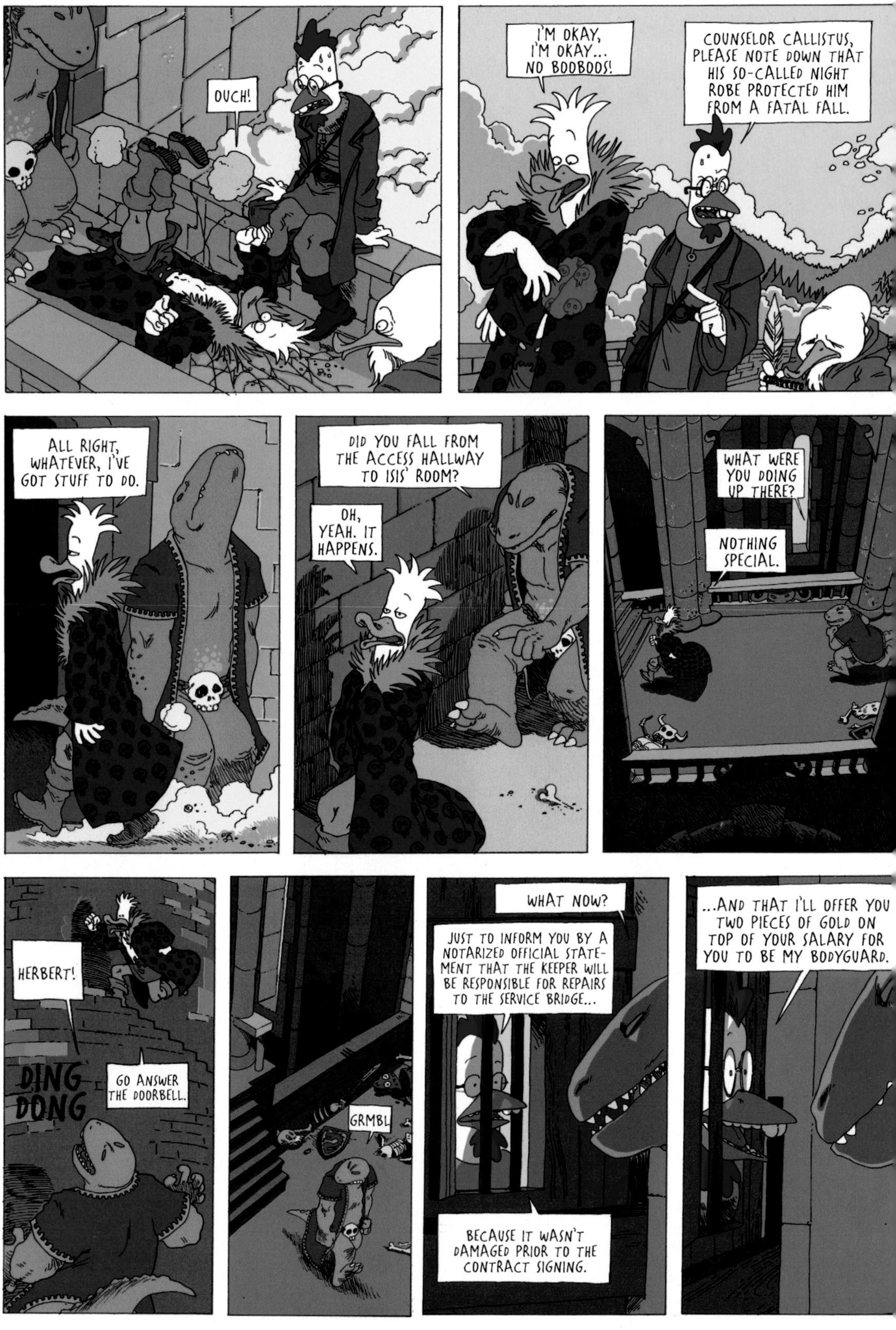
OUCH!
I'M OKAY, I'M OKAY... NO BOOBOOS!
COUNSELOR CALLISTUS, PLEASE NOTE DOWN THAT HIS SO-CALLED NIGHT ROBE PROTECTED HIM FROM A FATAL FALL.
ALL RIGHT, WHATEVER, I'VE GOT STUFF TO DO.
DID YOU FALL FROM THE ACCESS HALLWAY TO ISIS' ROOM?
OH, YEAH. IT HAPPENS.
WHAT WERE YOU DOING UP THERE?
NOTHING SPECIAL.
HERBERT!
DING DONG
GO ANSWER THE DOORBELL.
GRMBL
WHAT NOW?
JUST TO INFORM YOU BY A NOTARIZED OFFICIAL STATEMENT THAT THE KEEPER WILL BE RESPONSIBLE FOR REPAIRS TO THE SERVICE BRIDGE...
BECAUSE IT WASN'T DAMAGED PRIOR TO THE CONTRACT SIGNING.
...AND THAT I'LL OFFER YOU TWO PIECES OF GOLD ON TOP OF YOUR SALARY FOR YOU TO BE MY BODYGUARD.

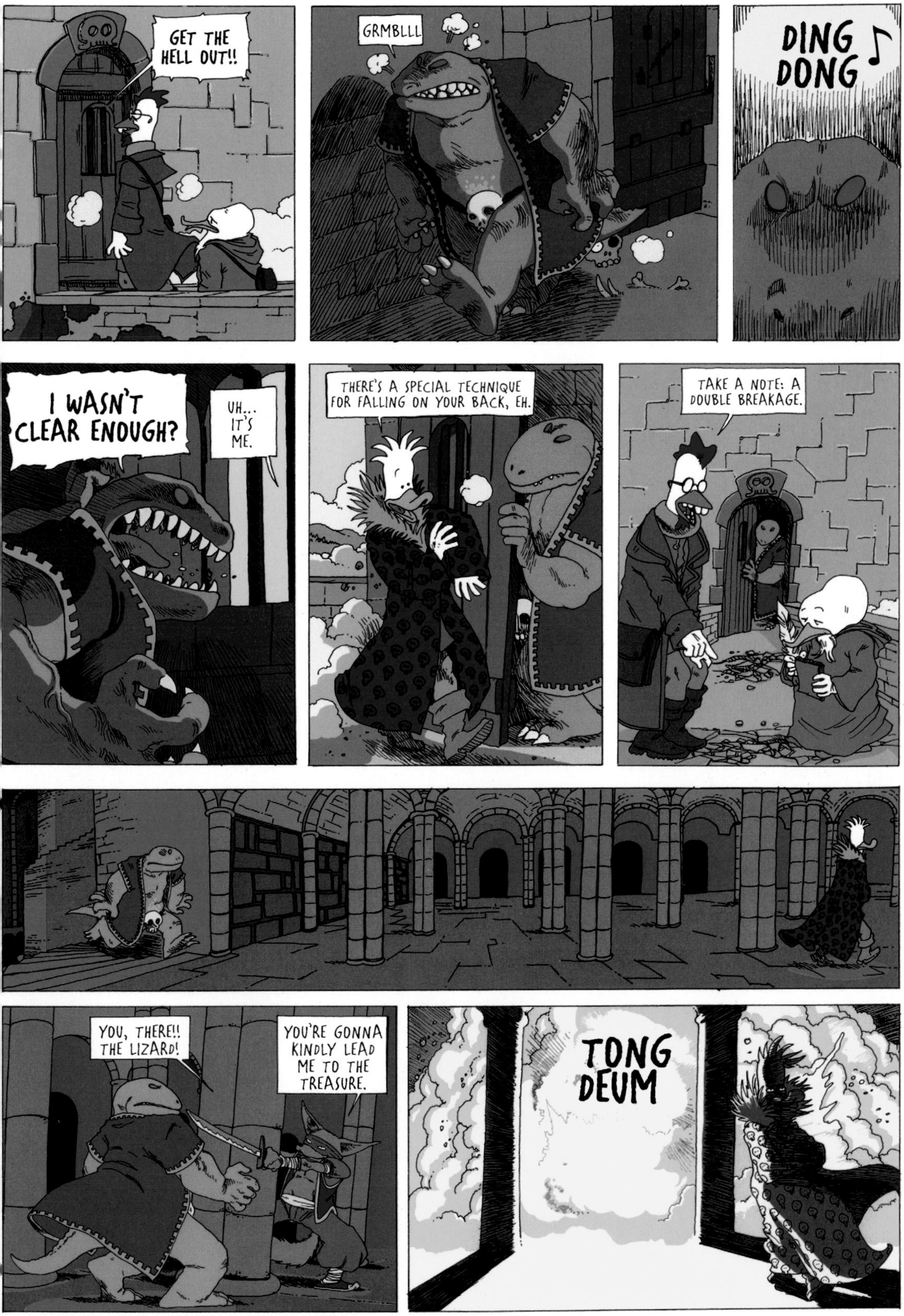
GET THE HELL OUT!!
GRMBLLL
DING DONG
I WASN'T CLEAR ENOUGH?
UH... IT'S ME.
THERE'S A SPECIAL TECHNIQUE FOR FALLING ON YOUR BACK, EH.
TAKE A NOTE: A DOUBLE BREAKAGE.
YOU, THERE!! THE LIZARD!
YOU'RE GONNA KINDLY LEAD ME TO THE TREASURE.
TONG DEUM

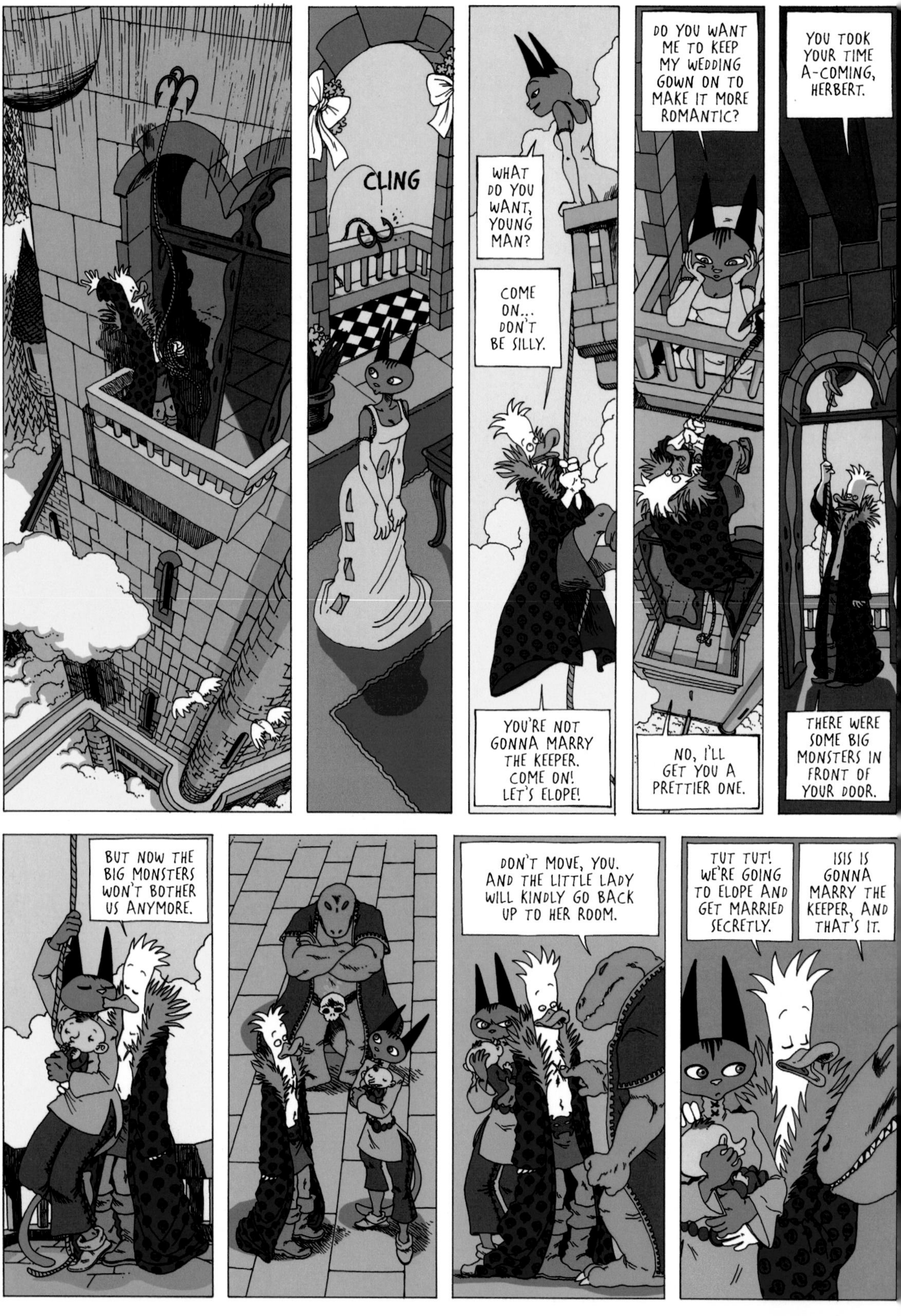
CLING
WHAT DO YOU WANT, YOUNG MAN?
COME ON... DON'T BE SILLY.
YOU'RE NOT GONNA MARRY THE KEEPER. COME ON! LET'S ELOPE!
DO YOU WANT ME TO KEEP MY WEDDING GOWN ON TO MAKE IT MORE ROMANTIC?
NO, I'LL GET YOU A PRETTIER ONE.
YOU TOOK YOUR TIME A-COMING, HERBERT.
THERE WERE SOME BIG MONSTERS IN FRONT OF YOUR DOOR.
BUT NOW THE BIG MONSTERS WON'T BOTHER US ANYMORE.
DON'T MOVE, YOU. AND THE LITTLE LADY WILL KINDLY GO BACK UP TO HER ROOM.
TUT TUT! WE'RE GOING TO ELOPE AND GET MARRIED SECRETLY.
ISIS IS GONNA MARRY THE KEEPER, AND THAT'S IT.

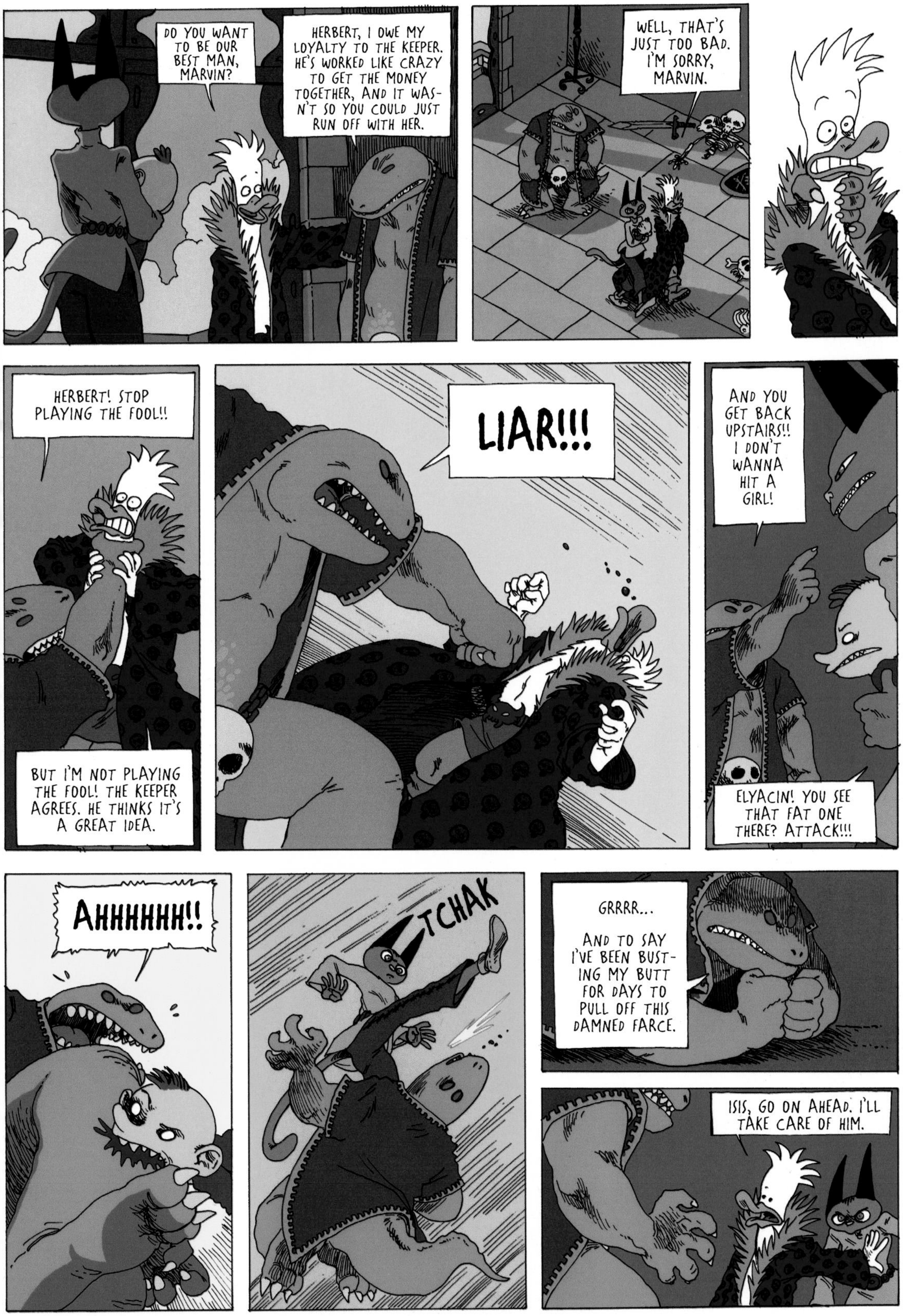

DO YOU WANT TO BE OUR BEST MAN, MARVIN?
HERBERT, I OWE MY LOYALTY TO THE KEEPER. HE'S WORKED LIKE CRAZY TO GET THE MONEY TOGETHER, AND IT WASN'T SO YOU COULD JUST RUN OFF WITH HER.
WELL, THAT'S JUST TOO BAD. I'M SORRY, MARVIN.
HERBERT! STOP PLAYING THE FOOL!!
BUT I'M NOT PLAYING THE FOOL! THE KEEPER AGREES. HE THINKS IT'S A GREAT IDEA.
LIAR!!!
AND YOU GET BACK UPSTAIRS!! I DON'T WANNA HIT A GIRL!
ELYACIN! YOU SEE THAT FAT ONE THERE? ATTACK!!!
AHHHHHH!!
TCHAK
GRRRR...
AND TO SAY I'VE BEEN BUSTING MY BUTT FOR DAYS TO PULL OFF THIS DAMNED FARCE.
ISIS, GO ON AHEAD. I'LL TAKE CARE OF HIM.

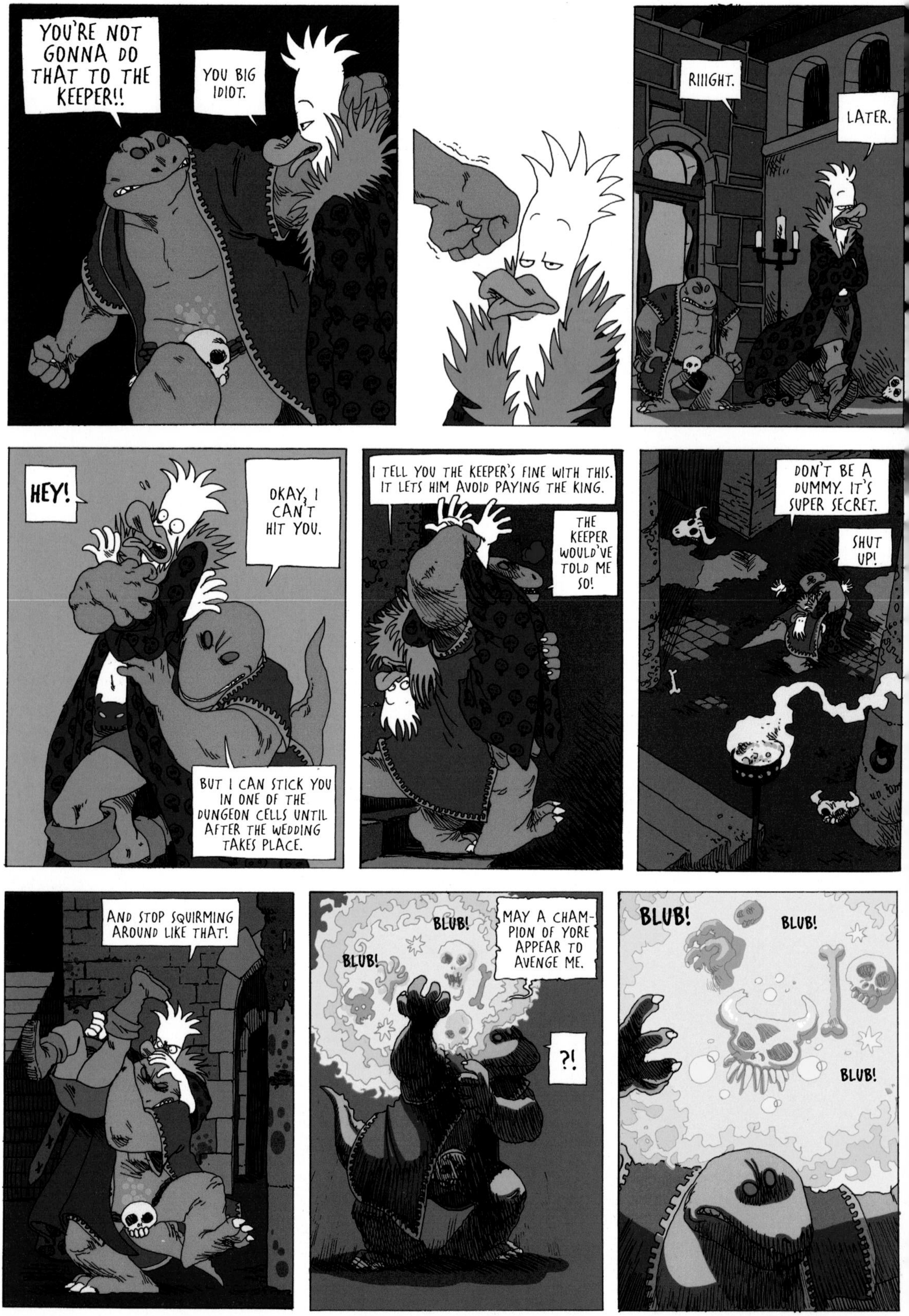

YOU'RE NOT GONNA DO THAT TO THE KEEPER!!
YOU BIG IDIOT.
RIIIGHT.
LATER.
HEY!
OKAY, I CAN'T HIT YOU.
BUT I CAN STICK YOU IN ONE OF THE DUNGEON CELLS UNTIL AFTER THE WEDDING TAKES PLACE.
I TELL YOU THE KEEPER'S FINE WITH THIS. IT LETS HIM AVOID PAYING THE KING.
THE KEEPER WOULD'VE TOLD ME SO!
DON'T BE A DUMMY. IT'S SUPER SECRET.
SHUT UP!
AND STOP SQUIRMING AROUND LIKE THAT!
BLUB!
BLUB!
MAY A CHAMPION OF YORE APPEAR TO AVENGE ME.
?!
BLUB!
BLUB!
BLUB!

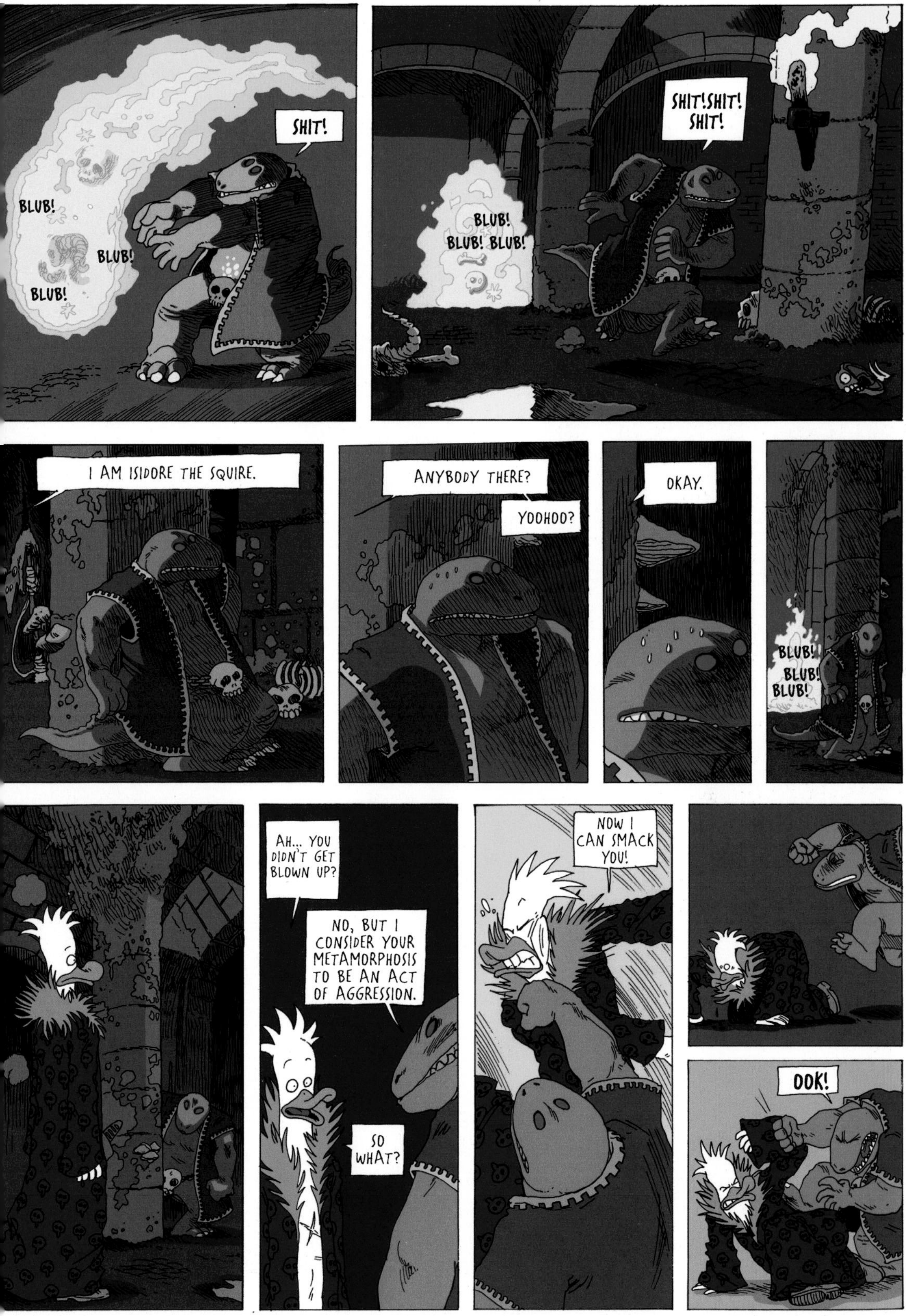
SHIT!
BLUB!
BLUB!
BLUB!
SHIT!SHIT! SHIT!
BLUB! BLUB! BLUB!
I AM ISIDORE THE SQUIRE.
ANYBODY THERE?
YOOHOO?
OKAY.
BLUB! BLUB! BLUB!
AH... YOU DIDN'T GET BLOWN UP?
NO, BUT I CONSIDER YOUR METAMORPHOSIS TO BE AN ACT OF AGGRESSION.
SO WHAT?
NOW I CAN SMACK YOU!
OOK!

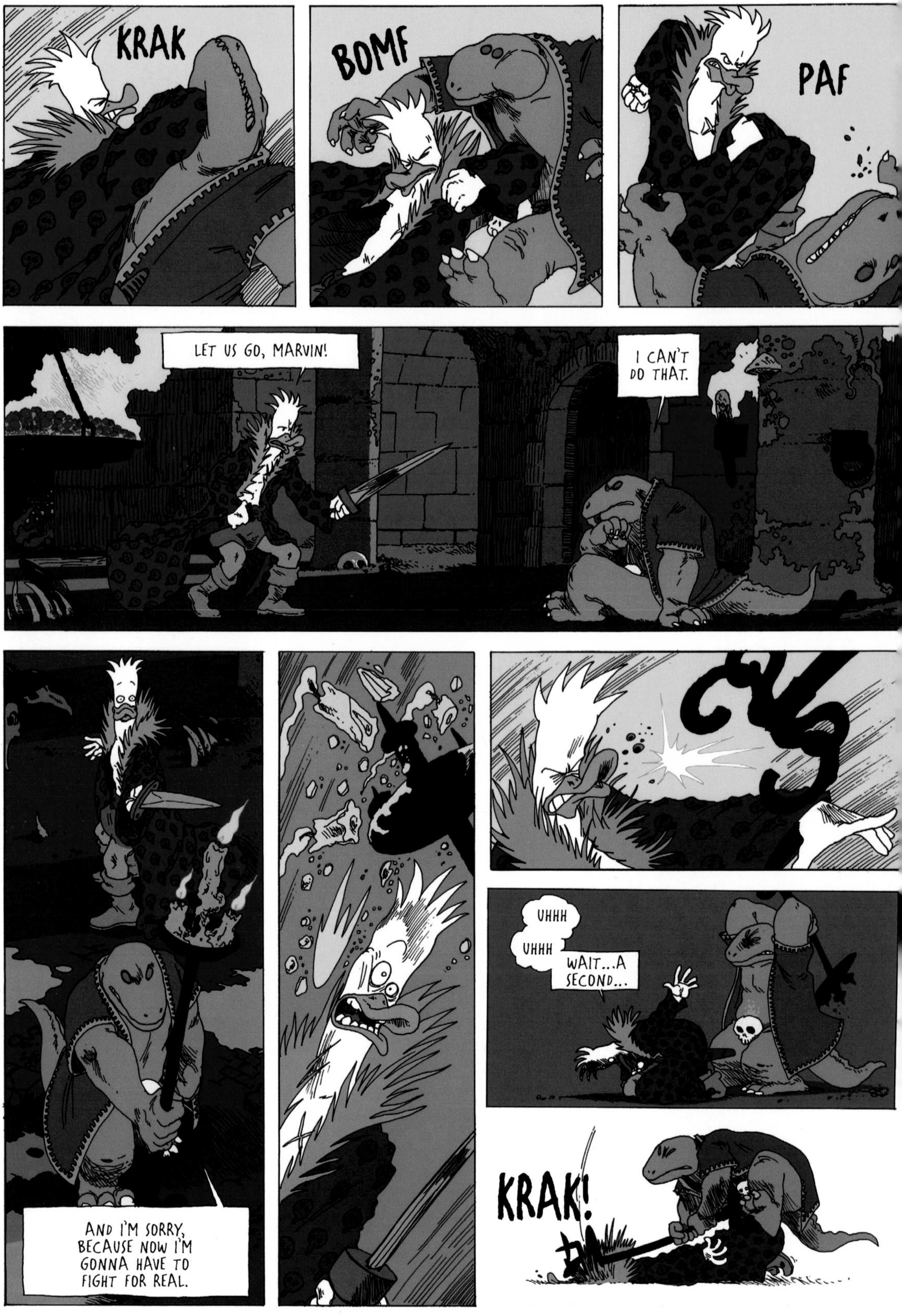
KRAK
BOMF
PAF
LET US GO, MARVIN!
I CAN'T DO THAT.
AND I'M SORRY, BECAUSE NOW I'M GONNA HAVE TO FIGHT FOR REAL.
UHHH
UHHH
WAIT...A SECOND...
KRAK!

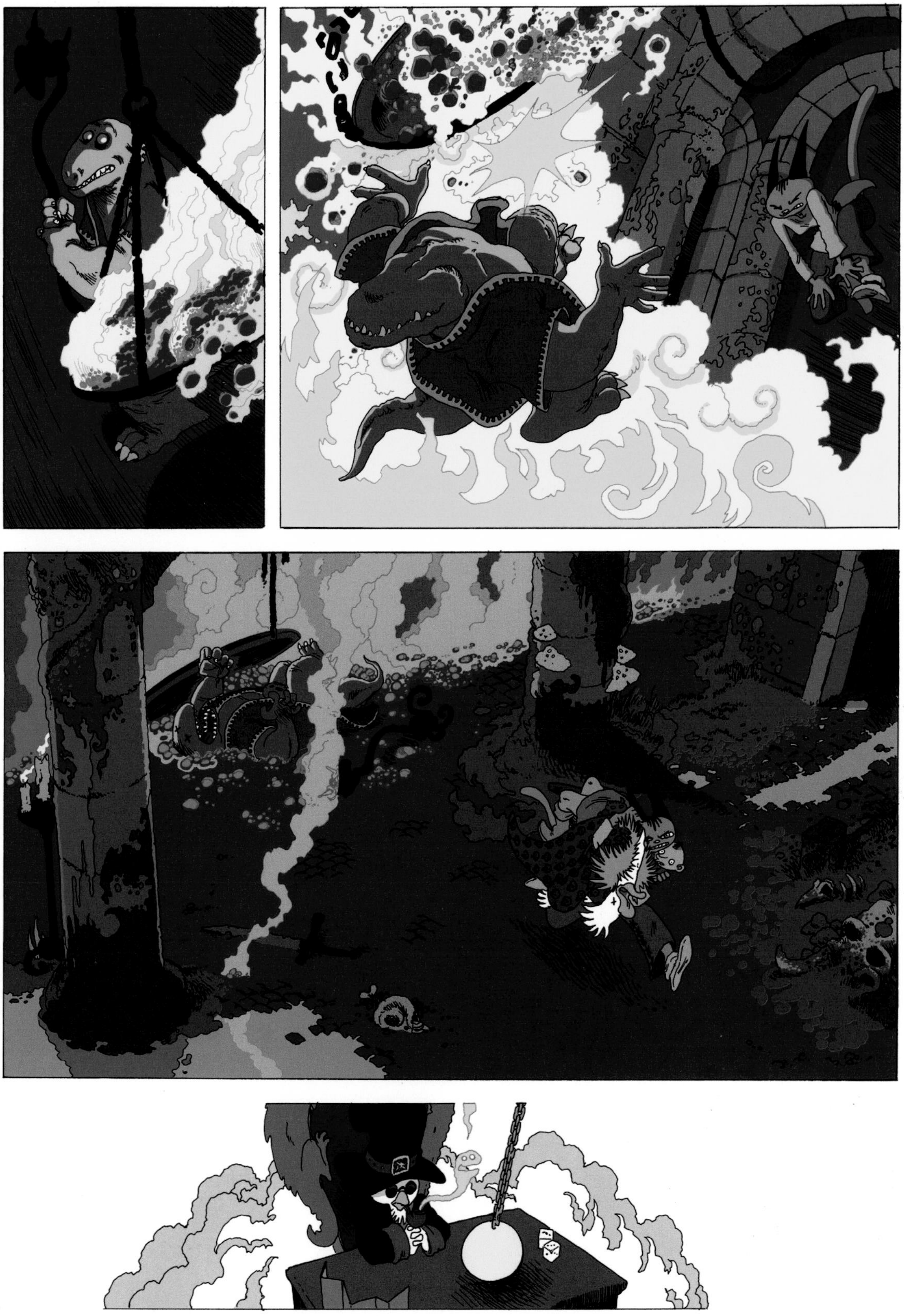

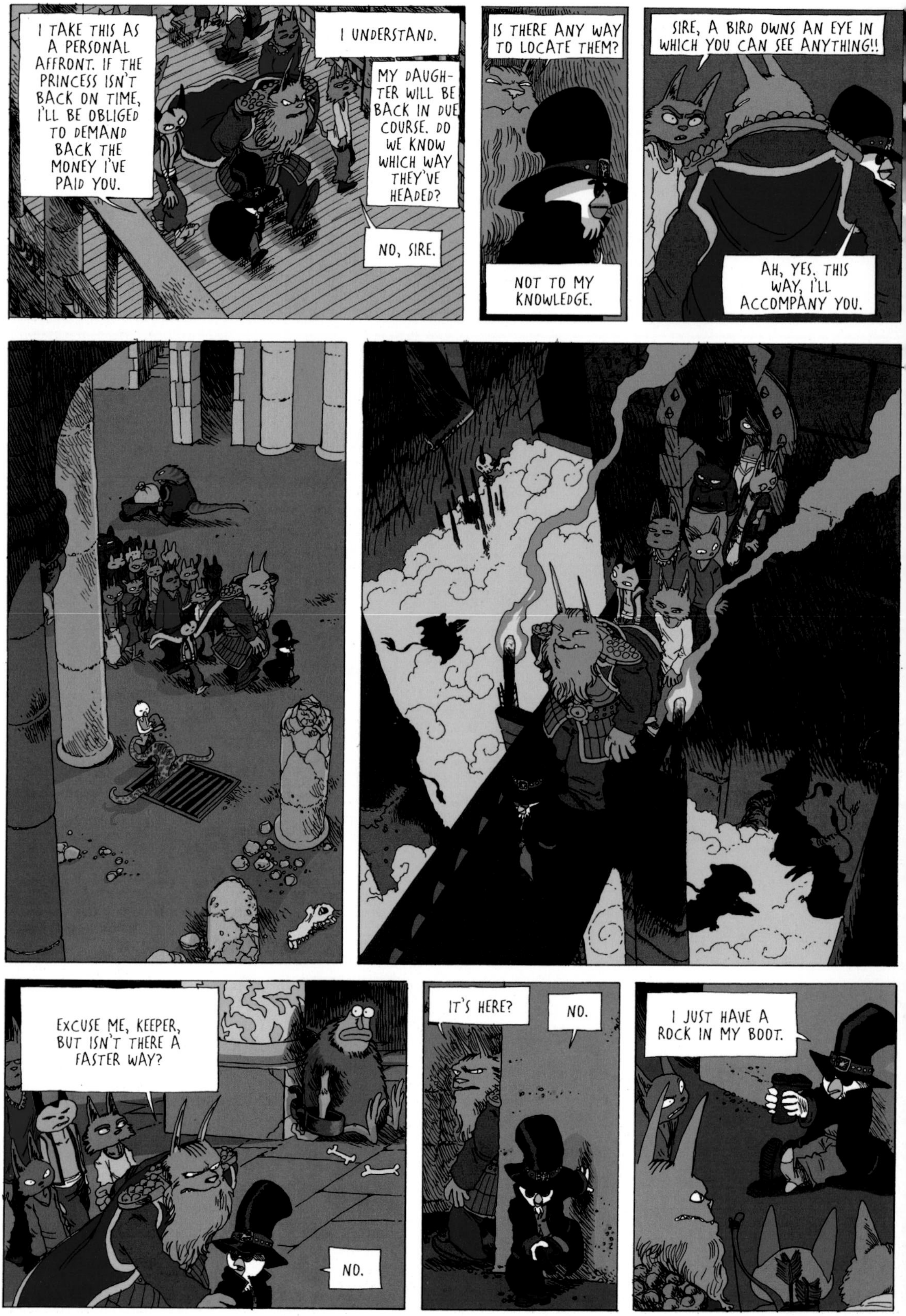
I TAKE THIS AS A PERSONAL AFFRONT. IF THE PRINCESS ISN'T BACK ON TIME, I'LL BE OBLIGED TO DEMAND BACK THE MONEY I'VE PAID YOU.
I UNDERSTAND.
MY DAUGHTER WILL BE BACK IN DUE COURSE. DO WE KNOW WHICH WAY THEY'VE HEADED?
NO, SIRE.
IS THERE ANY WAY TO LOCATE THEM?
NOT TO MY KNOWLEDGE.
SIRE, A BIRD OWNS AN EYE IN WHICH YOU CAN SEE ANYTHING!!
AH, YES. THIS WAY, I'LL ACCOMPANY YOU.
EXCUSE ME, KEEPER, BUT ISN'T THERE A FASTER WAY?
NO.
IT'S HERE?
NO.
I JUST HAVE A ROCK IN MY BOOT.

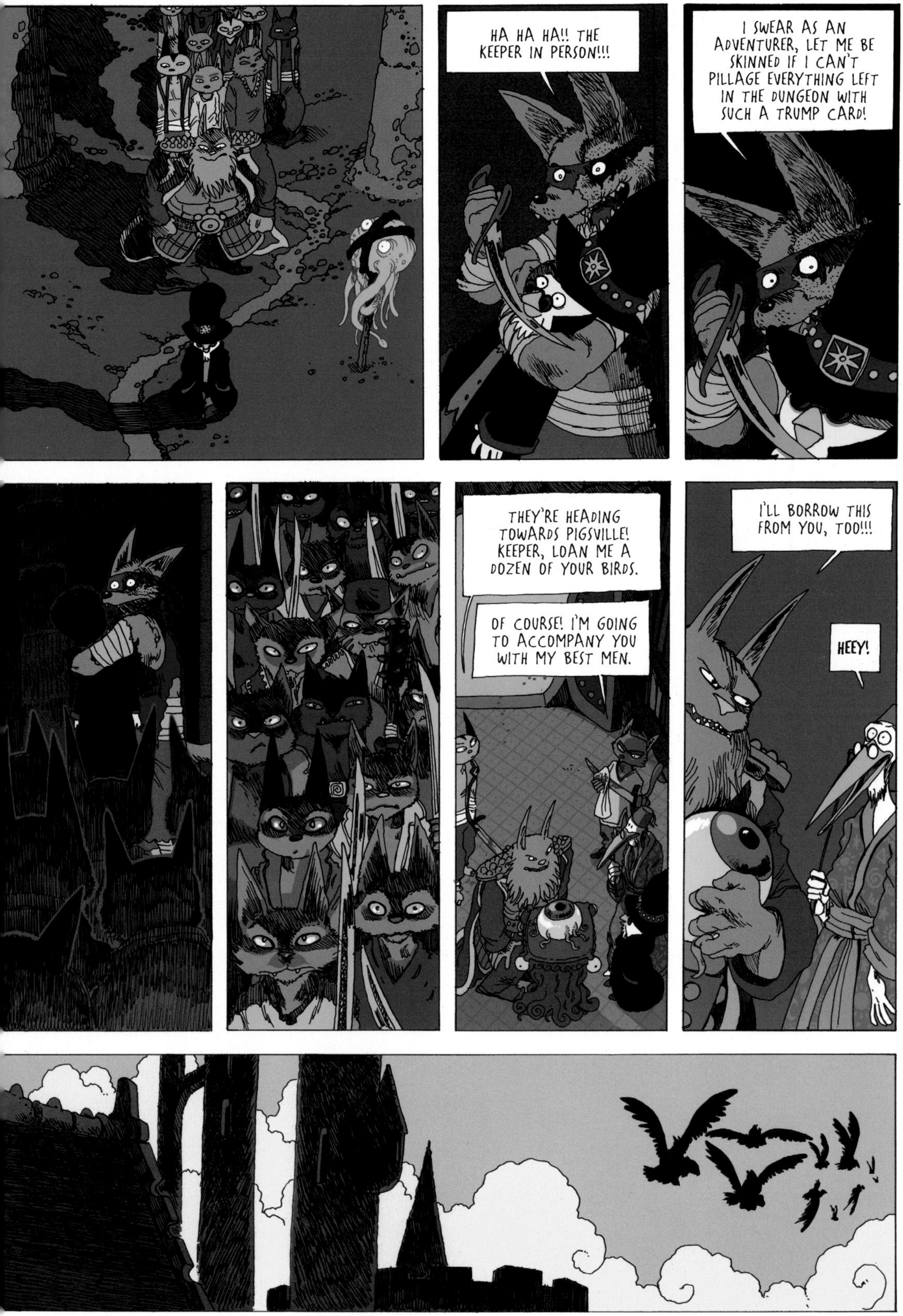
HA HA HA!! THE KEEPER IN PERSON!!!
I SWEAR AS AN ADVENTURER, LET ME BE SKINNED IF I CAN'T PILLAGE EVERYTHING LEFT IN THE DUNGEON WITH SUCH A TRUMP CARD!
THEY'RE HEADING TOWARDS PIGSVILLE! KEEPER, LOAN ME A DOZEN OF YOUR BIRDS.
OF COURSE! I'M GOING TO ACCOMPANY YOU WITH MY BEST MEN.
I'LL BORROW THIS FROM YOU, TOO!!!
HEEY!

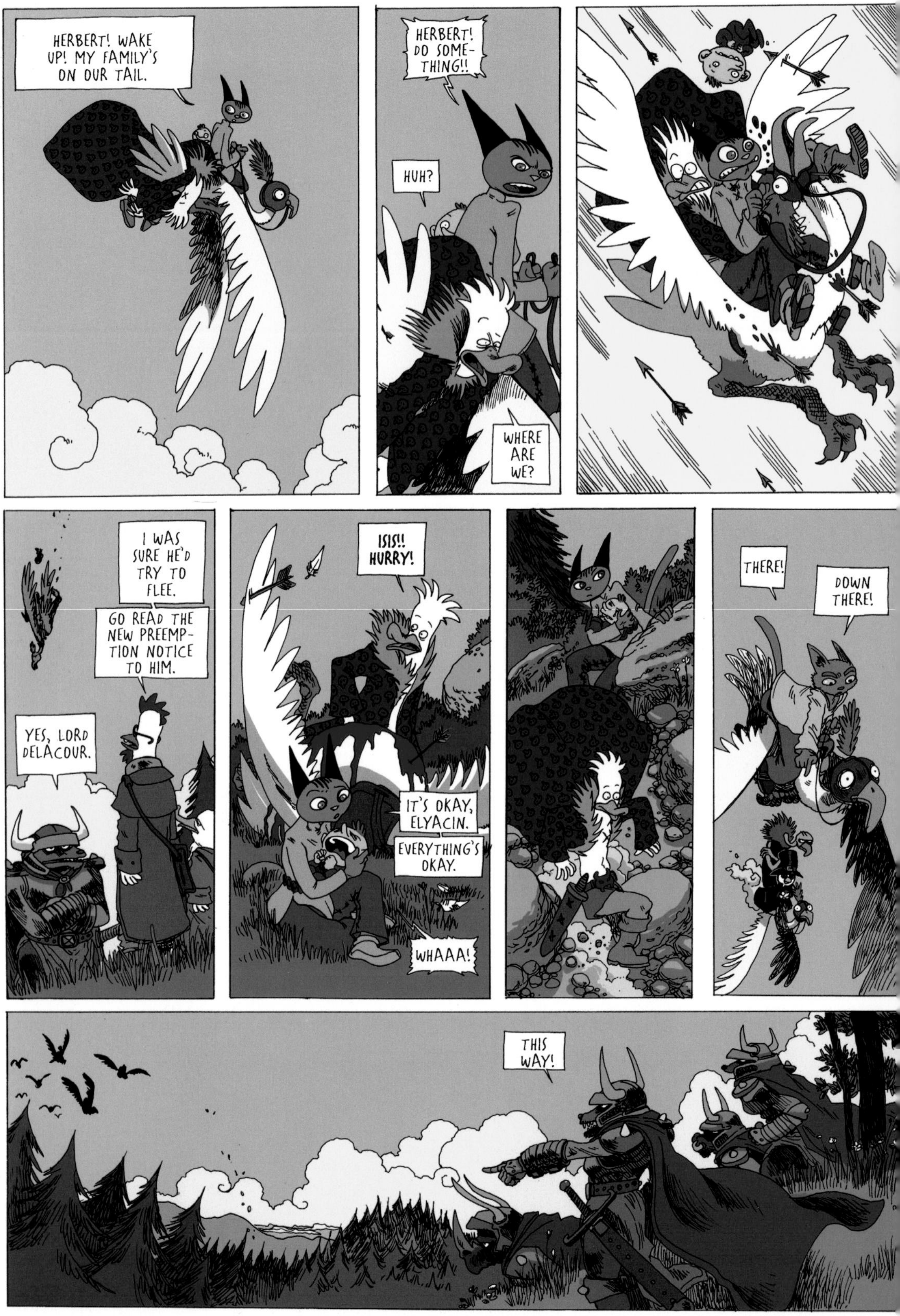
HERBERT! WAKE UP! MY FAMILY'S ON OUR TAIL.
HERBERT! DO SOME-THING!!
HUH?
WHERE ARE WE?
I WAS SURE HE'D TRY TO FLEE.
GO READ THE NEW PREEMP-TION NOTICE TO HIM.
YES, LORD DELACOUR.
ISIS!! HURRY!
IT'S OKAY, ELYACIN.
EVERYTHING'S OKAY.
WHAAA!
THERE!
DOWN THERE!
THIS WAY!

HORUS, COULD YOU DISCREET-LY PREVENT THEM FROM CATCHING THE FUGITIVES?

OH? BUT...

DO AS I TELL YOU!

?

WHAT'S WITH THIS FOG?

WHAAA!

WE'LL GO TRACK THEM ON THE GROUND!!!

WHAAAA!

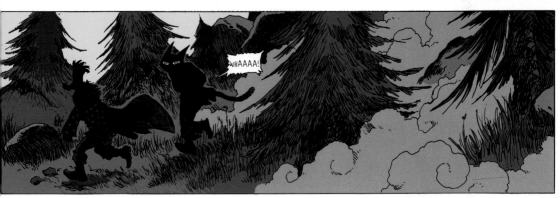

WHAAAA!

GIVE HIM TO ME!

WHAAAA!

NO! YOU!! GIMME THAT BABY!!

WHAAAAA!

DON'T DO IT! TROLLS EAT BABIES!

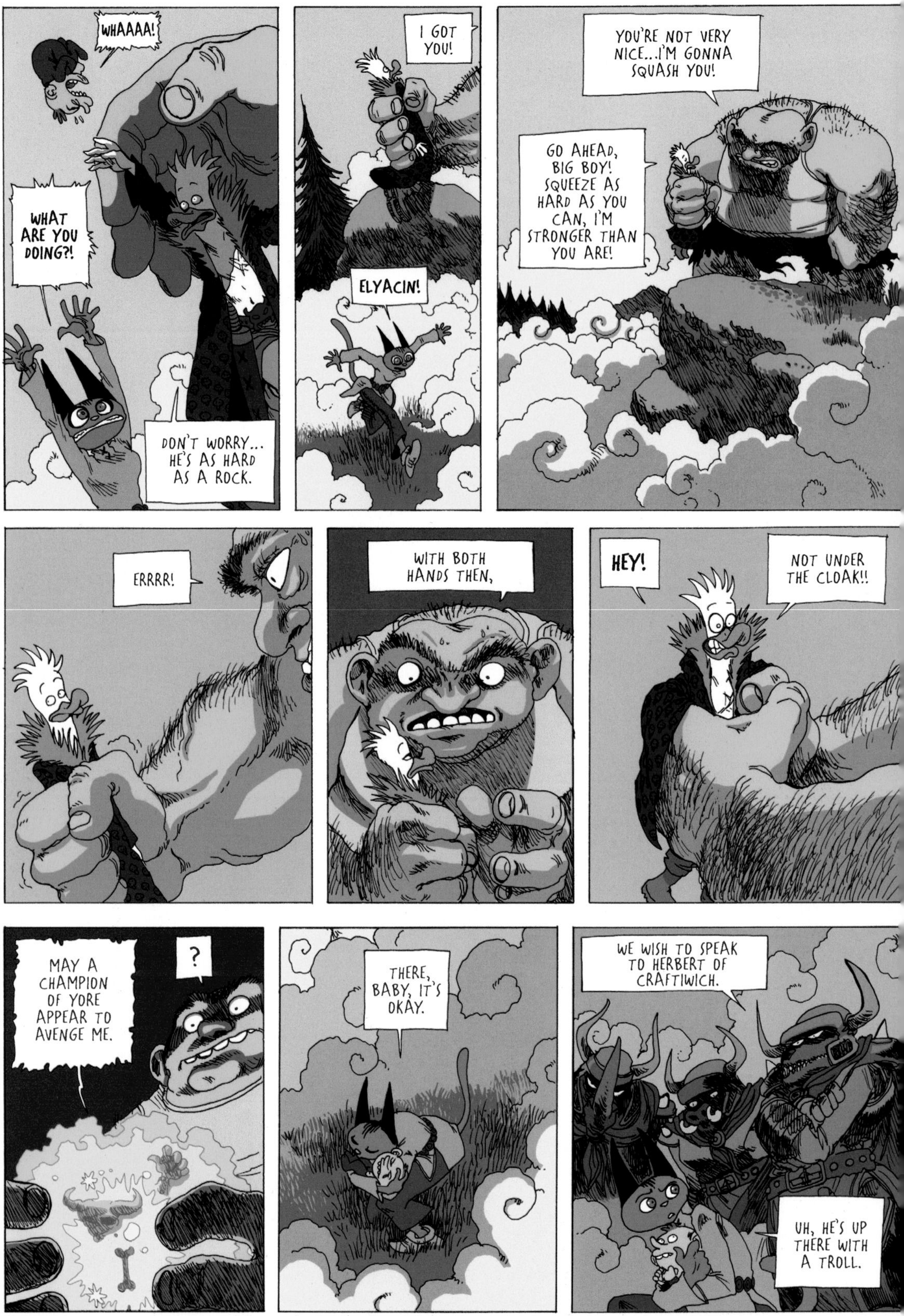

WHAAAA!
WHAT ARE YOU DOING?!
DON'T WORRY... HE'S AS HARD AS A ROCK.
I GOT YOU!
ELYACIN!
YOU'RE NOT VERY NICE...I'M GONNA SQUASH YOU!
GO AHEAD, BIG BOY! SQUEEZE AS HARD AS YOU CAN, I'M STRONGER THAN YOU ARE!
ERRRR!
WITH BOTH HANDS THEN,
HEY!
NOT UNDER THE CLOAK!!
MAY A CHAMPION OF YORE APPEAR TO AVENGE ME.
?
THERE, BABY, IT'S OKAY.
WE WISH TO SPEAK TO HERBERT OF CRAFTIWICH.
UH, HE'S UP THERE WITH A TROLL.

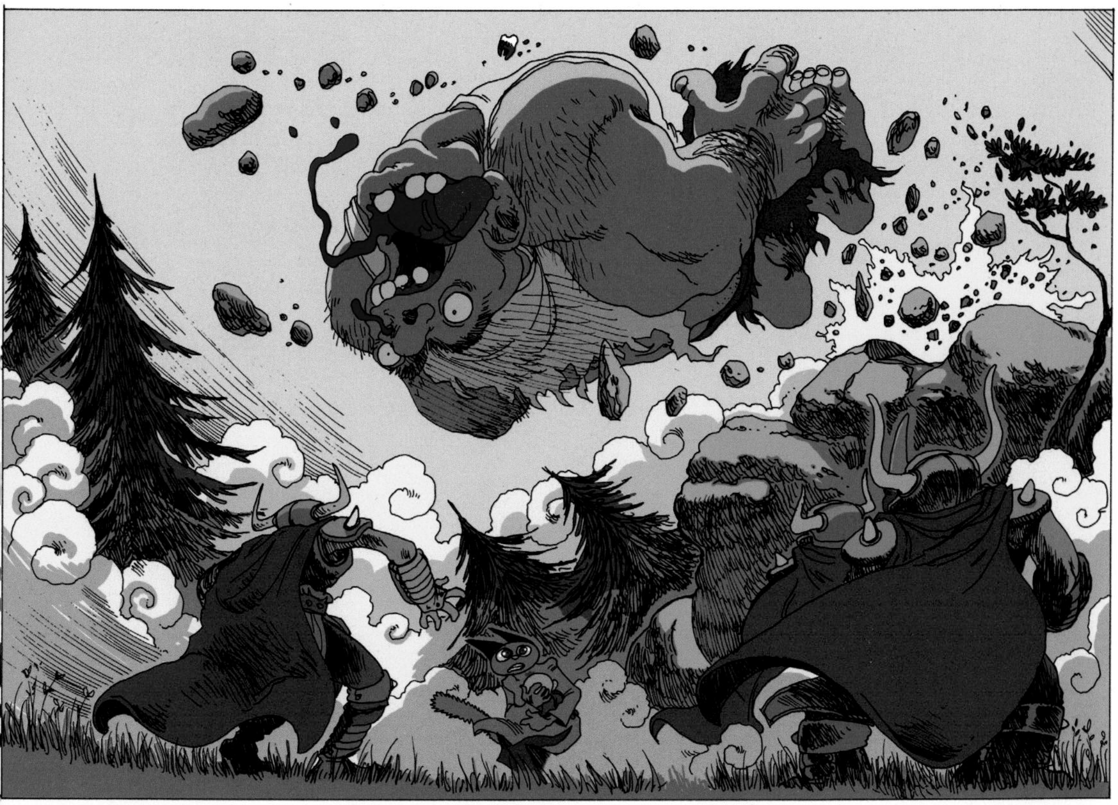

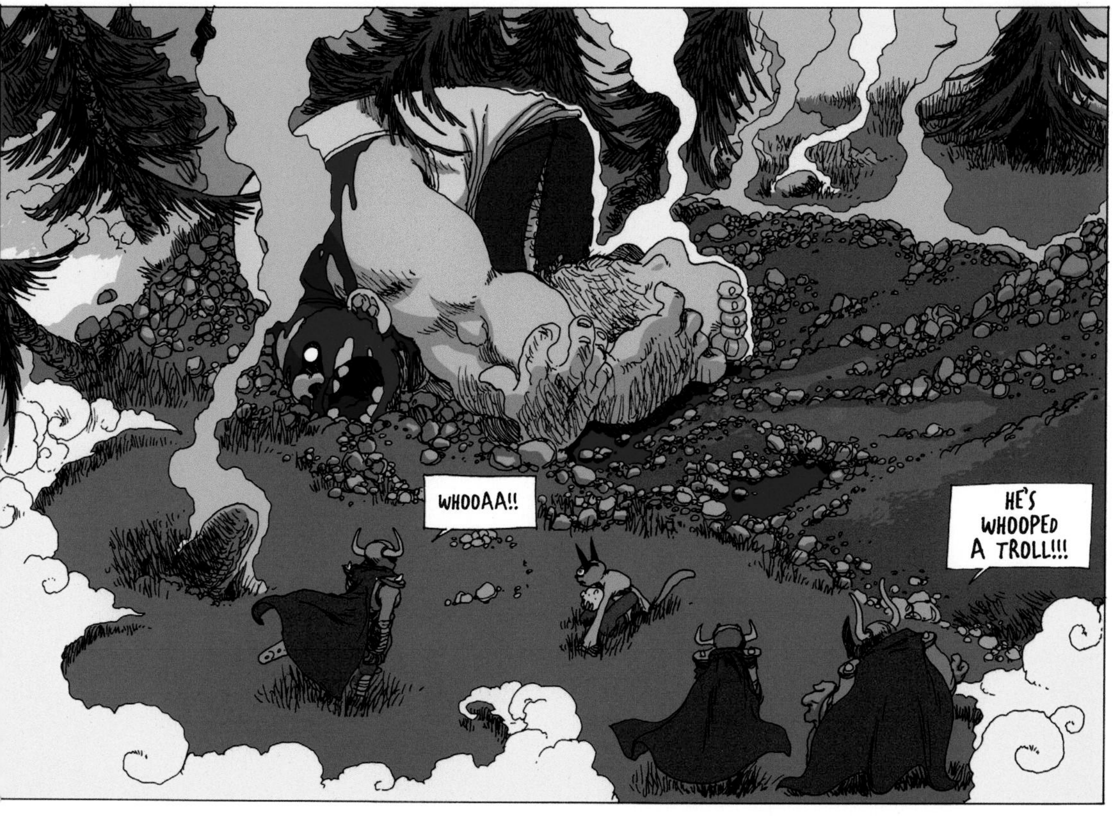
WHOOAA!!
HE'S WHOOPED A TROLL!!!

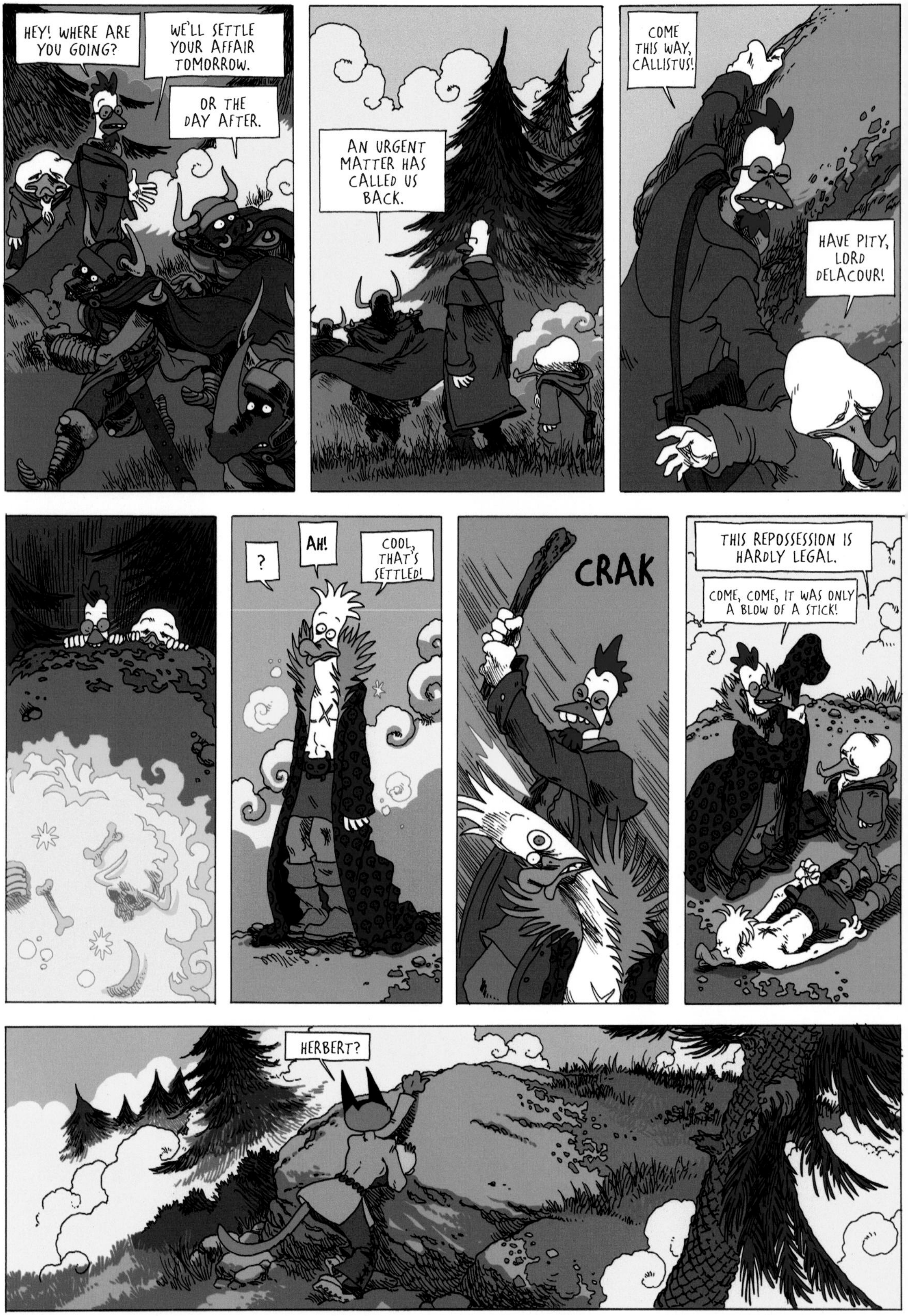
HEY! WHERE ARE YOU GOING?
WE'LL SETTLE YOUR AFFAIR TOMORROW.
OR THE DAY AFTER.
AN URGENT MATTER HAS CALLED US BACK.
COME THIS WAY, CALLISTUS!
HAVE PITY, LORD DELACOUR!
?
AH!
COOL, THAT'S SETTLED!
CRAK
THIS REPOSSESSION IS HARDLY LEGAL.
COME, COME, IT WAS ONLY A BLOW OF A STICK!
HERBERT?

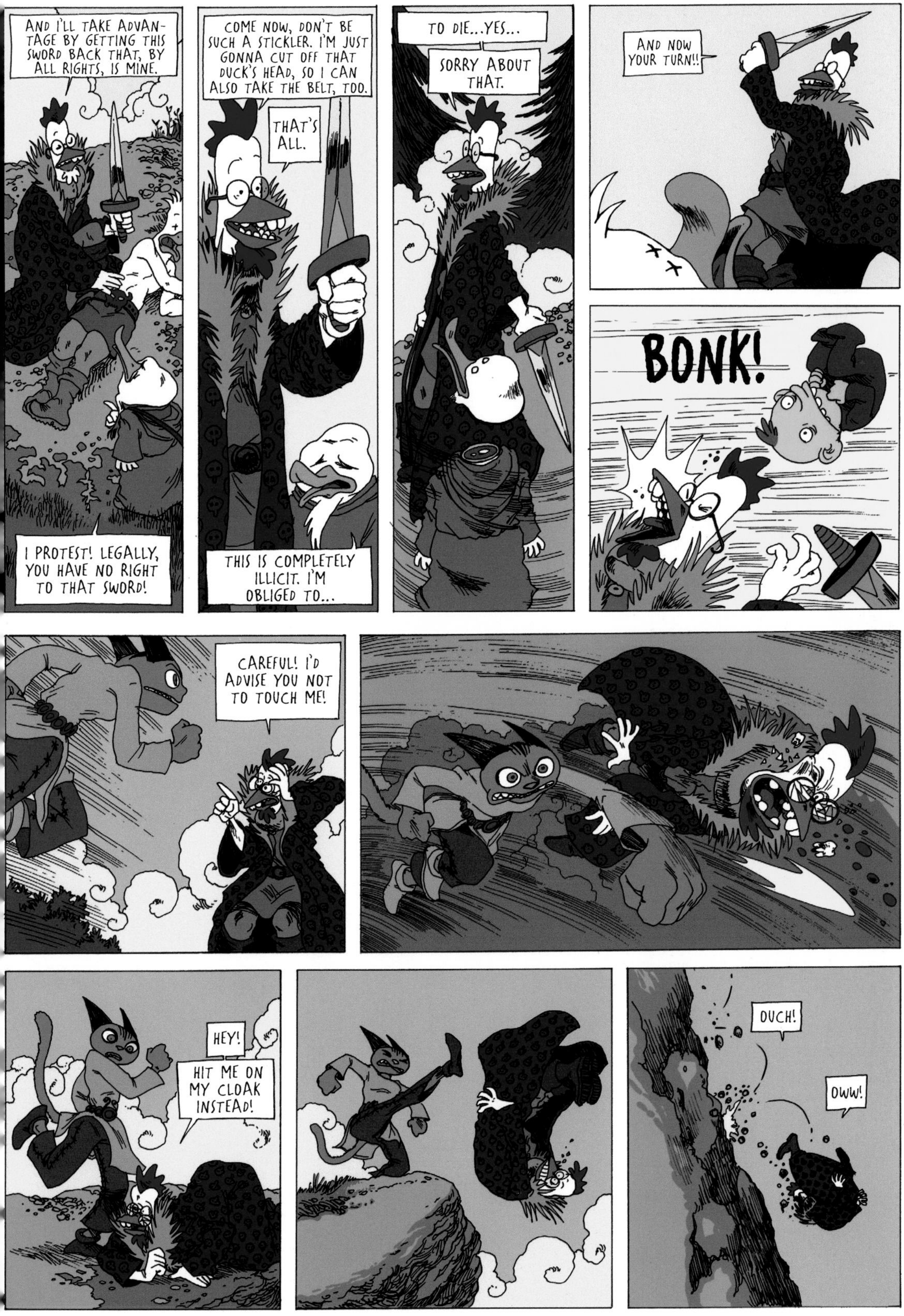
AND I'LL TAKE ADVANTAGE BY GETTING THIS SWORD BACK THAT, BY ALL RIGHTS, IS MINE.
I PROTEST! LEGALLY, YOU HAVE NO RIGHT TO THAT SWORD!
COME NOW, DON'T BE SUCH A STICKLER. I'M JUST GONNA CUT OFF THAT DUCK'S HEAD, SO I CAN ALSO TAKE THE BELT, TOO.
THAT'S ALL.
THIS IS COMPLETELY ILLICIT. I'M OBLIGED TO...
TO DIE...YES...
SORRY ABOUT THAT.
AND NOW YOUR TURN!!
BONK!
CAREFUL! I'D ADVISE YOU NOT TO TOUCH ME!
HEY!
HIT ME ON MY CLOAK INSTEAD!
OUCH!
OWW!

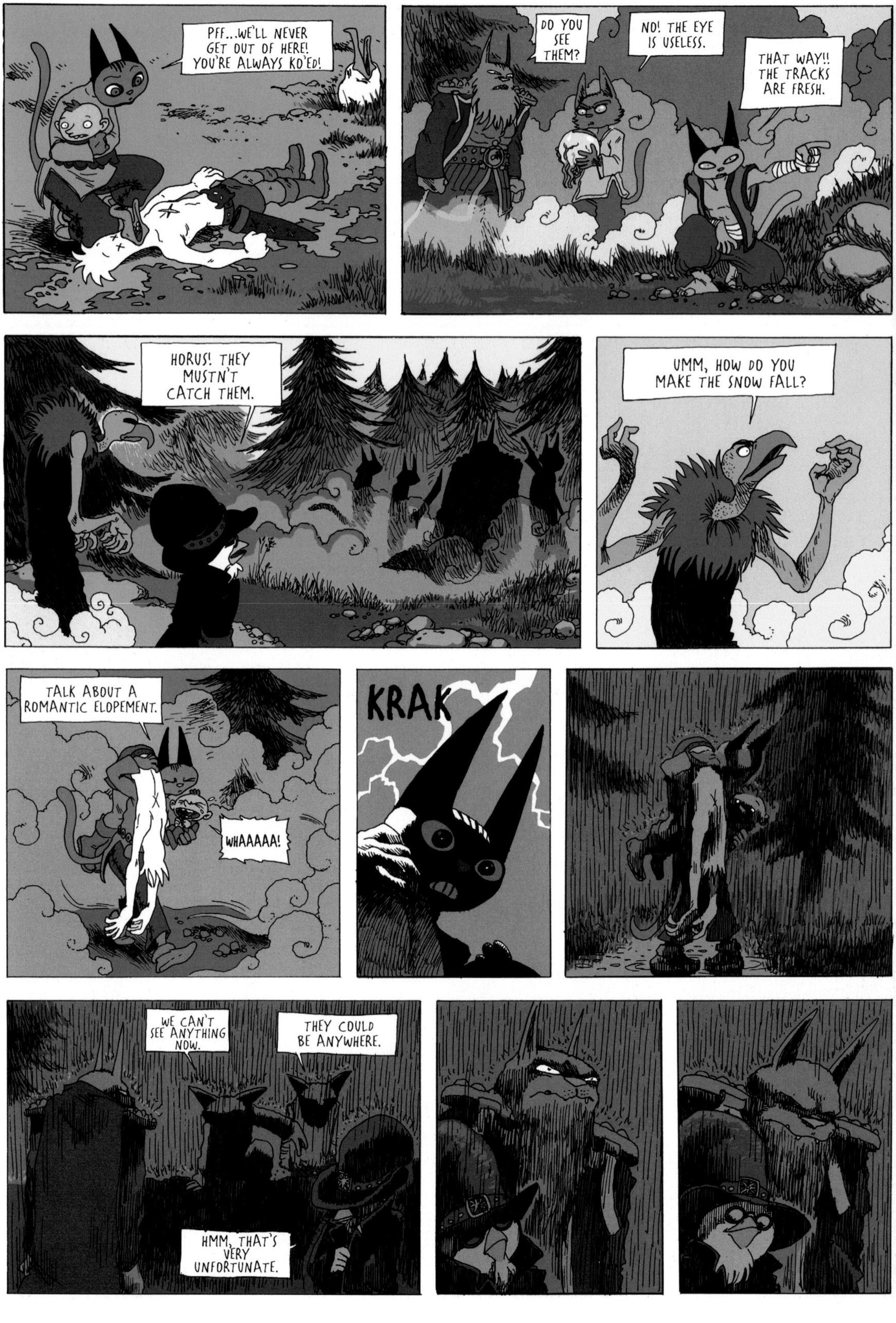
PFF...WE'LL NEVER GET OUT OF HERE! YOU'RE ALWAYS KO'ED!
DO YOU SEE THEM?
NO! THE EYE IS USELESS.
THAT WAY!! THE TRACKS ARE FRESH.
HORUS! THEY MUSTN'T CATCH THEM.
UMM, HOW DO YOU MAKE THE SNOW FALL?
TALK ABOUT A ROMANTIC ELOPEMENT.
WHAAAAA!
KRAK
WE CAN'T SEE ANYTHING NOW.
THEY COULD BE ANYWHERE.
HMM, THAT'S VERY UNFORTUNATE.

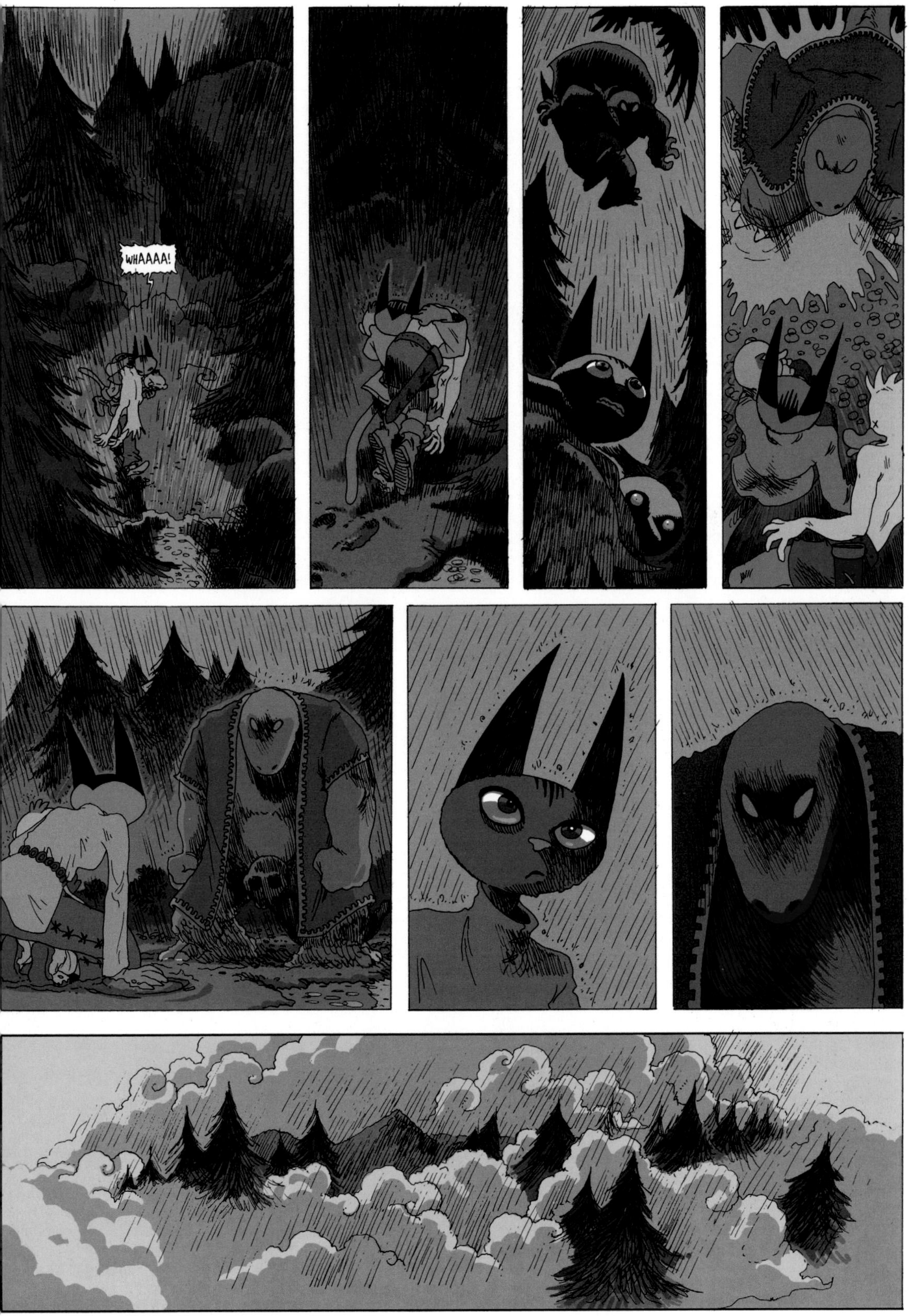
WHAAAA!

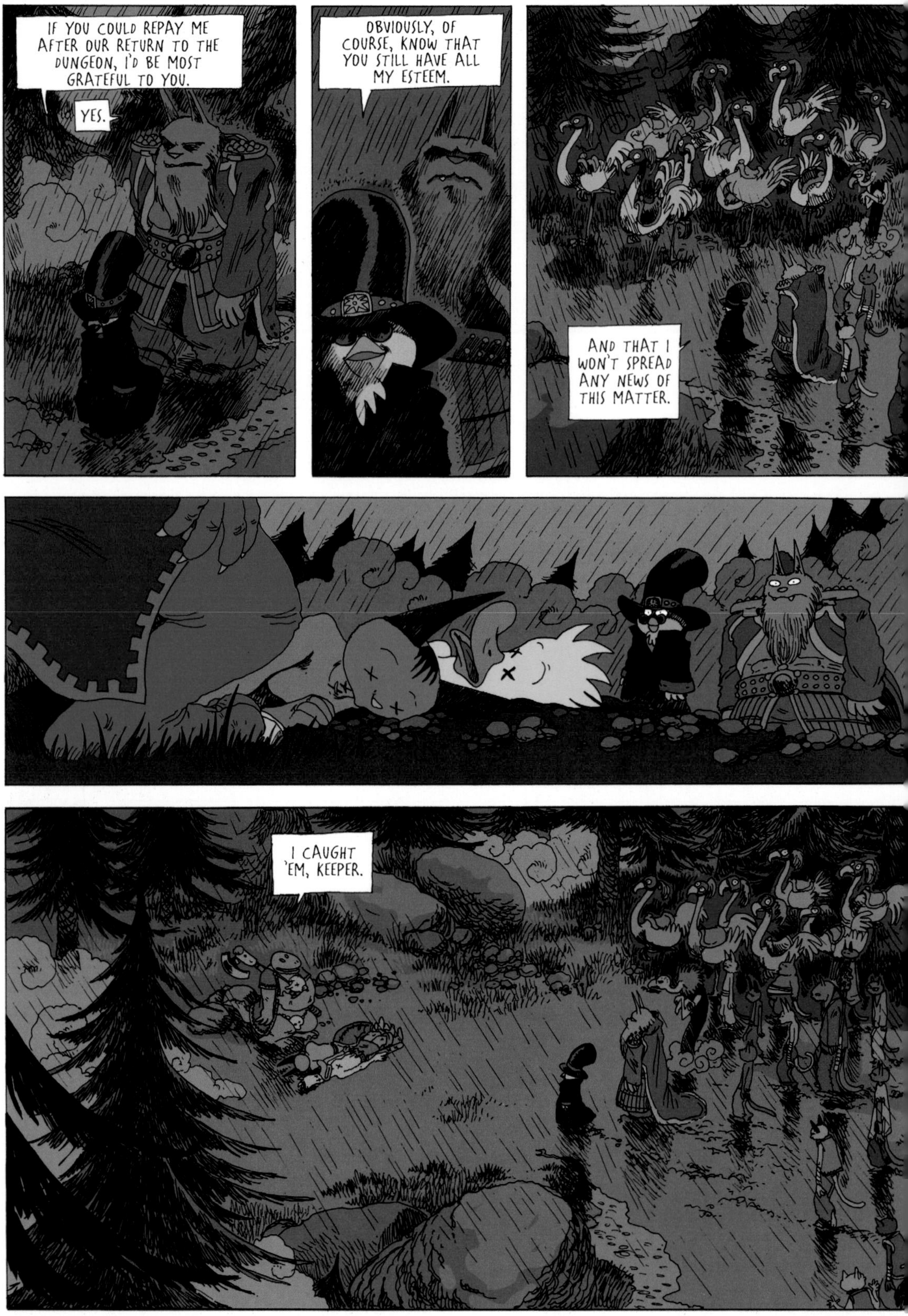
IF YOU COULD REPAY ME AFTER OUR RETURN TO THE DUNGEON, I'D BE MOST GRATEFUL TO YOU.
YES.
OBVIOUSLY, OF COURSE, KNOW THAT YOU STILL HAVE ALL MY ESTEEM.
AND THAT I WON'T SPREAD ANY NEWS OF THIS MATTER.
I CAUGHT 'EM, KEEPER.

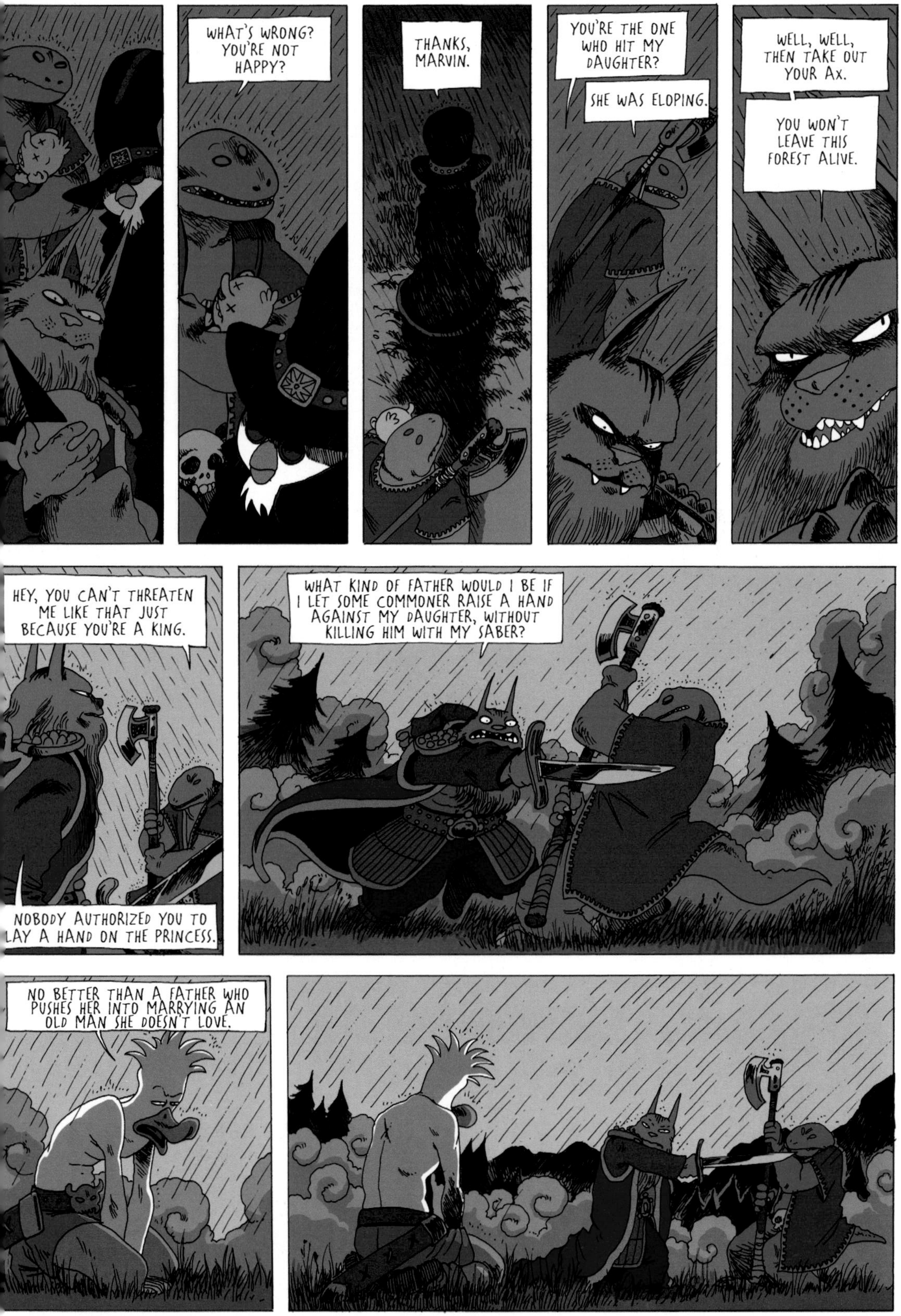

WHAT'S WRONG? YOU'RE NOT HAPPY?
THANKS, MARVIN.
YOU'RE THE ONE WHO HIT MY DAUGHTER?
SHE WAS ELOPING.
WELL, WELL, THEN TAKE OUT YOUR AX.
YOU WON'T LEAVE THIS FOREST ALIVE.
HEY, YOU CAN'T THREATEN ME LIKE THAT JUST BECAUSE YOU'RE A KING.
NOBODY AUTHORIZED YOU TO LAY A HAND ON THE PRINCESS.
WHAT KIND OF FATHER WOULD I BE IF I LET SOME COMMONER RAISE A HAND AGAINST MY DAUGHTER, WITHOUT KILLING HIM WITH MY SABER?
NO BETTER THAN A FATHER WHO PUSHES HER INTO MARRYING AN OLD MAN SHE DOESN'T LOVE.

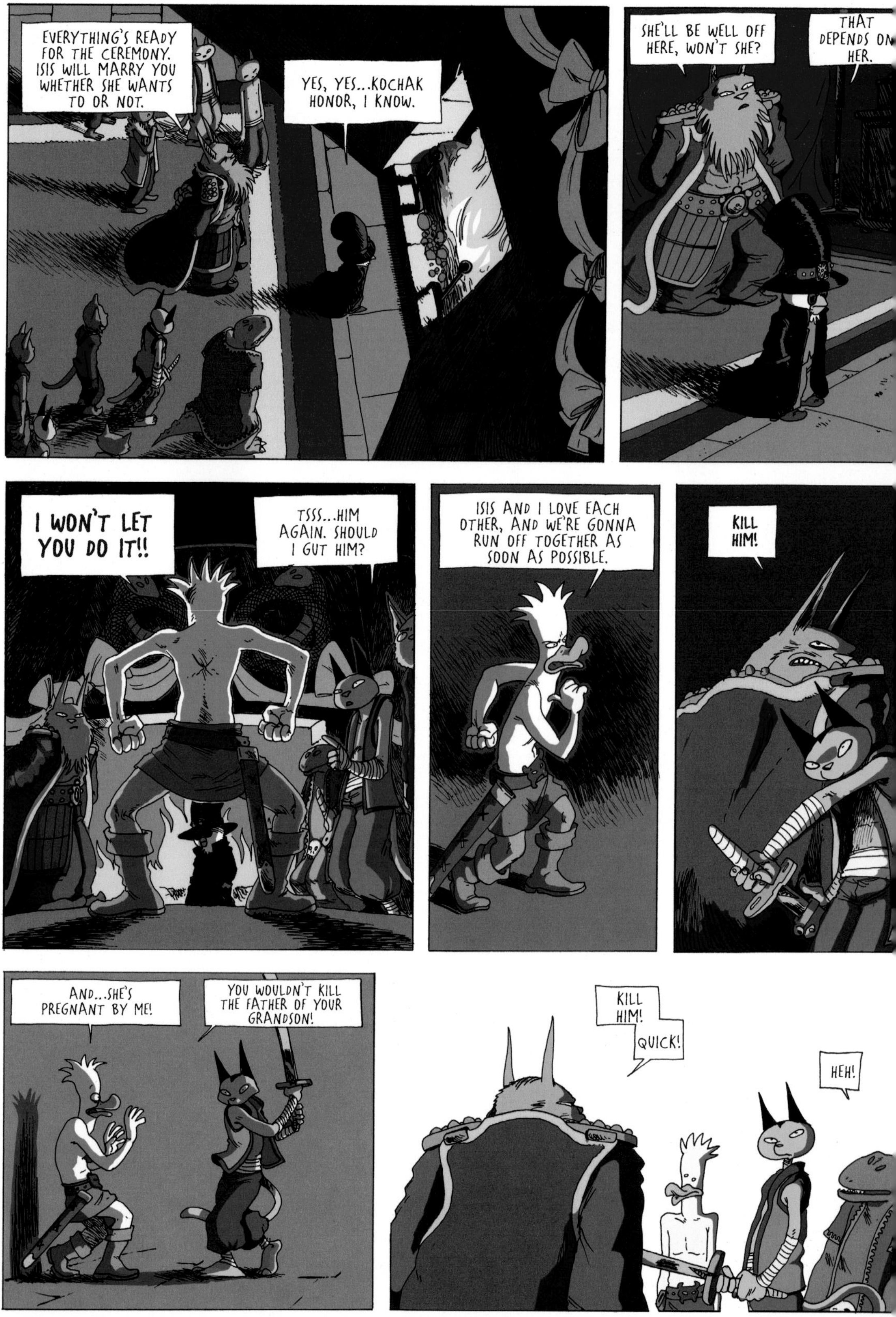
EVERYTHING'S READY FOR THE CEREMONY. ISIS WILL MARRY YOU WHETHER SHE WANTS TO OR NOT.
YES, YES...KOCHAK HONOR, I KNOW.
SHE'LL BE WELL OFF HERE, WON'T SHE?
THAT DEPENDS ON HER.
I WON'T LET YOU DO IT!!
TSSS...HIM AGAIN. SHOULD I GUT HIM?
ISIS AND I LOVE EACH OTHER, AND WE'RE GONNA RUN OFF TOGETHER AS SOON AS POSSIBLE.
KILL HIM!
AND...SHE'S PREGNANT BY ME!
YOU WOULDN'T KILL THE FATHER OF YOUR GRANDSON!
KILL HIM!
QUICK!
HEH!

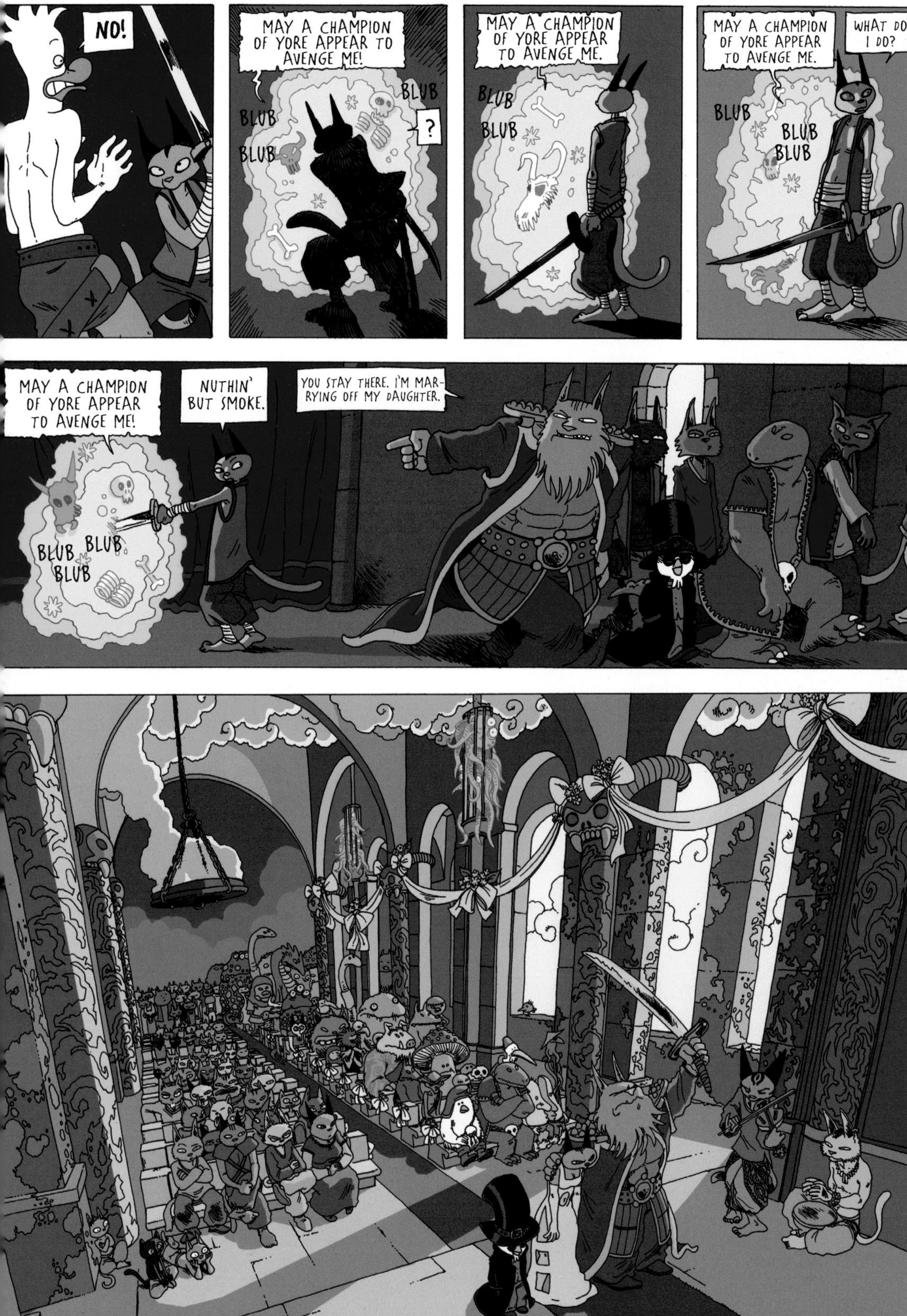
NO!
MAY A CHAMPION OF YORE APPEAR TO AVENGE ME!
BLUB
BLUB
BLUB
?
MAY A CHAMPION OF YORE APPEAR TO AVENGE ME.
BLUB
BLUB
MAY A CHAMPION OF YORE APPEAR TO AVENGE ME.
WHAT DO I DO?
BLUB
BLUB
BLUB
MAY A CHAMPION OF YORE APPEAR TO AVENGE ME!
BLUB BLUB
BLUB
NUTHIN' BUT SMOKE.
YOU STAY THERE. I'M MARRYING OFF MY DAUGHTER.

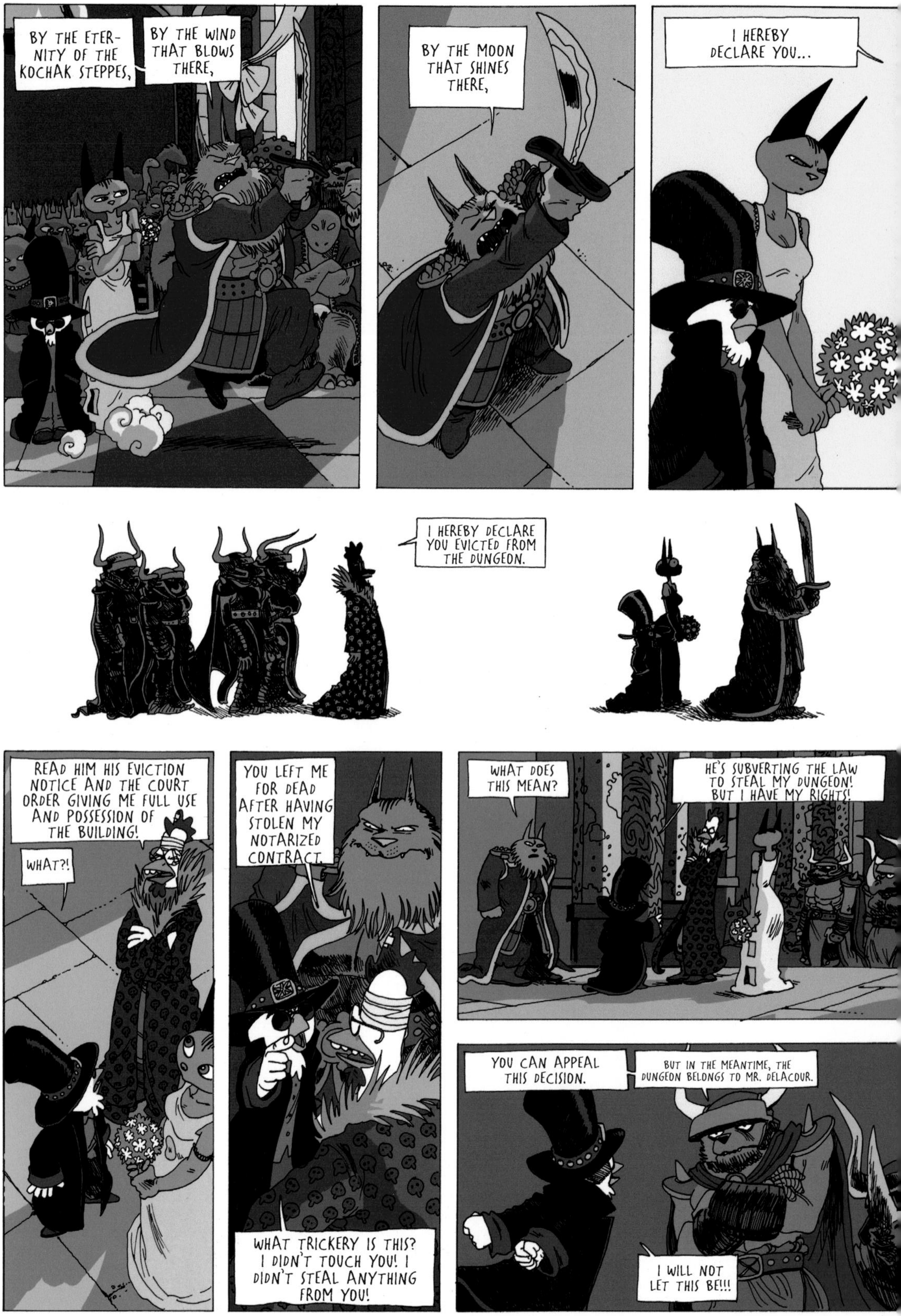
BY THE ETERNITY OF THE KOCHAK STEPPES,
BY THE WIND THAT BLOWS THERE,
BY THE MOON THAT SHINES THERE,
I HEREBY DECLARE YOU...
I HEREBY DECLARE YOU EVICTED FROM THE DUNGEON.
READ HIM HIS EVICTION NOTICE AND THE COURT ORDER GIVING ME FULL USE AND POSSESSION OF THE BUILDING!
WHAT?!
YOU LEFT ME FOR DEAD AFTER HAVING STOLEN MY NOTARIZED CONTRACT.
WHAT TRICKERY IS THIS? I DIDN'T TOUCH YOU! I DIDN'T STEAL ANYTHING FROM YOU!
WHAT DOES THIS MEAN?
HE'S SUBVERTING THE LAW TO STEAL MY DUNGEON! BUT I HAVE MY RIGHTS!
YOU CAN APPEAL THIS DECISION.
BUT IN THE MEANTIME, THE DUNGEON BELONGS TO MR. DELACOUR.
I WILL NOT LET THIS BE!!!

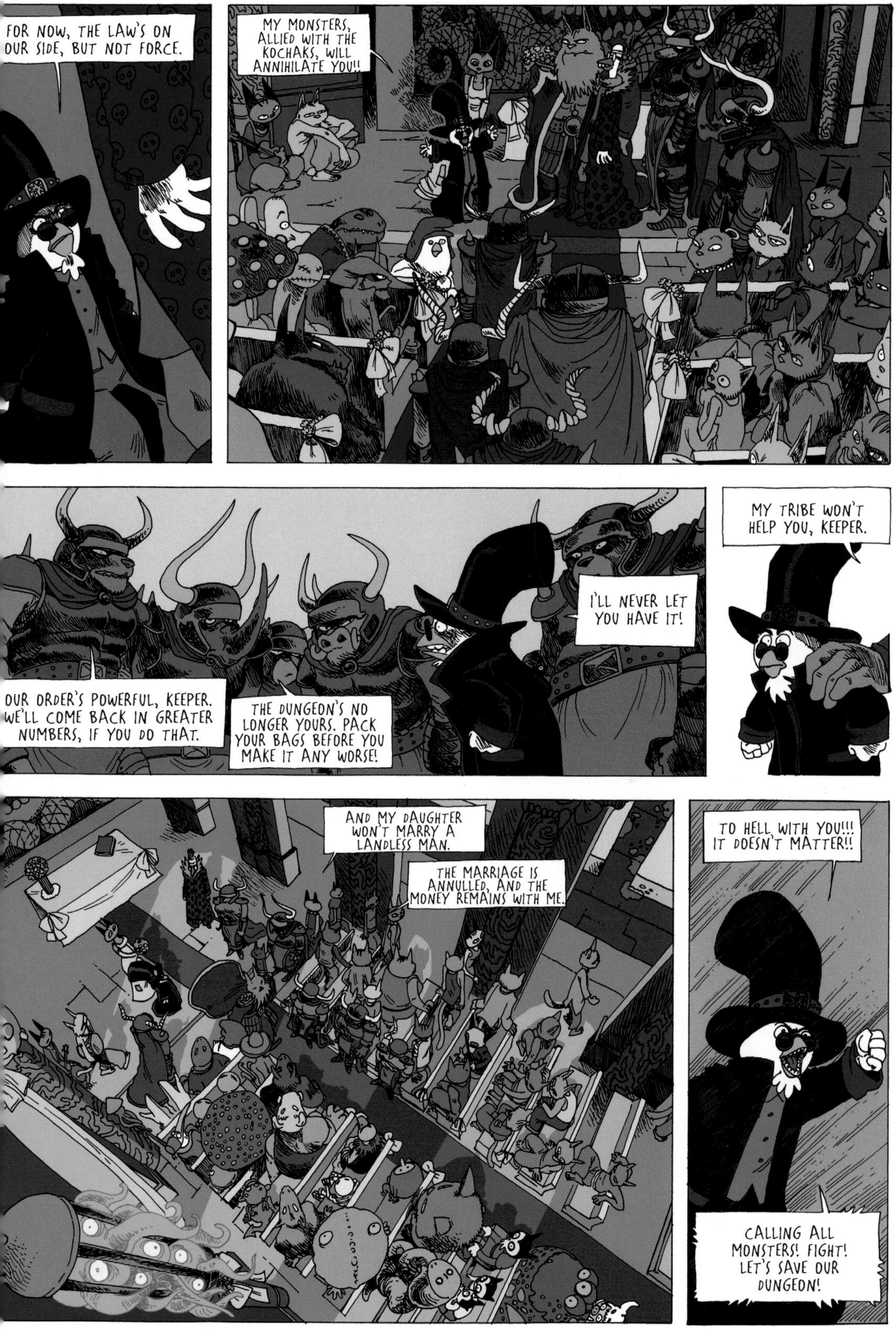

FOR NOW, THE LAW'S ON OUR SIDE, BUT NOT FORCE.
MY MONSTERS, ALLIED WITH THE KOCHAKS, WILL ANNIHILATE YOU!!
OUR ORDER'S POWERFUL, KEEPER. WE'LL COME BACK IN GREATER NUMBERS, IF YOU DO THAT.
THE DUNGEON'S NO LONGER YOURS. PACK YOUR BAGS BEFORE YOU MAKE IT ANY WORSE!
I'LL NEVER LET YOU HAVE IT!
MY TRIBE WON'T HELP YOU, KEEPER.
AND MY DAUGHTER WON'T MARRY A LANDLESS MAN.
THE MARRIAGE IS ANNULLED, AND THE MONEY REMAINS WITH ME.
TO HELL WITH YOU!!! IT DOESN'T MATTER!!
CALLING ALL MONSTERS! FIGHT! LET'S SAVE OUR DUNGEON!

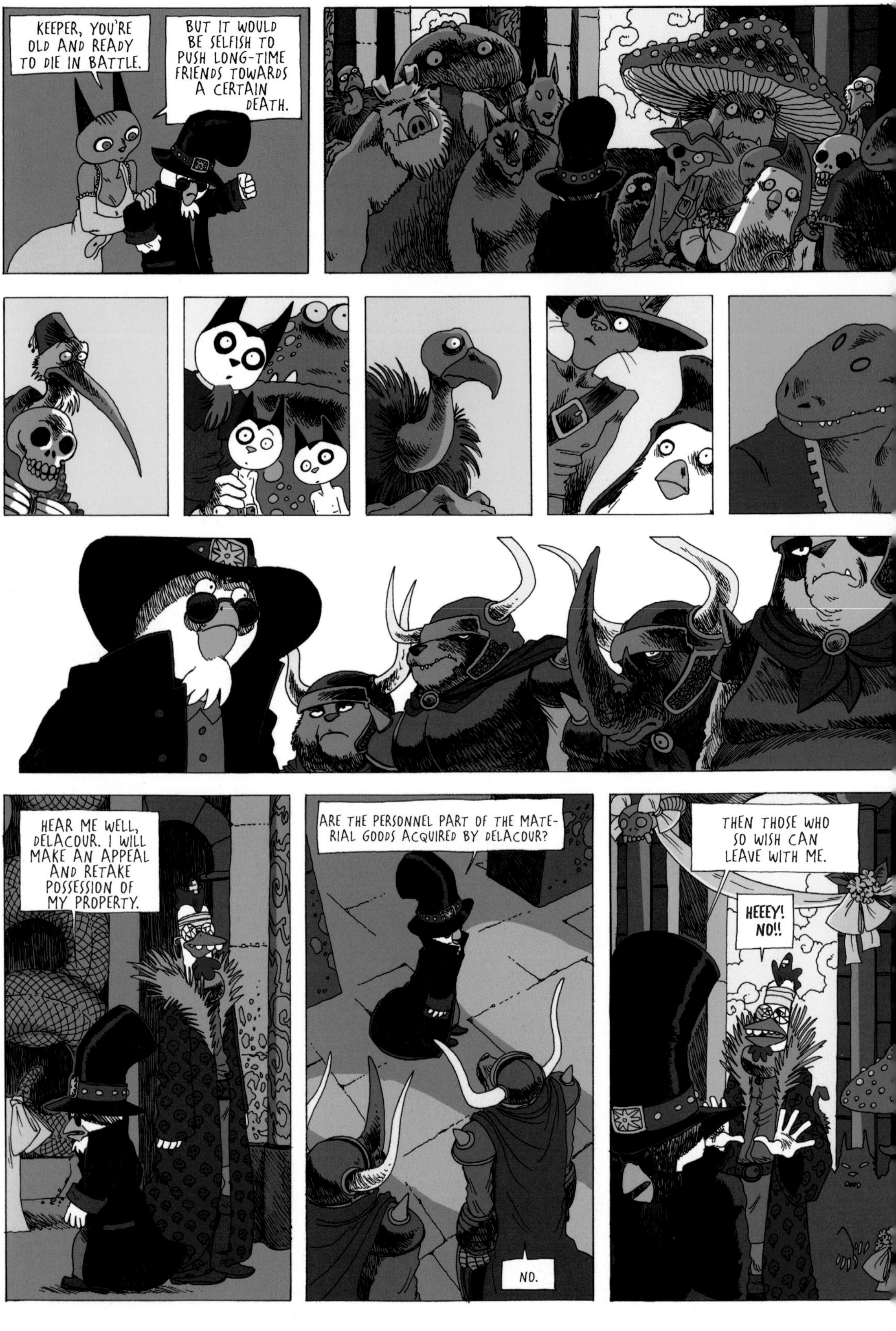
KEEPER, YOU'RE OLD AND READY TO DIE IN BATTLE.
BUT IT WOULD BE SELFISH TO PUSH LONG-TIME FRIENDS TOWARDS A CERTAIN DEATH.
HEAR ME WELL, DELACOUR. I WILL MAKE AN APPEAL AND RETAKE POSSESSION OF MY PROPERTY.
ARE THE PERSONNEL PART OF THE MATERIAL GOODS ACQUIRED BY DELACOUR?
NO.
THEN THOSE WHO SO WISH CAN LEAVE WITH ME.
HEEEY! NO!!

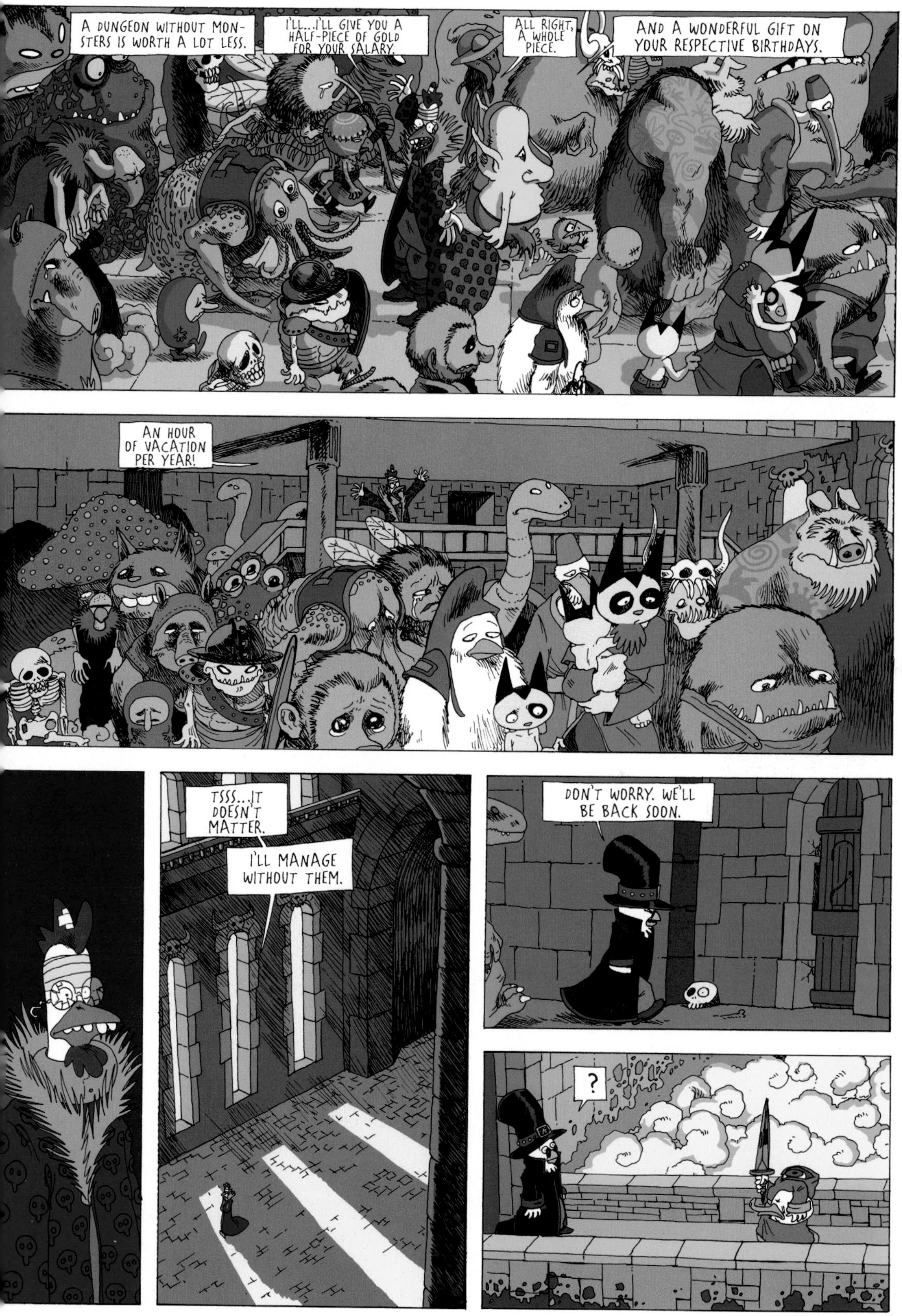
A DUNGEON WITHOUT MONSTERS IS WORTH A LOT LESS.
I'LL...I'LL GIVE YOU A HALF-PIECE OF GOLD FOR YOUR SALARY.
ALL RIGHT, A WHOLE PIECE.
AND A WONDERFUL GIFT ON YOUR RESPECTIVE BIRTHDAYS.
AN HOUR OF VACATION PER YEAR!
TSSS...IT DOESN'T MATTER.
I'LL MANAGE WITHOUT THEM.
DON'T WORRY. WE'LL BE BACK SOON.
?

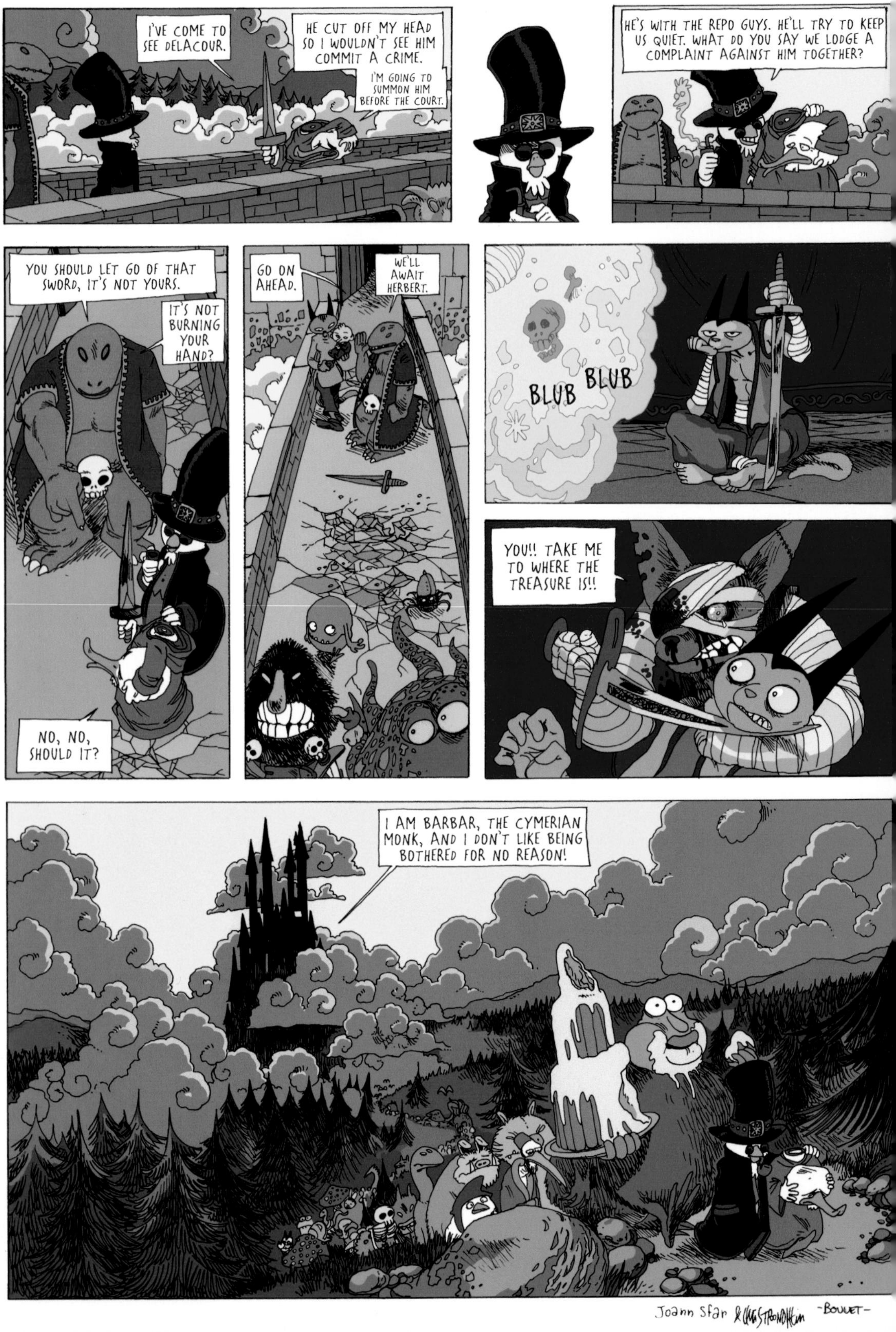
I'VE COME TO SEE DELACOUR.
HE CUT OFF MY HEAD SO I WOULDN'T SEE HIM COMMIT A CRIME.
I'M GOING TO SUMMON HIM BEFORE THE COURT.
HE'S WITH THE REPO GUYS. HE'LL TRY TO KEEP US QUIET. WHAT DO YOU SAY WE LODGE A COMPLAINT AGAINST HIM TOGETHER?
YOU SHOULD LET GO OF THAT SWORD, IT'S NOT YOURS.
IT'S NOT BURNING YOUR HAND?
NO, NO, SHOULD IT?
GO ON AHEAD.
WE'LL AWAIT HERBERT.
BLUB BLUB
YOU!! TAKE ME TO WHERE THE TREASURE IS!!
I AM BARBAR, THE CYMERIAN MONK, AND I DON'T LIKE BEING BOTHERED FOR NO REASON!
Joann Sfar

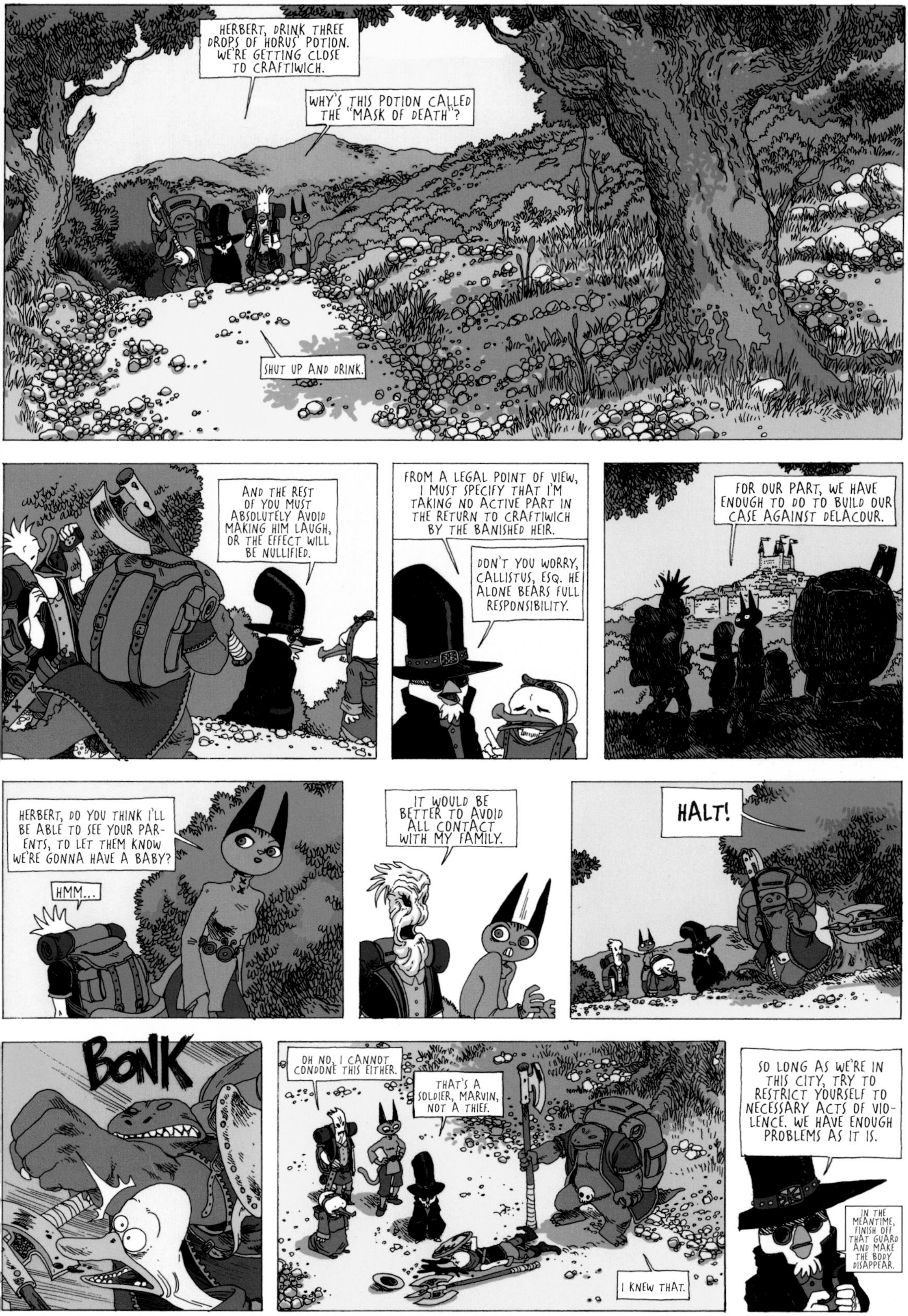
HERBERT, DRINK THREE DROPS OF HORUS' POTION. WE'RE GETTING CLOSE TO CRAFTIWICH.
WHY'S THIS POTION CALLED THE "MASK OF DEATH"?
SHUT UP AND DRINK.
AND THE REST OF YOU MUST ABSOLUTELY AVOID MAKING HIM LAUGH, OR THE EFFECT WILL BE NULLIFIED.
FROM A LEGAL POINT OF VIEW, I MUST SPECIFY THAT I'M TAKING NO ACTIVE PART IN THE RETURN TO CRAFTIWICH BY THE BANISHED HEIR.
DON'T YOU WORRY, CALLISTUS, ESQ. HE ALONE BEARS FULL RESPONSIBILITY.
FOR OUR PART, WE HAVE ENOUGH TO DO TO BUILD OUR CASE AGAINST DELACOUR.
HERBERT, DO YOU THINK I'LL BE ABLE TO SEE YOUR PARENTS, TO LET THEM KNOW WE'RE GONNA HAVE A BABY?
HMM...
IT WOULD BE BETTER TO AVOID ALL CONTACT WITH MY FAMILY.
HALT!
BONK
OH NO, I CANNOT CONDONE THIS EITHER.
THAT'S A SOLDIER, MARVIN, NOT A THIEF.
I KNEW THAT.
SO LONG AS WE'RE IN THIS CITY, TRY TO RESTRICT YOURSELF TO NECESSARY ACTS OF VIOLENCE. WE HAVE ENOUGH PROBLEMS AS IT IS.
IN THE MEANTIME, FINISH OFF THAT GUARD AND MAKE THE BODY DISAPPEAR.

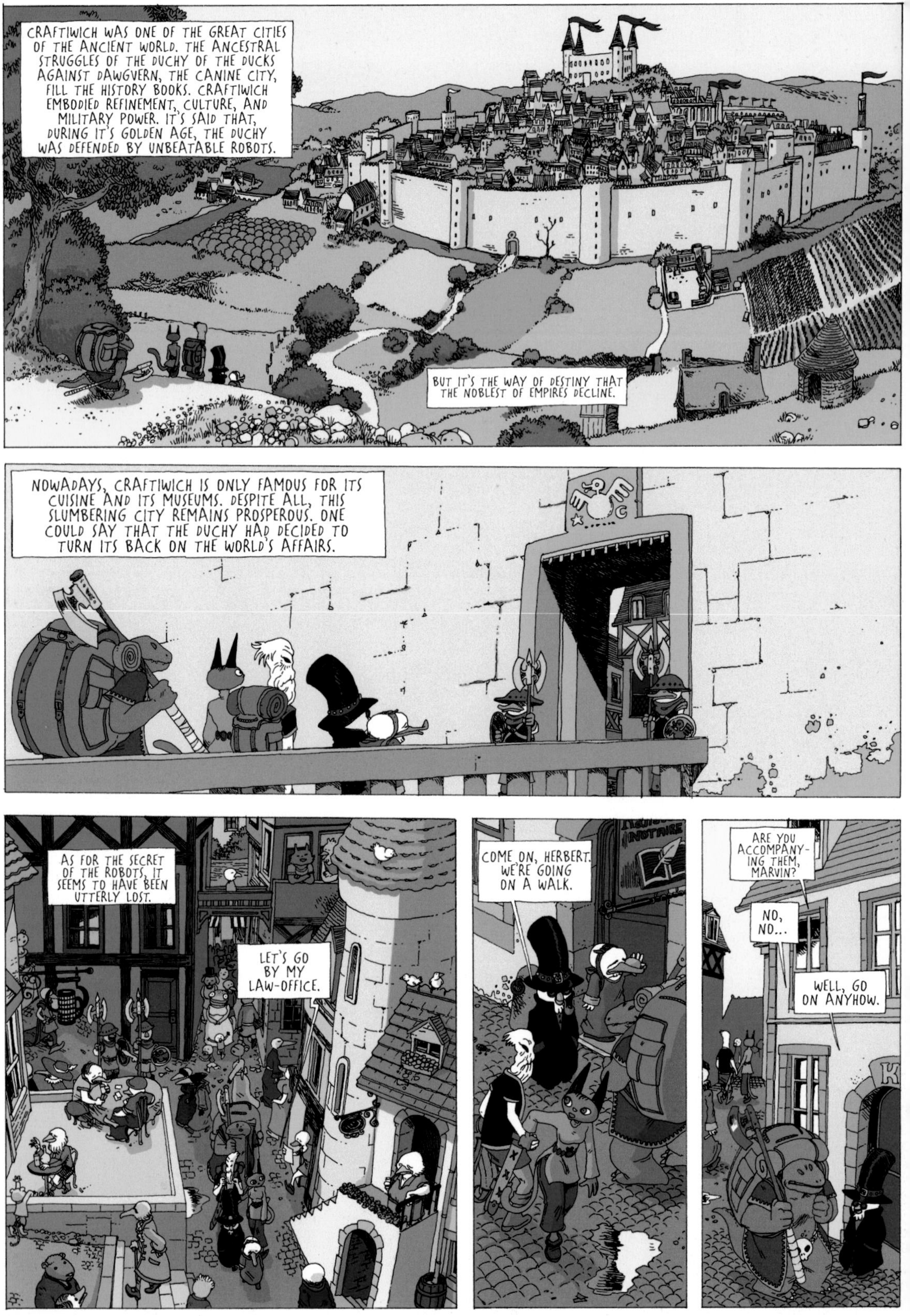
CRAFTIWICH WAS ONE OF THE GREAT CITIES OF THE ANCIENT WORLD. THE ANCESTRAL STRUGGLES OF THE DUCHY OF THE DUCKS AGAINST DAWGVERN, THE CANINE CITY, FILL THE HISTORY BOOKS. CRAFTIWICH EMBODIED REFINEMENT, CULTURE, AND MILITARY POWER. IT'S SAID THAT, DURING IT'S GOLDEN AGE, THE DUCHY WAS DEFENDED BY UNBEATABLE ROBOTS.
BUT IT'S THE WAY OF DESTINY THAT THE NOBLEST OF EMPIRES DECLINE.
NOWADAYS, CRAFTIWICH IS ONLY FAMOUS FOR ITS CUISINE AND ITS MUSEUMS. DESPITE ALL, THIS SLUMBERING CITY REMAINS PROSPEROUS. ONE COULD SAY THAT THE DUCHY HAD DECIDED TO TURN ITS BACK ON THE WORLD'S AFFAIRS.
AS FOR THE SECRET OF THE ROBOTS, IT SEEMS TO HAVE BEEN UTTERLY LOST.
LET'S GO BY MY LAW-OFFICE.
NOTAIRE
COME ON, HERBERT. WE'RE GOING ON A WALK.
ARE YOU ACCOMPANYING THEM, MARVIN?
NO, NO...
WELL, GO ON ANYHOW.

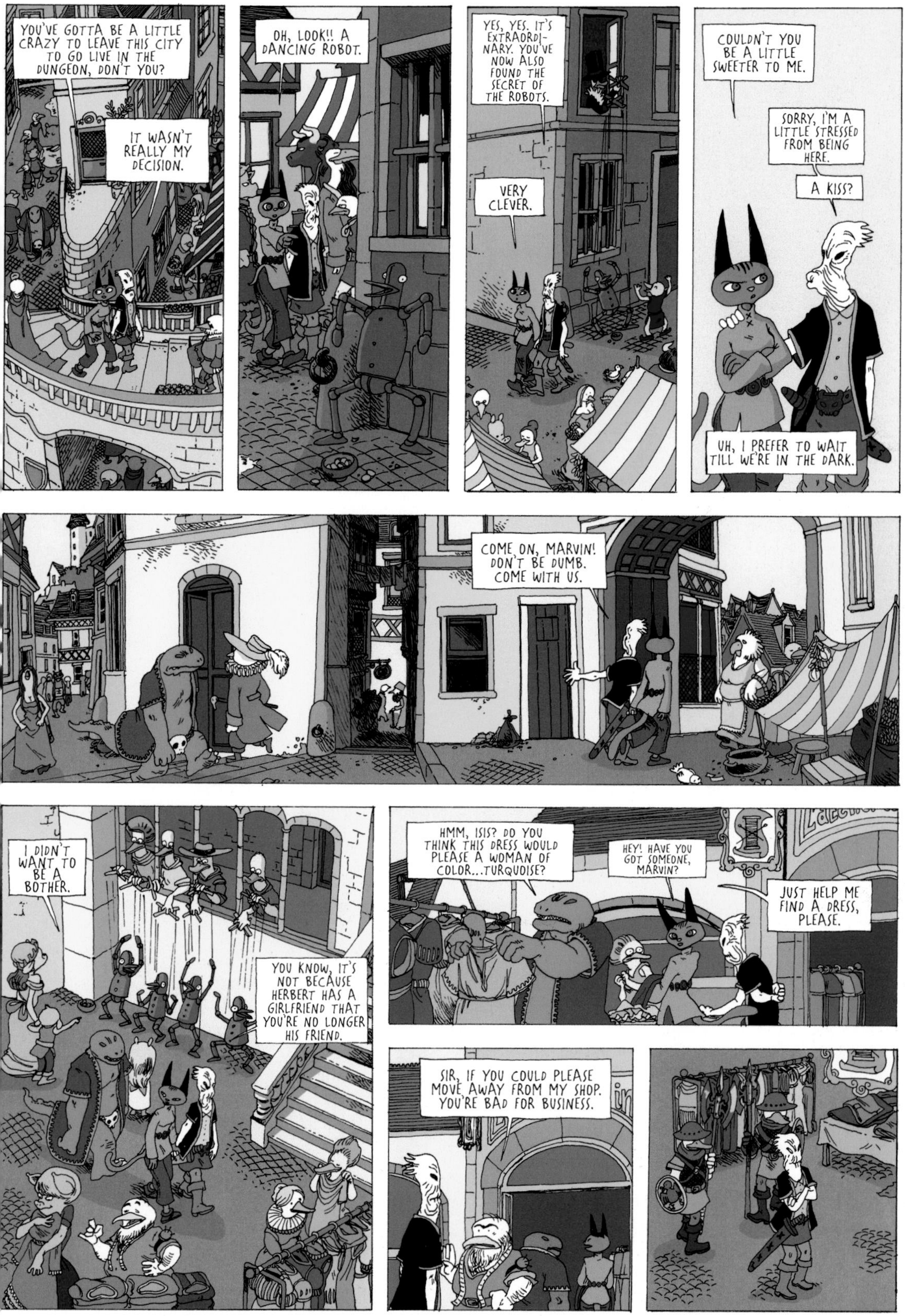
YOU'VE GOTTA BE A LITTLE CRAZY TO LEAVE THIS CITY TO GO LIVE IN THE DUNGEON, DON'T YOU?
IT WASN'T REALLY MY DECISION.
OH, LOOK!! A DANCING ROBOT.
YES, YES. IT'S EXTRAORDI-NARY. YOU'VE NOW ALSO FOUND THE SECRET OF THE ROBOTS.
VERY CLEVER.
COULDN'T YOU BE A LITTLE SWEETER TO ME.
SORRY, I'M A LITTLE STRESSED FROM BEING HERE.
A KISS?
UH, I PREFER TO WAIT TILL WE'RE IN THE DARK.
COME ON, MARVIN! DON'T BE DUMB. COME WITH US.
I DIDN'T WANT TO BE A BOTHER.
YOU KNOW, IT'S NOT BECAUSE HERBERT HAS A GIRLFRIEND THAT YOU'RE NO LONGER HIS FRIEND.
HMM, ISIS? DO YOU THINK THIS DRESS WOULD PLEASE A WOMAN OF COLOR...TURQUDISE?
HEY! HAVE YOU GOT SOMEONE, MARVIN?
JUST HELP ME FIND A DRESS, PLEASE.
SIR, IF YOU COULD PLEASE MOVE AWAY FROM MY SHOP. YOU'RE BAD FOR BUSINESS.

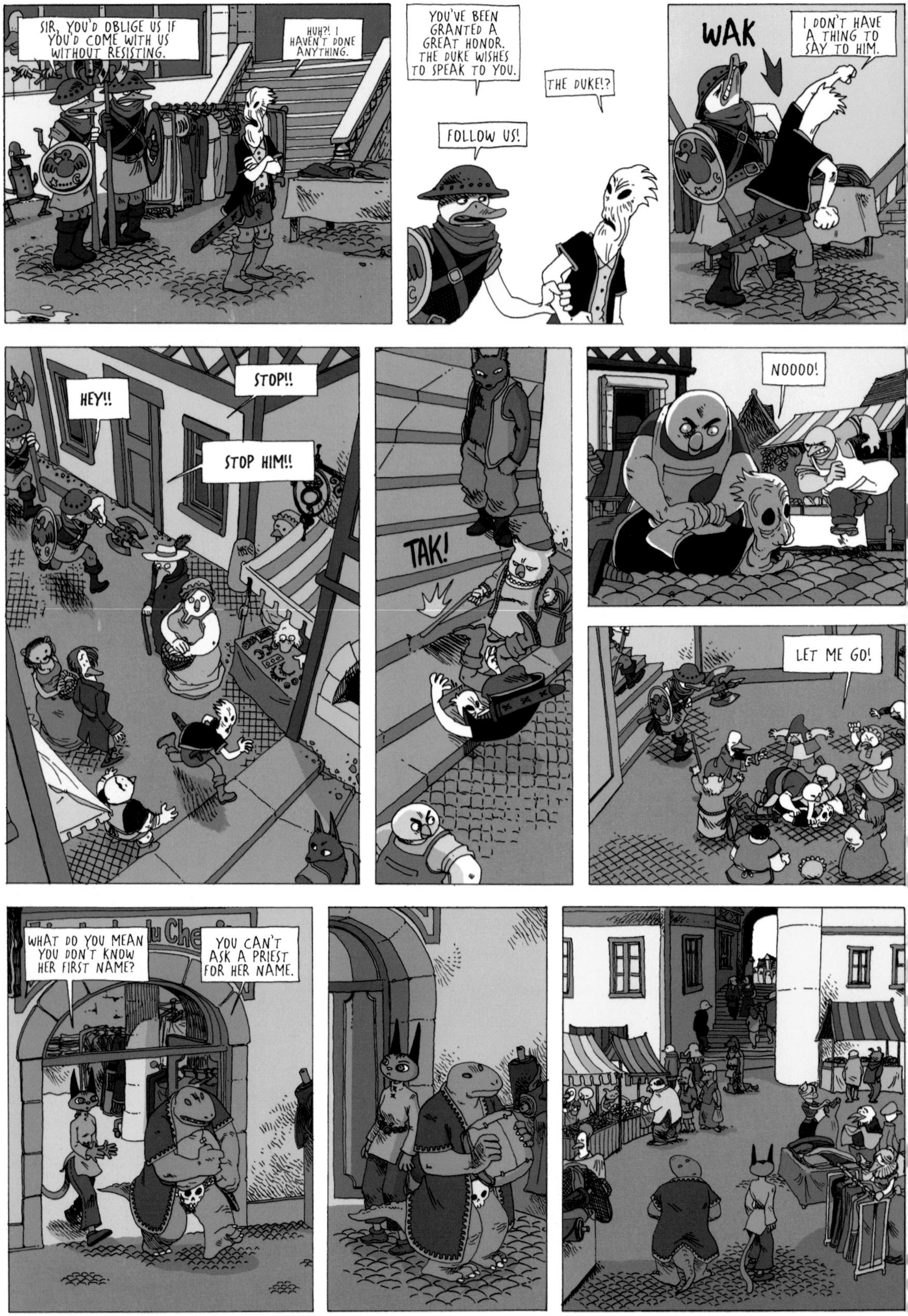
SIR, YOU'D OBLIGE US IF YOU'D COME WITH US WITHOUT RESISTING.
HUH?! I HAVEN'T DONE ANYTHING.
YOU'VE BEEN GRANTED A GREAT HONOR. THE DUKE WISHES TO SPEAK TO YOU.
THE DUKE!?
FOLLOW US!
WAK
I DON'T HAVE A THING TO SAY TO HIM.
HEY!!
STOP!!
STOP HIM!!
TAK!
NOOOO!
LET ME GO!
WHAT DO YOU MEAN YOU DON'T KNOW HER FIRST NAME?
YOU CAN'T ASK A PRIEST FOR HER NAME.

AND TRY TO KEEP CALM WHILE YOU'RE IN THE PRESENCE OF THE DUKE.

BROLOMBROMLOMBRROOLOM

BROLOMBROMLOMBRROOLOM

COMING, COMING...

HERE I AM.

BROLOMBROLOM

BROLOMM

I'D LIKE TO GET STRAIGHT TO THE POINT.

YES.

YOU'RE ONE OF THE LACKEYS FROM CAVALLERE'S DUNGEON.

YES.

I NEED SOME INFORMATION.

PAF!

BLANG!

YES, YES!! I'LL TELL YOU WHAT YOU WANT TO KNOW!!

OH...I'M COMPLETELY EMBARRASSED. THIS MECHANICAL ARM IS TOTALLY UNCONTROLLABLE.

REMOVE THIS CONTRAPTION.

LISTEN, MY ONLY SON IS AT THE DUNGEON.

HE'S A GOOD BOY, BUT HE'S FRAGILE AND CLUMSY. I NEED NEWS OF HIM.

THE LAWS OF OUR CITY AREN'T NEGOTIABLE, EVEN FOR THE DUKE. MY SON WAS CHASED AWAY FROM THE FAMILY LANDS. TELL HIM THAT, EVEN FROM AFAR, WE CAN HELP HIM.

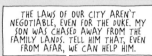

UH...

WHAT?! DO YOU KNOW ANYTHING? IS HE ALIVE? IS HE WELL?

YOU KNOW, YOUR SON HAS BECOME A GREAT WARRIOR.

YOU MUST BE MISTAKEN, MY SON IS A DUCK. HE LOOKS A LITTLE LIKE ME, BUT HE HAS HIS MOTHER'S EYES.

NO, NO...HE'S A GREAT WARRIOR, I ASSURE YOU.

HE'S IN CHARGE OF THE DUNGEON'S SECURITY, AND THE KEEPER ENTRUSTS HIM WITH LOTS OF MISSIONS.

AH YES, THAT WOULD EXPLAIN A GREAT DEAL. I HEARD THAT THE DUNGEON WENT BANKRUPT RECENTLY.

THAT'S NOT HIS FAULT. BUT, ON THE OTHER HAND, HE CONFIDED TO ME HIS WISH TO ONE DAY RETURN TO CRAFTIWICH.

GOD FORBID. I'D BE FORCED TO HAVE HIS HEAD CHOPPED OFF IMMEDIATELY.

STILL, IF I COULD SEE HIM IF ONLY FOR AN INSTANT, IN THE FOREST OUTSIDE THE CITY...

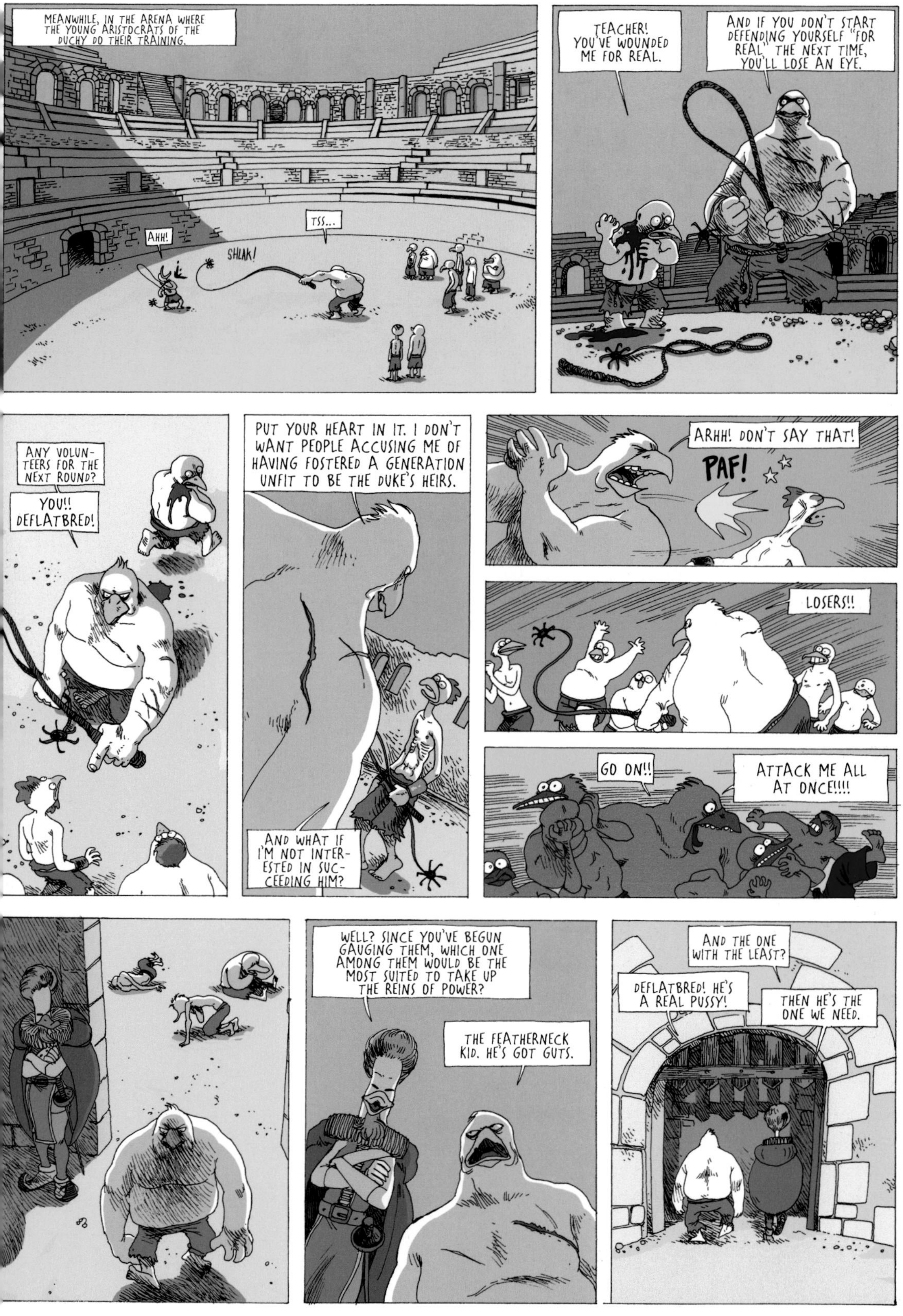
MEANWHILE, IN THE ARENA WHERE THE YOUNG ARISTOCRATS OF THE DUCHY DO THEIR TRAINING.
AHH!
SHLAK!
TSS...
TEACHER! YOU'VE WOUNDED ME FOR REAL.
AND IF YOU DON'T START DEFENDING YOURSELF "FOR REAL" THE NEXT TIME, YOU'LL LOSE AN EYE.
ANY VOLUNTEERS FOR THE NEXT ROUND?
YOU!! DEFLATBRED!
PUT YOUR HEART IN IT. I DON'T WANT PEOPLE ACCUSING ME OF HAVING FOSTERED A GENERATION UNFIT TO BE THE DUKE'S HEIRS.
AND WHAT IF I'M NOT INTERESTED IN SUCCEEDING HIM?
ARHH! DON'T SAY THAT!
PAF!
LOSERS!!
GO ON!!
ATTACK ME ALL AT ONCE!!!!
WELL? SINCE YOU'VE BEGUN GAUGING THEM, WHICH ONE AMONG THEM WOULD BE THE MOST SUITED TO TAKE UP THE REINS OF POWER?
THE FEATHERNECK KID. HE'S GOT GUTS.
AND THE ONE WITH THE LEAST?
DEFLATBRED! HE'S A REAL PUSSY!
THEN HE'S THE ONE WE NEED.

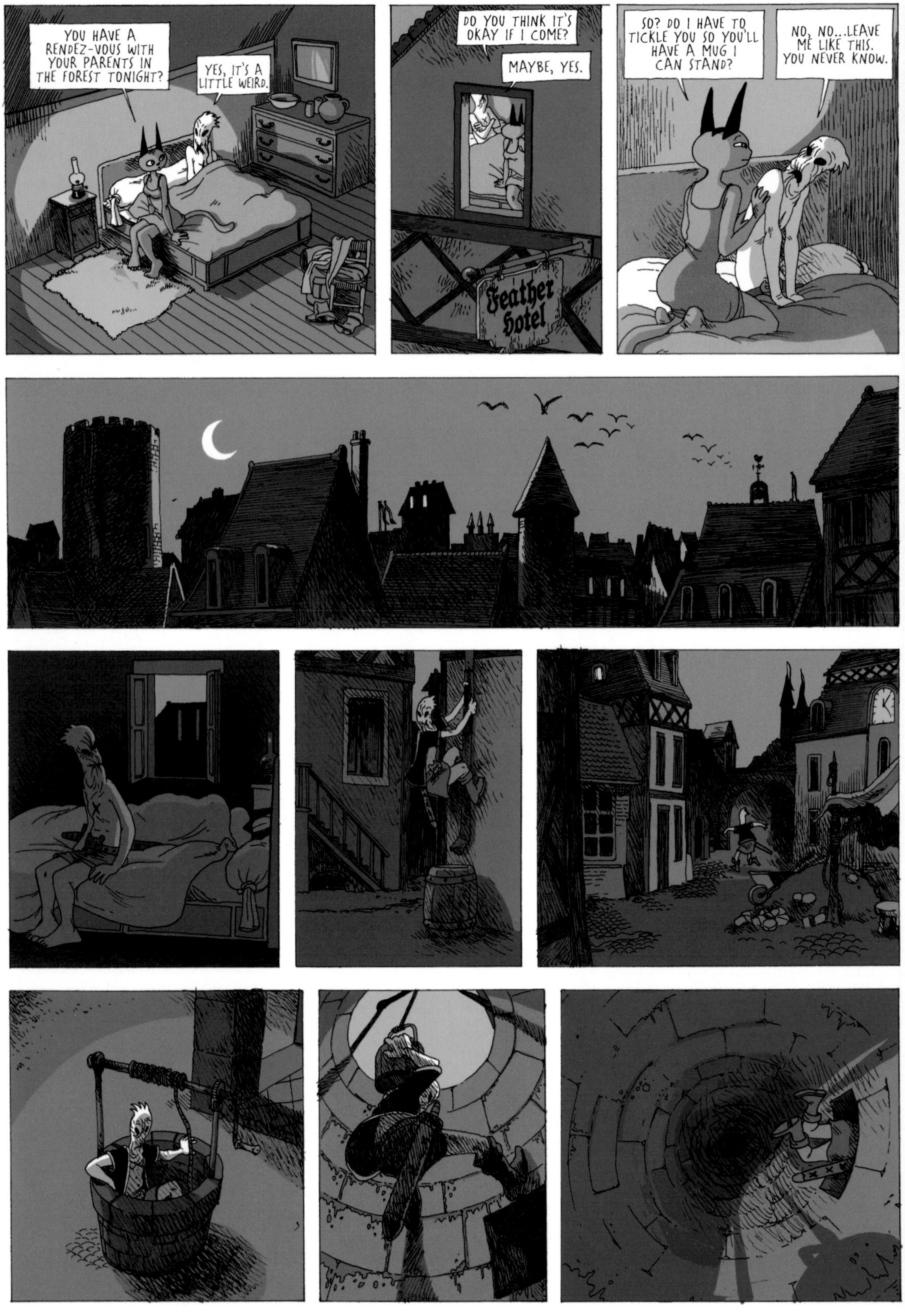

YOU HAVE A RENDEZ-VOUS WITH YOUR PARENTS IN THE FOREST TONIGHT?
YES, IT'S A LITTLE WEIRD.
DO YOU THINK IT'S OKAY IF I COME?
MAYBE, YES.
Feather Hotel
SO? DO I HAVE TO TICKLE YOU SO YOU'LL HAVE A MUG I CAN STAND?
NO, NO...LEAVE ME LIKE THIS. YOU NEVER KNOW.

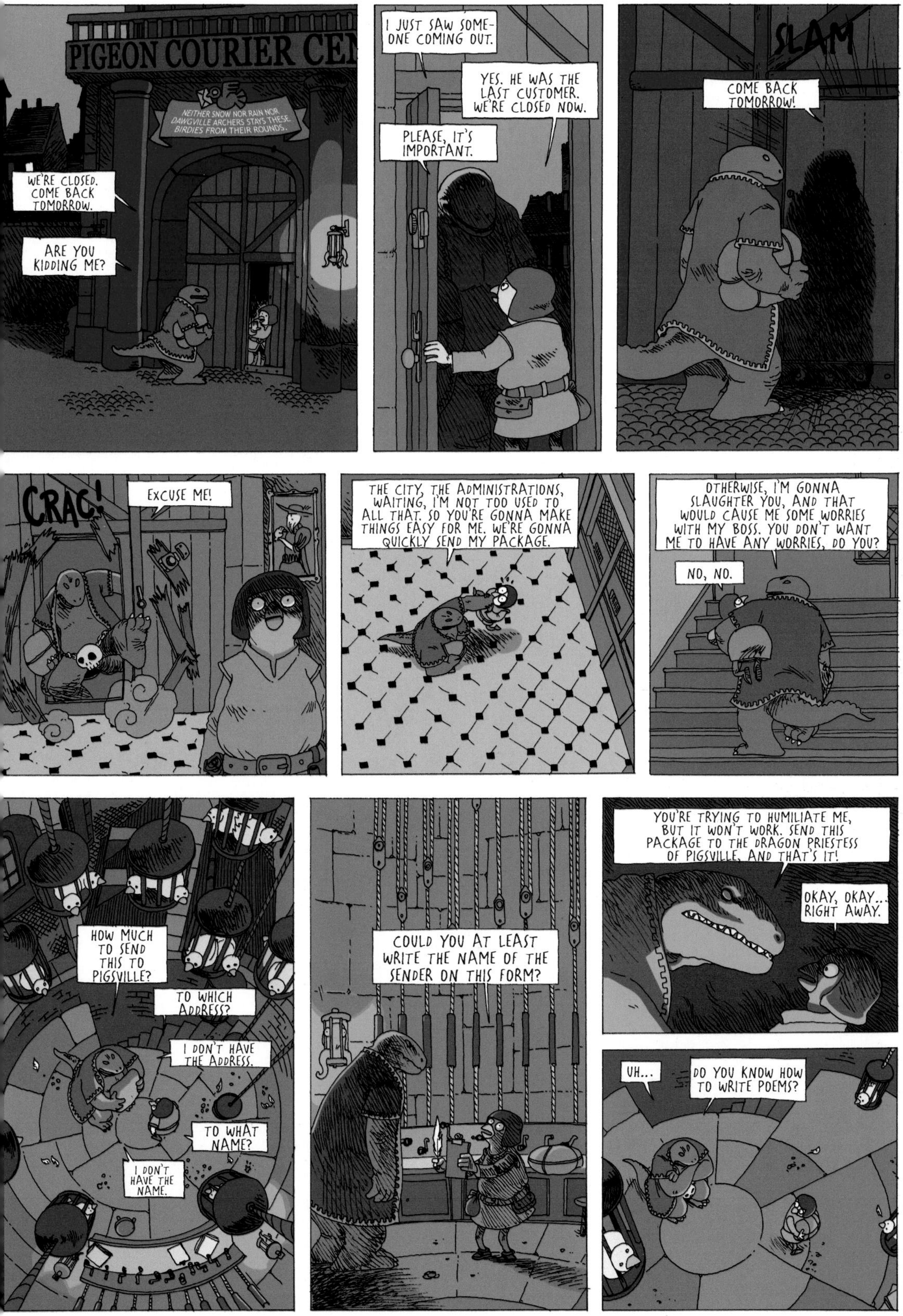
PIGEON COURIER CEN
NEITHER SNOW NOR RAIN NOR DAWGVILLE ARCHERS STAYS THESE BIRDIES FROM THEIR ROUNDS.
WE'RE CLOSED. COME BACK TOMORROW.
ARE YOU KIDDING ME?
I JUST SAW SOME-ONE COMING OUT.
YES. HE WAS THE LAST CUSTOMER. WE'RE CLOSED NOW.
PLEASE, IT'S IMPORTANT.
SLAM
COME BACK TOMORROW!
CRAC!
EXCUSE ME!
THE CITY, THE ADMINISTRATIONS, WAITING, I'M NOT TOO USED TO ALL THAT. SO YOU'RE GONNA MAKE THINGS EASY FOR ME. WE'RE GONNA QUICKLY SEND MY PACKAGE.
OTHERWISE, I'M GONNA SLAUGHTER YOU, AND THAT WOULD CAUSE ME SOME WORRIES WITH MY BOSS. YOU DON'T WANT ME TO HAVE ANY WORRIES, DO YOU?
NO, NO.
HOW MUCH TO SEND THIS TO PIGSVILLE?
TO WHICH ADDRESS?
I DON'T HAVE THE ADDRESS.
TO WHAT NAME?
I DON'T HAVE THE NAME.
COULD YOU AT LEAST WRITE THE NAME OF THE SENDER ON THIS FORM?
YOU'RE TRYING TO HUMILIATE ME, BUT IT WON'T WORK. SEND THIS PACKAGE TO THE DRAGON PRIESTESS OF PIGSVILLE, AND THAT'S IT!
OKAY, OKAY... RIGHT AWAY.
UH...
DO YOU KNOW HOW TO WRITE POEMS?

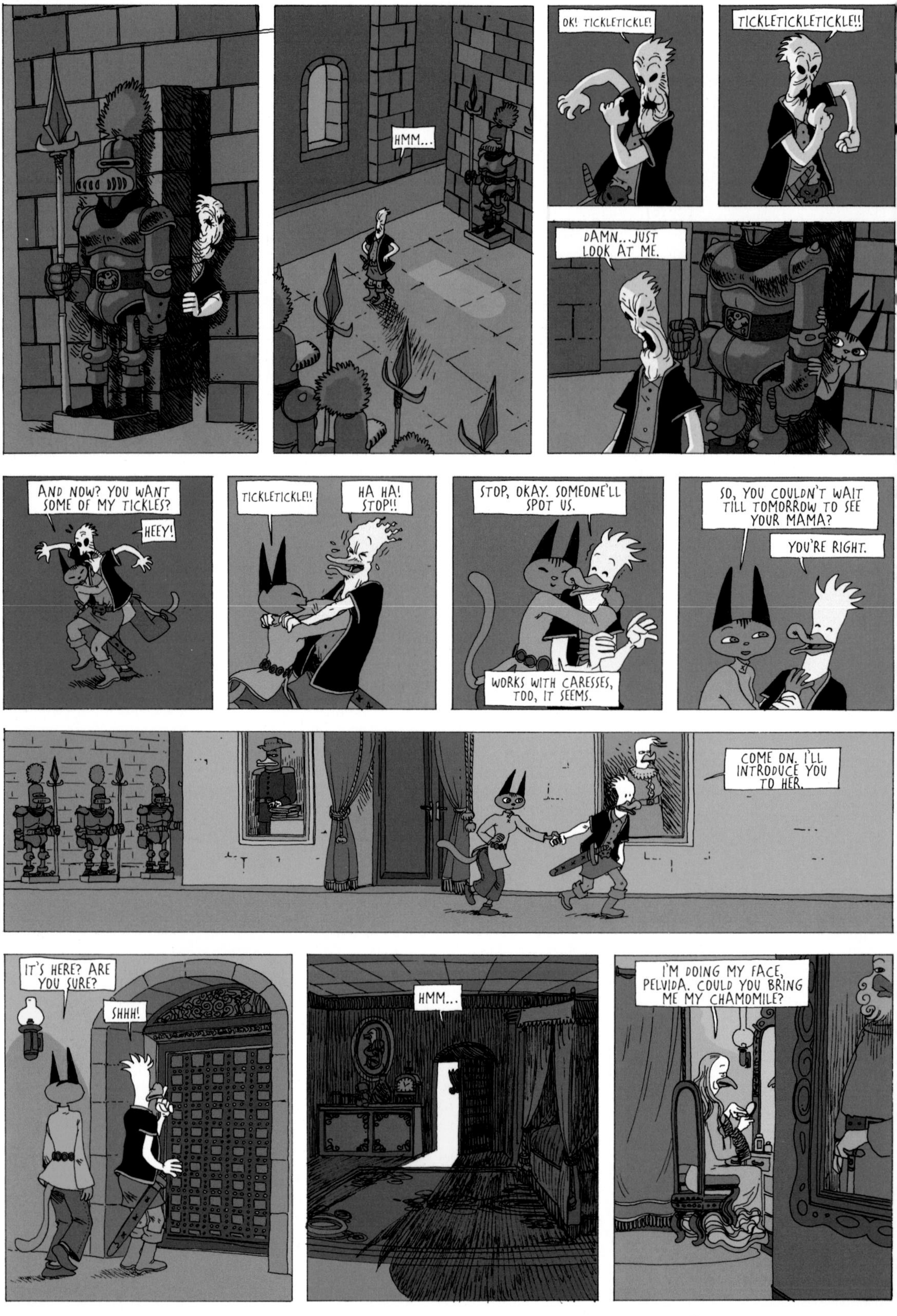
HMM...
OK! TICKLETICKLE!
TICKLETICKLETICKLE!!
DAMN...JUST LOOK AT ME.
AND NOW? YOU WANT SOME OF MY TICKLES?
HEEY!
TICKLETICKLE!!
HA HA! STOP!!
STOP, OKAY. SOMEONE'LL SPOT US.
WORKS WITH CARESSES, TOO, IT SEEMS.
SO, YOU COULDN'T WAIT TILL TOMORROW TO SEE YOUR MAMA?
YOU'RE RIGHT.
COME ON. I'LL INTRODUCE YOU TO HER.
IT'S HERE? ARE YOU SURE?
SHHH!
HMM...
I'M DOING MY FACE, PELVIDA. COULD YOU BRING ME MY CHAMOMILE?

IT'S NOT PELVIDA, MAMA.

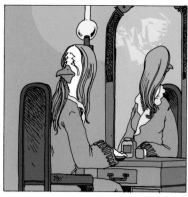

LET ME INTRODUCE...

OH, MY GOD!

MR. HERBERT!

EVENING, PELVIDA!

YOU KNOW, PELVIDA, YOU MUST-N'T TELL ANYONE I'M HERE. I'M RISKING MY HEAD IN THIS.

OF COURSE, MR. HERBERT, SIR. I'VE KNOWN YOU SINCE...

EEEEE...

MAMA.

IT'S TOO GRAVE A SECRET, MY CHILD.

YOUR MOTHER'S RIGHT, HERBERT. WE'LL HAVE TO CARRY OFF THE BODY AND HURRY ALONG BEFORE CHANCING UPON ANYONE ELSE.

YOU'LL SEE EACH OTHER TOMORROW IN THE FOREST.

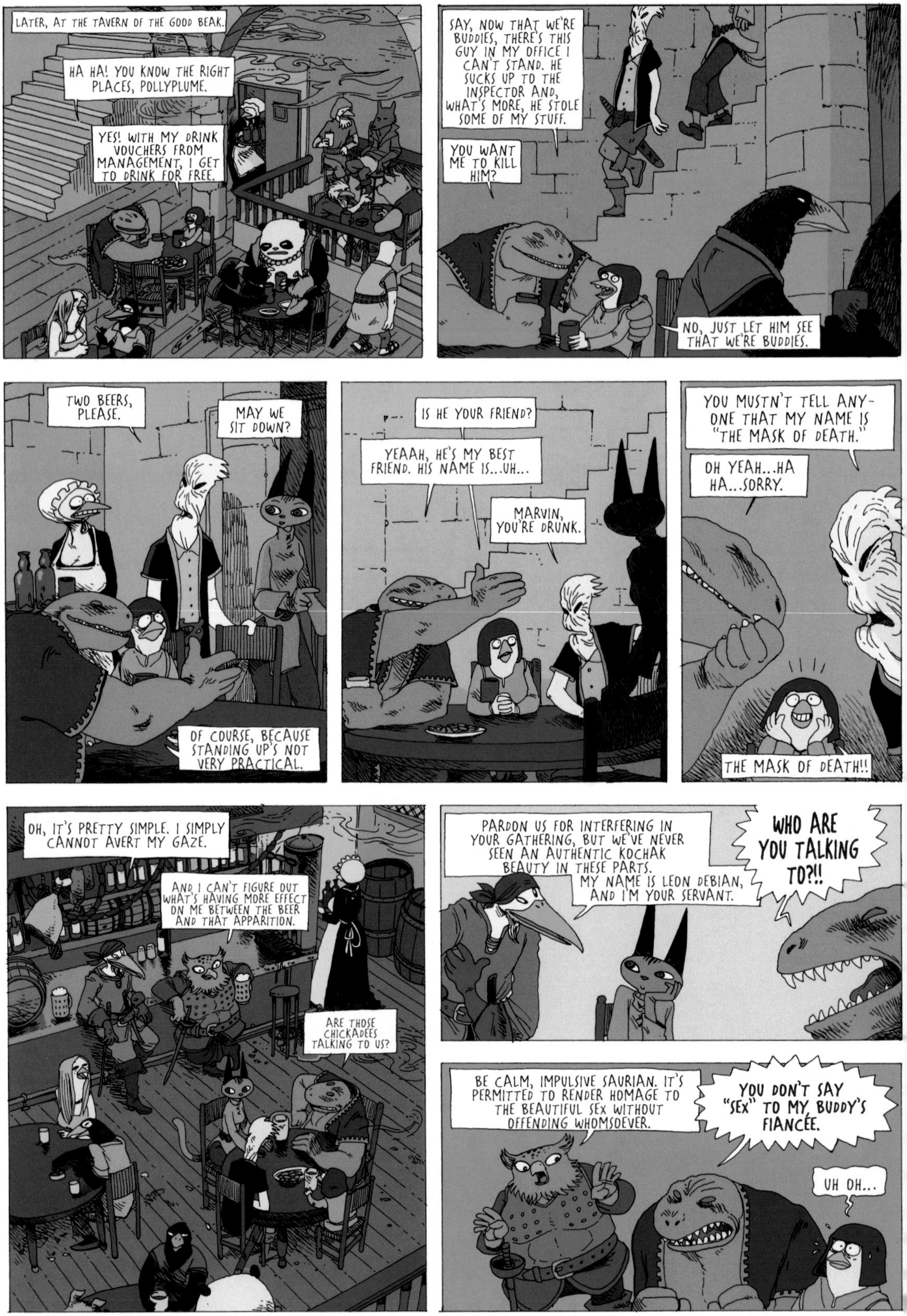
LATER, AT THE TAVERN OF THE GOOD BEAK.
HA HA! YOU KNOW THE RIGHT PLACES, POLLYPLUME.
YES! WITH MY DRINK VOUCHERS FROM MANAGEMENT, I GET TO DRINK FOR FREE.
SAY, NOW THAT WE'RE BUDDIES, THERE'S THIS GUY IN MY OFFICE I CAN'T STAND. HE SUCKS UP TO THE INSPECTOR AND, WHAT'S MORE, HE STOLE SOME OF MY STUFF.
YOU WANT ME TO KILL HIM?
NO, JUST LET HIM SEE THAT WE'RE BUDDIES.
TWO BEERS, PLEASE.
MAY WE SIT DOWN?
OF COURSE, BECAUSE STANDING UP'S NOT VERY PRACTICAL.
IS HE YOUR FRIEND?
YEAAH, HE'S MY BEST FRIEND. HIS NAME IS...UH...
MARVIN, YOU'RE DRUNK.
YOU MUSTN'T TELL ANYONE THAT MY NAME IS "THE MASK OF DEATH."
OH YEAH...HA HA...SORRY.
THE MASK OF DEATH!!
OH, IT'S PRETTY SIMPLE. I SIMPLY CANNOT AVERT MY GAZE.
AND I CAN'T FIGURE OUT WHAT'S HAVING MORE EFFECT ON ME BETWEEN THE BEER AND THAT APPARITION.
ARE THOSE CHICKADEES TALKING TO US?
PARDON US FOR INTERFERING IN YOUR GATHERING, BUT WE'VE NEVER SEEN AN AUTHENTIC KOCHAK BEAUTY IN THESE PARTS.
MY NAME IS LEON DEBIAN, AND I'M YOUR SERVANT.
WHO ARE YOU TALKING TO?!!
BE CALM, IMPULSIVE SAURIAN. IT'S PERMITTED TO RENDER HOMAGE TO THE BEAUTIFUL SEX WITHOUT OFFENDING WHOMSOEVER.
YOU DON'T SAY "SEX" TO MY BUDDY'S FIANCÉE.
UH OH...

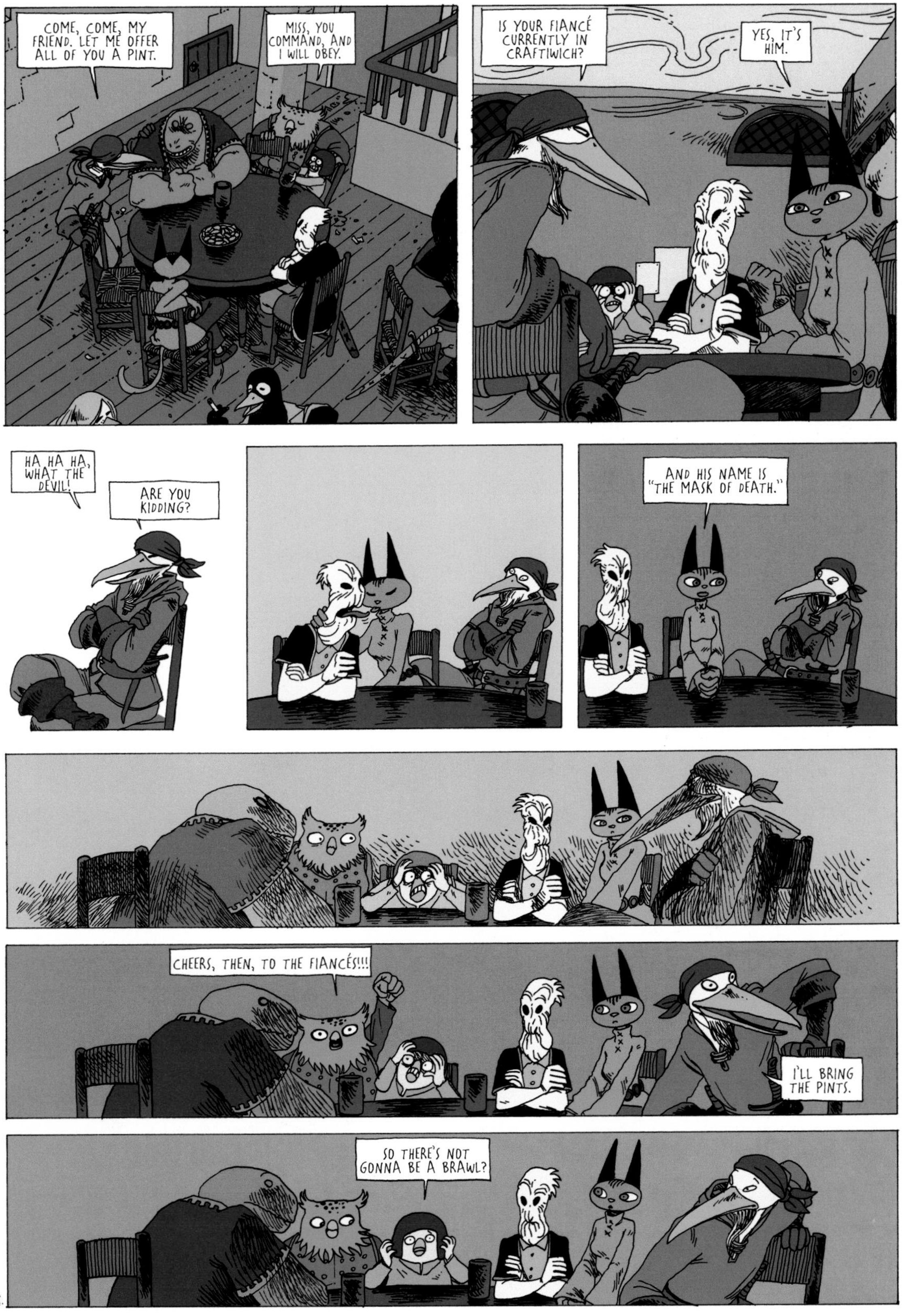
COME, COME, MY FRIEND. LET ME OFFER ALL OF YOU A PINT.
MISS, YOU COMMAND, AND I WILL OBEY.
IS YOUR FIANCÉ CURRENTLY IN CRAFTIWICH?
YES, IT'S HIM.
HA HA HA, WHAT THE DEVIL!
ARE YOU KIDDING?
AND HIS NAME IS "THE MASK OF DEATH."
CHEERS, THEN, TO THE FIANCÉS!!!
I'LL BRING THE PINTS.
SO THERE'S NOT GONNA BE A BRAWL?

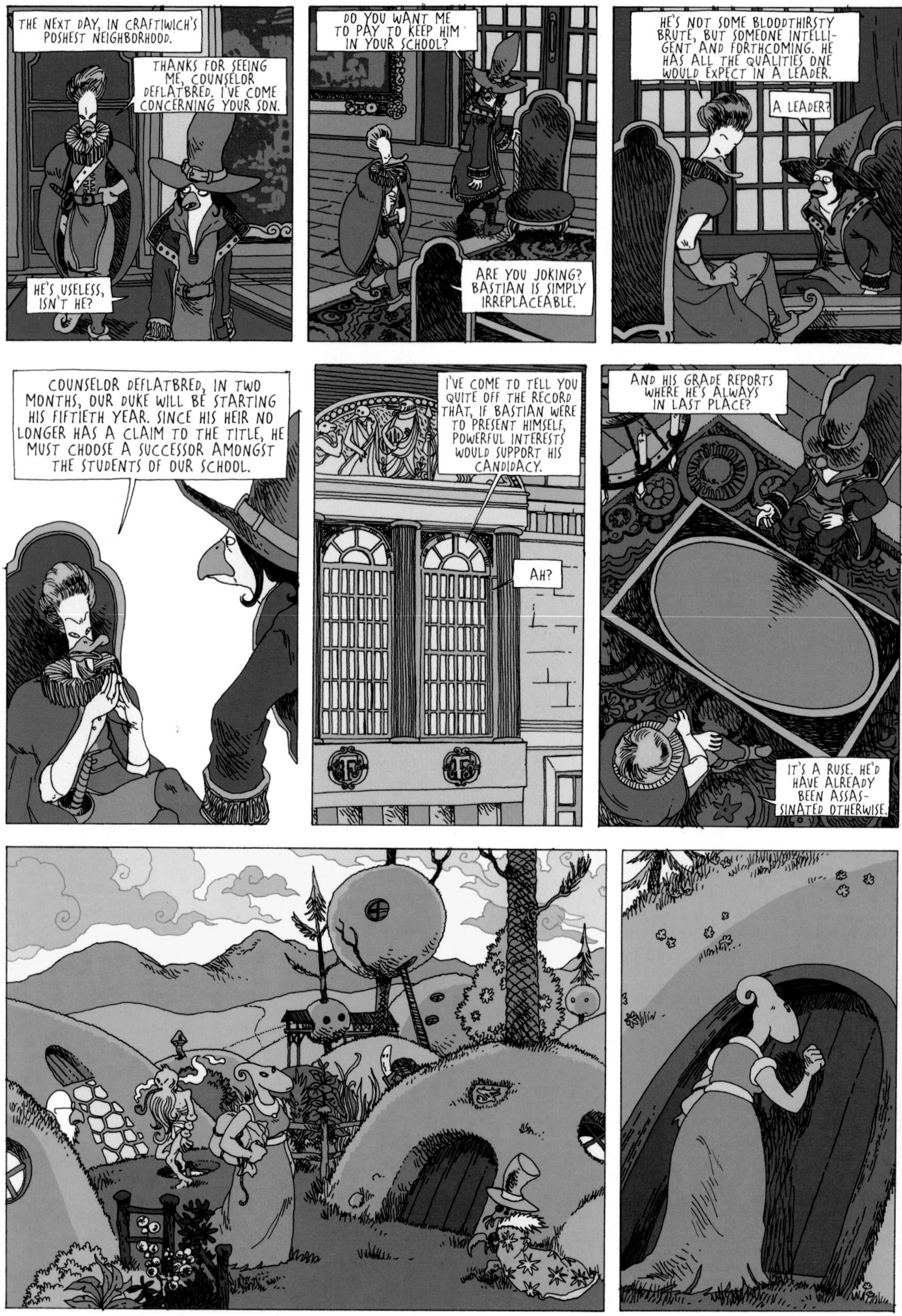
THE NEXT DAY, IN CRAFTIWICH'S POSHEST NEIGHBORHOOD.
THANKS FOR SEEING ME, COUNSELOR DEFLATBRED. I'VE COME CONCERNING YOUR SON.
HE'S USELESS, ISN'T HE?
DO YOU WANT ME TO PAY TO KEEP HIM IN YOUR SCHOOL?
ARE YOU JOKING? BASTIAN IS SIMPLY IRREPLACEABLE.
HE'S NOT SOME BLOODTHIRSTY BRUTE, BUT SOMEONE INTELLIGENT AND FORTHCOMING. HE HAS ALL THE QUALITIES ONE WOULD EXPECT IN A LEADER.
A LEADER?
COUNSELOR DEFLATBRED, IN TWO MONTHS, OUR DUKE WILL BE STARTING HIS FIFTIETH YEAR. SINCE HIS HEIR NO LONGER HAS A CLAIM TO THE TITLE, HE MUST CHOOSE A SUCCESSOR AMONGST THE STUDENTS OF OUR SCHOOL.
I'VE COME TO TELL YOU QUITE OFF THE RECORD THAT, IF BASTIAN WERE TO PRESENT HIMSELF, POWERFUL INTERESTS WOULD SUPPORT HIS CANDIDACY.
AH?
AND HIS GRADE REPORTS WHERE HE'S ALWAYS IN LAST PLACE?
IT'S A RUSE. HE'D HAVE ALREADY BEEN ASSASSINATED OTHERWISE.

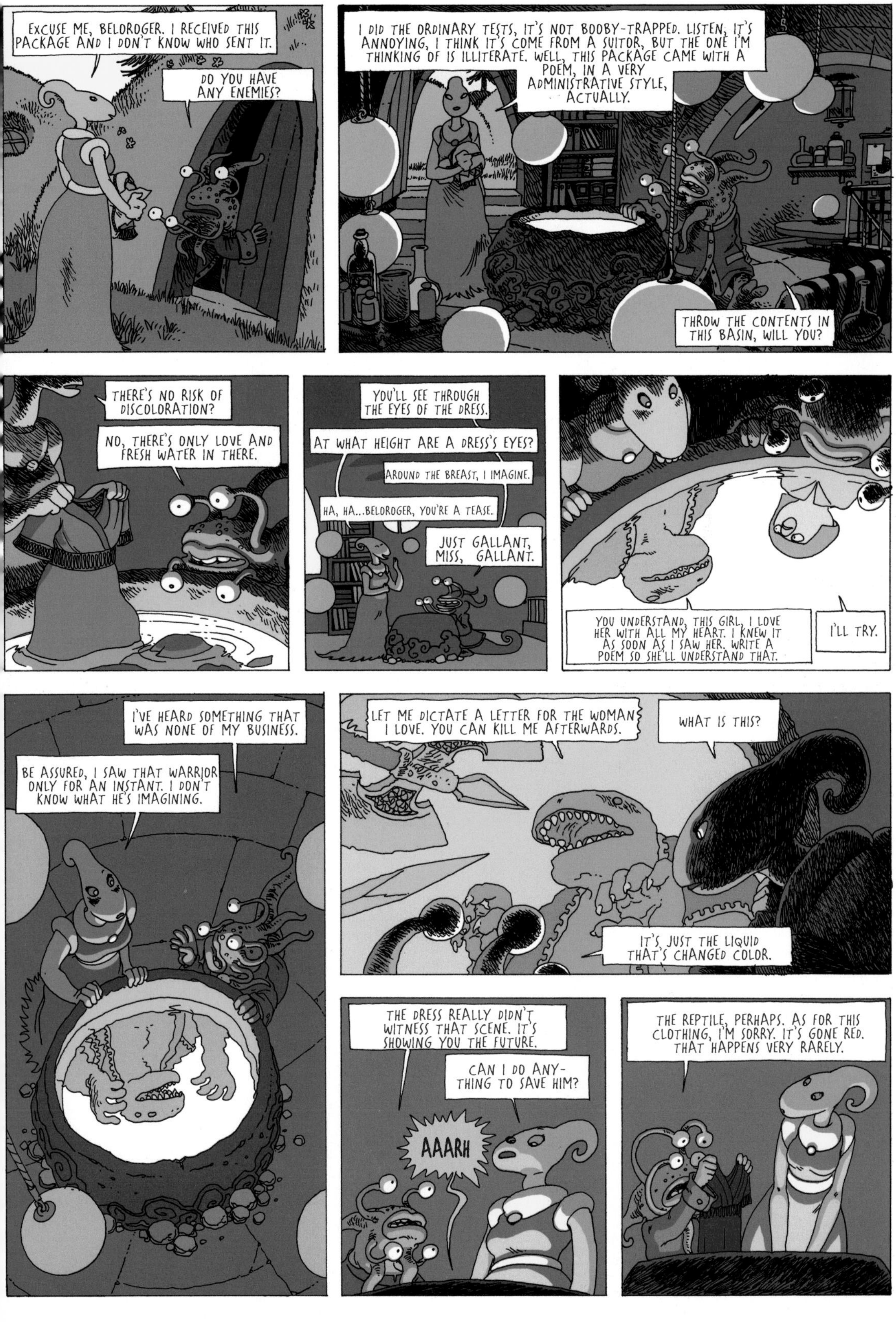
EXCUSE ME, BELOROGER. I RECEIVED THIS PACKAGE AND I DON'T KNOW WHO SENT IT.
DO YOU HAVE ANY ENEMIES?
I DID THE ORDINARY TESTS, IT'S NOT BOOBY-TRAPPED. LISTEN, IT'S ANNOYING, I THINK IT'S COME FROM A SUITOR, BUT THE ONE I'M THINKING OF IS ILLITERATE. WELL, THIS PACKAGE CAME WITH A POEM, IN A VERY ADMINISTRATIVE STYLE, ACTUALLY.
THROW THE CONTENTS IN THIS BASIN, WILL YOU?
THERE'S NO RISK OF DISCOLORATION?
NO, THERE'S ONLY LOVE AND FRESH WATER IN THERE.
YOU'LL SEE THROUGH THE EYES OF THE DRESS.
AT WHAT HEIGHT ARE A DRESS'S EYES?
AROUND THE BREAST, I IMAGINE.
HA, HA...BELOROGER, YOU'RE A TEASE.
JUST GALLANT, MISS, GALLANT.
YOU UNDERSTAND, THIS GIRL, I LOVE HER WITH ALL MY HEART. I KNEW IT AS SOON AS I SAW HER. WRITE A POEM SO SHE'LL UNDERSTAND THAT.
I'LL TRY.
I'VE HEARD SOMETHING THAT WAS NONE OF MY BUSINESS.
BE ASSURED, I SAW THAT WARRIOR ONLY FOR AN INSTANT. I DON'T KNOW WHAT HE'S IMAGINING.
LET ME DICTATE A LETTER FOR THE WOMAN I LOVE. YOU CAN KILL ME AFTERWARDS.
WHAT IS THIS?
IT'S JUST THE LIQUID THAT'S CHANGED COLOR.
THE DRESS REALLY DIDN'T WITNESS THAT SCENE. IT'S SHOWING YOU THE FUTURE.
CAN I DO ANYTHING TO SAVE HIM?
AAARH
THE REPTILE, PERHAPS. AS FOR THIS CLOTHING, I'M SORRY. IT'S GONE RED. THAT HAPPENS VERY RARELY.

DAD!

I HAVE VERY LITTLE TIME, HERBERT.

DO YOU WANT TO TAKE OVER THE DUCHY OF CRAFTIWICH?

UH...I DON'T KNOW. IS THAT POSSIBLE?

I'LL SOON BE FIFTY AND I HAVE SERIOUS FEARS FOR MY SAFETY.

IF YOU WANT CRAFTIWICH, YOU CAN HAVE IT...BUT BY FORCE!!

I'LL GATHER FOR YOU ALL OF MY TRUSTWORTHY HENCHMEN, MY MOST DEVOTED SOLDIERS, AND IT'S UP TO YOU TO BRING ABOUT A COUP D'ÉTAT!

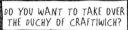

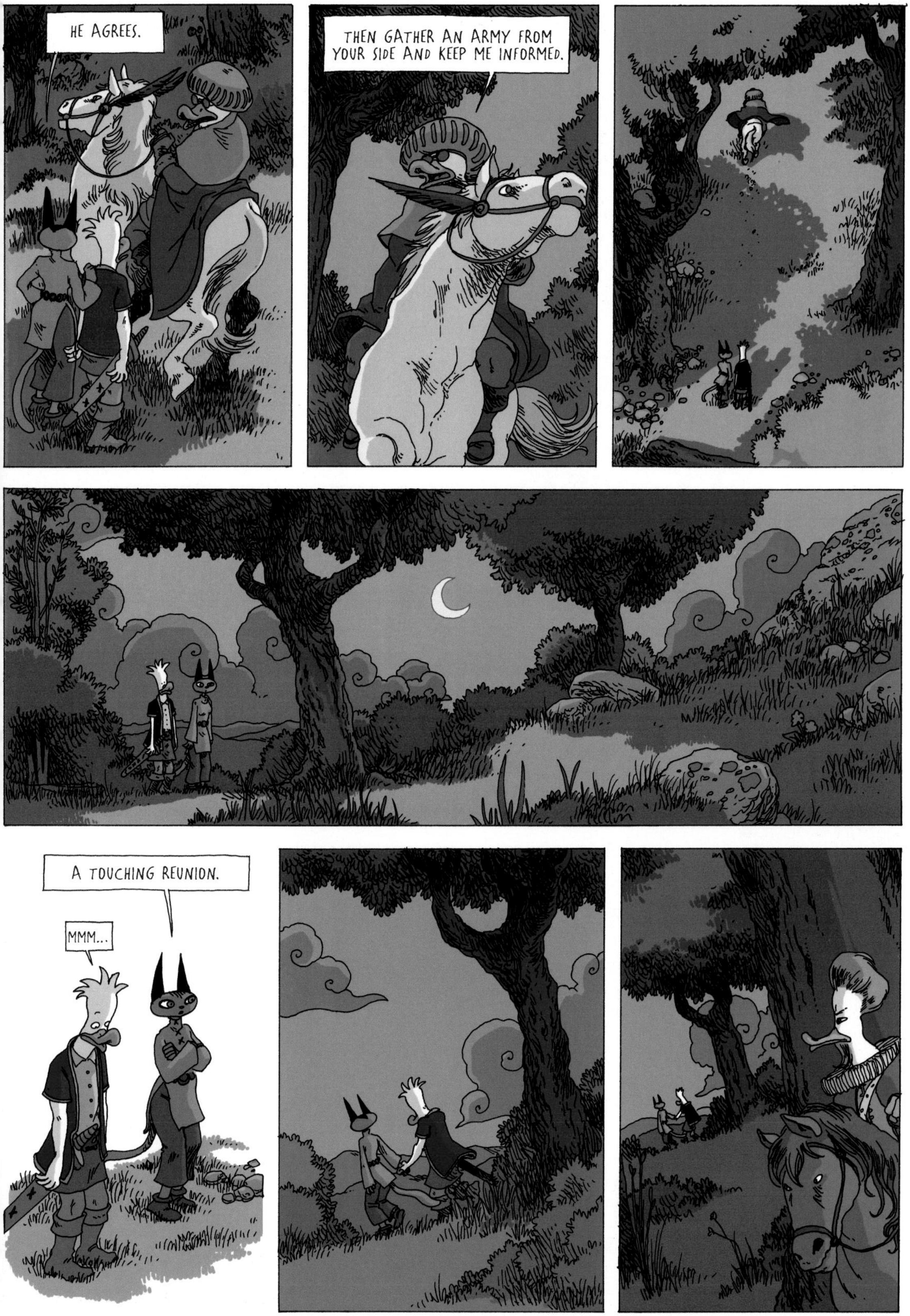

HE AGREES.
THEN GATHER AN ARMY FROM YOUR SIDE AND KEEP ME INFORMED.
A TOUCHING REUNION.
MMM...

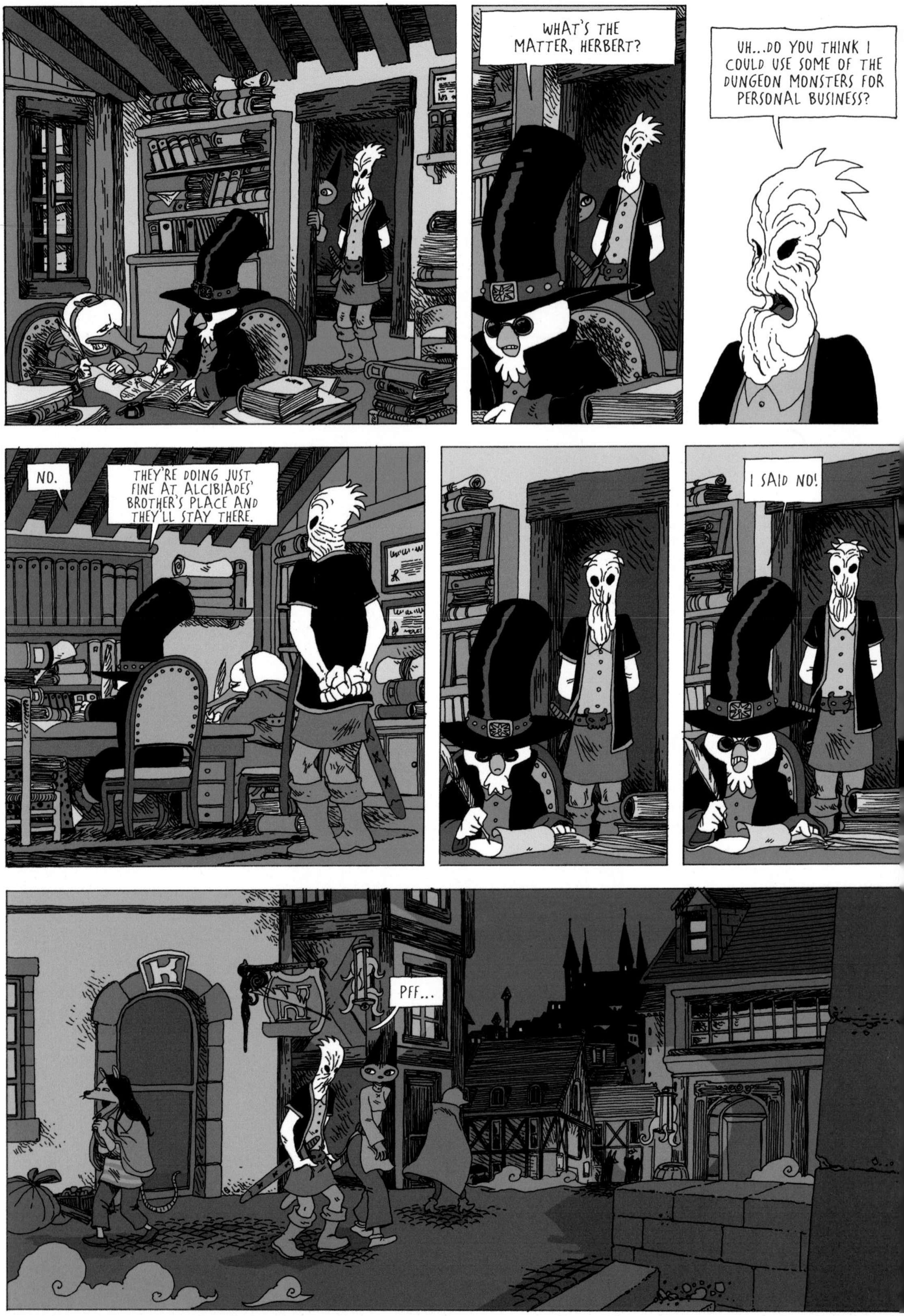
WHAT'S THE MATTER, HERBERT?
UH...DO YOU THINK I COULD USE SOME OF THE DUNGEON MONSTERS FOR PERSONAL BUSINESS?
NO.
THEY'RE DOING JUST FINE AT ALCIBIADES' BROTHER'S PLACE AND THEY'LL STAY THERE.
I SAID NO!
PFF...

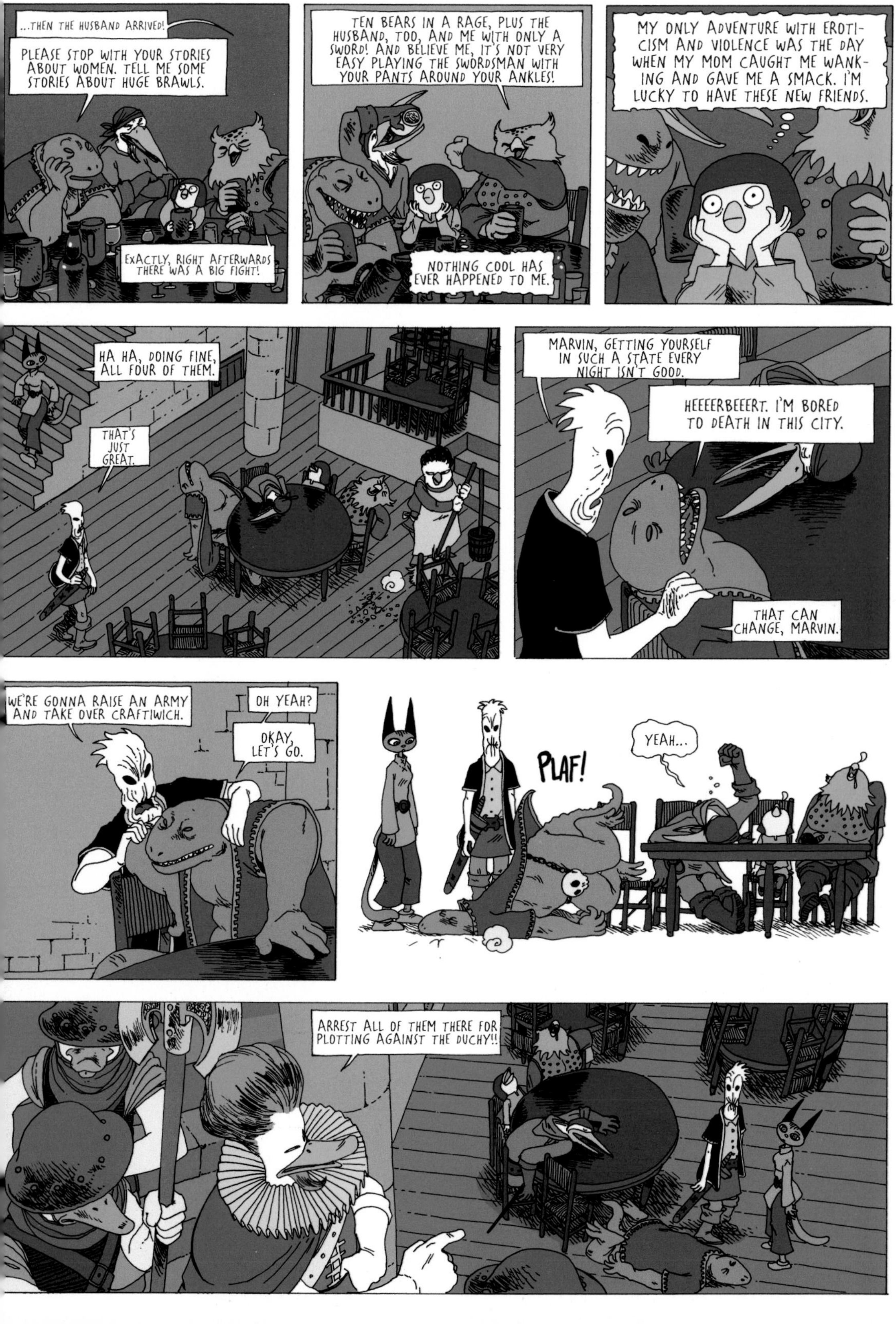
...THEN THE HUSBAND ARRIVED!
PLEASE STOP WITH YOUR STORIES ABOUT WOMEN. TELL ME SOME STORIES ABOUT HUGE BRAWLS.
EXACTLY, RIGHT AFTERWARDS THERE WAS A BIG FIGHT!
TEN BEARS IN A RAGE, PLUS THE HUSBAND, TOO, AND ME WITH ONLY A SWORD! AND BELIEVE ME, IT'S NOT VERY EASY PLAYING THE SWORDSMAN WITH YOUR PANTS AROUND YOUR ANKLES!
NOTHING COOL HAS EVER HAPPENED TO ME.
MY ONLY ADVENTURE WITH EROTI-CISM AND VIOLENCE WAS THE DAY WHEN MY MOM CAUGHT ME WANK-ING AND GAVE ME A SMACK. I'M LUCKY TO HAVE THESE NEW FRIENDS.
HA HA, DOING FINE, ALL FOUR OF THEM.
THAT'S JUST GREAT.
MARVIN, GETTING YOURSELF IN SUCH A STATE EVERY NIGHT ISN'T GOOD.
HEEEERBEEERT. I'M BORED TO DEATH IN THIS CITY.
THAT CAN CHANGE, MARVIN.
WE'RE GONNA RAISE AN ARMY AND TAKE OVER CRAFTIWICH.
OH YEAH?
OKAY, LET'S GO.
PLAF!
YEAH...
ARREST ALL OF THEM THERE FOR PLOTTING AGAINST THE DUCHY!!

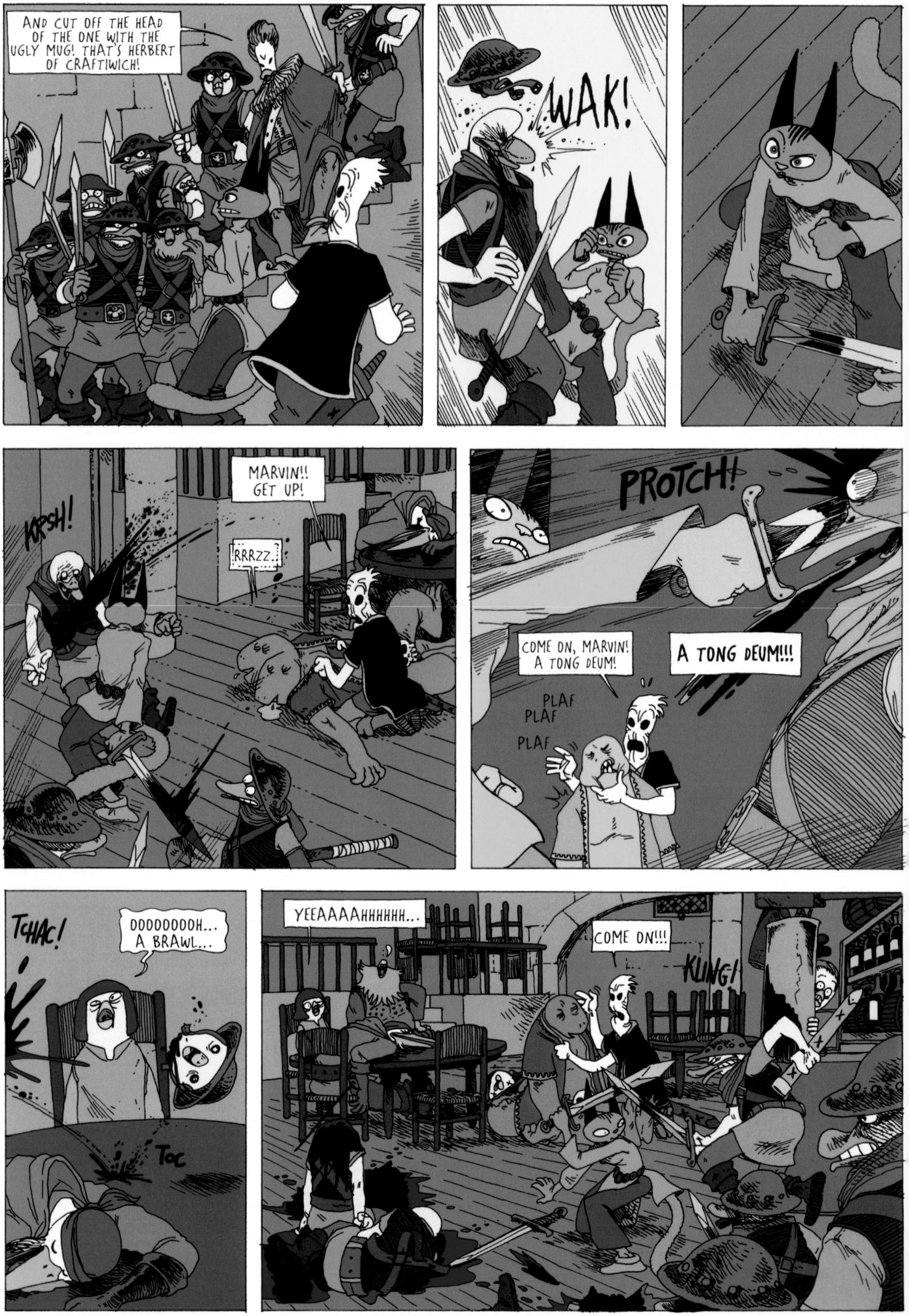

AND CUT OFF THE HEAD OF THE ONE WITH THE UGLY MUG! THAT'S HERBERT OF CRAFTIWICH!
WAK!
KRSH!
MARVIN!! GET UP!
RRRZZ...
PROTCH!
COME ON, MARVIN! A TONG DEUM!
A TONG DEUM!!!
PLAF
PLAF
PLAF
TCHAC!
OOOOOOOOH... A BRAWL...
TOC
YEEAAAAHHHHHH...
COME ON!!!
KLING!

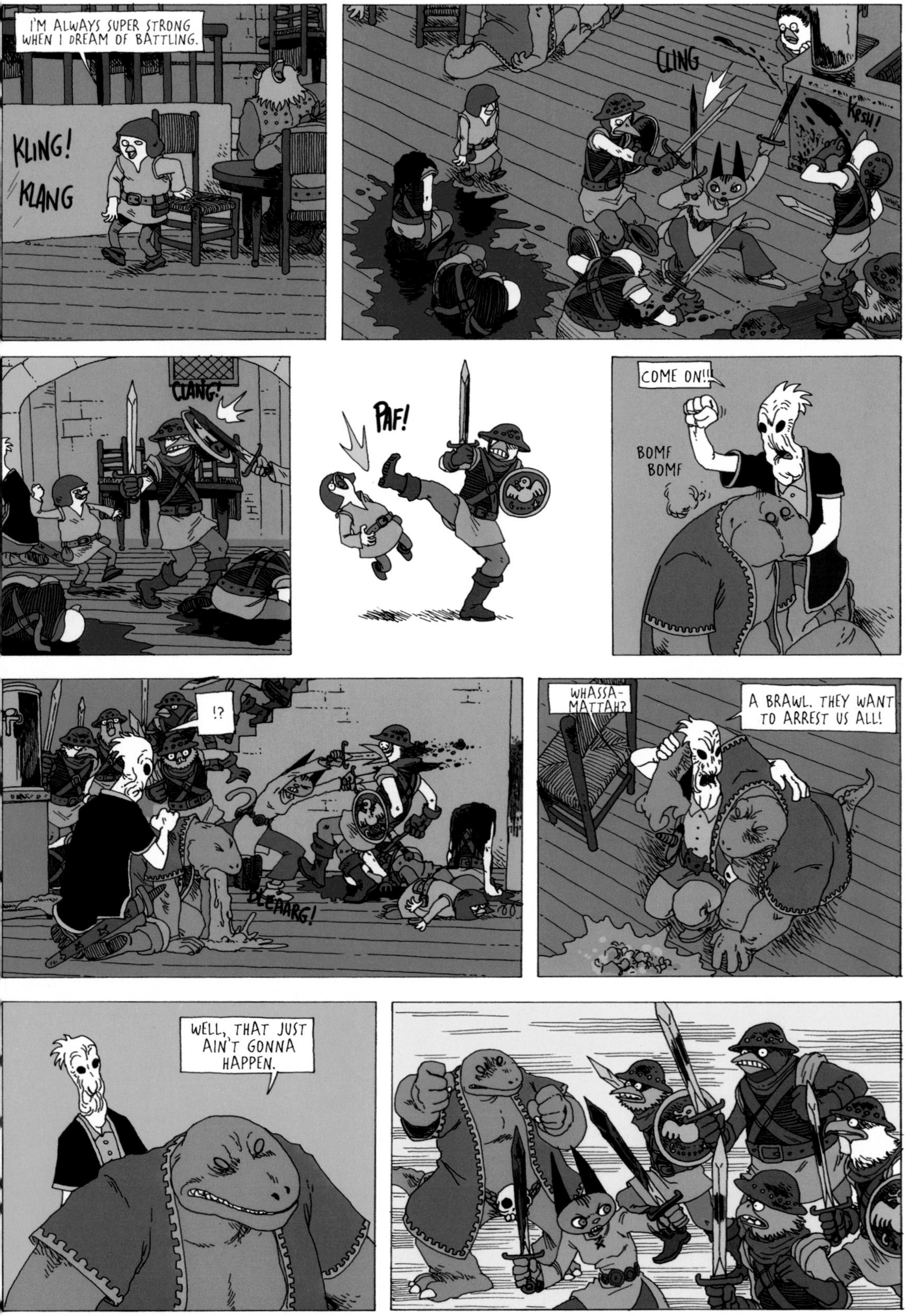
I'M ALWAYS SUPER STRONG WHEN I DREAM OF BATTLING.
KLING!
KLANG
CLING
KRSH!
CLANG!
PAF!
COME ON!!
BOMF BOMF
!?
BLEAARG!
WHASSA-MATTAH?
A BRAWL. THEY WANT TO ARREST US ALL!
WELL, THAT JUST AIN'T GONNA HAPPEN.

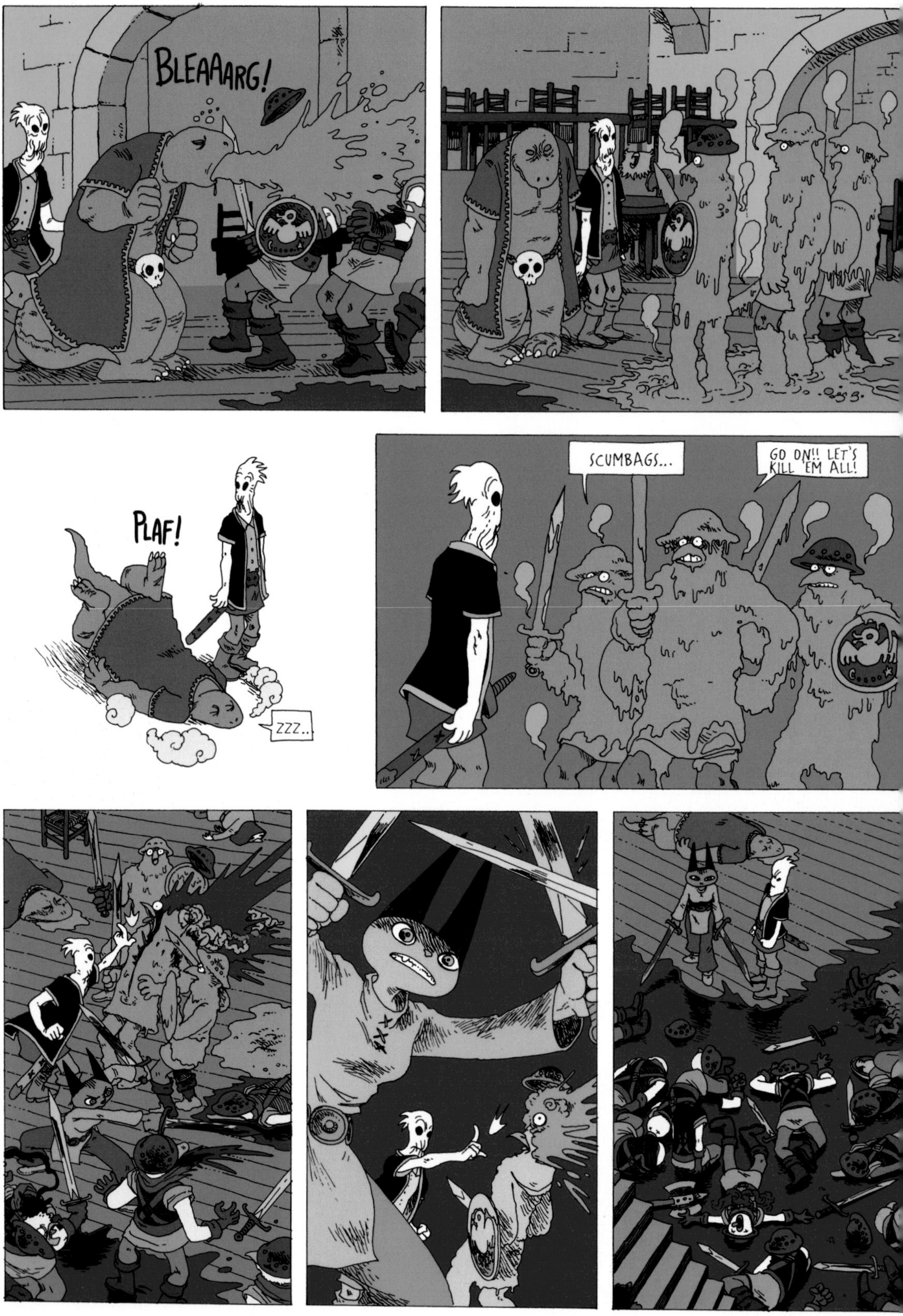
BLEAAARG!
PLAF!
ZZZ..
SCUMBAGS...
GO ON!! LET'S KILL 'EM ALL!

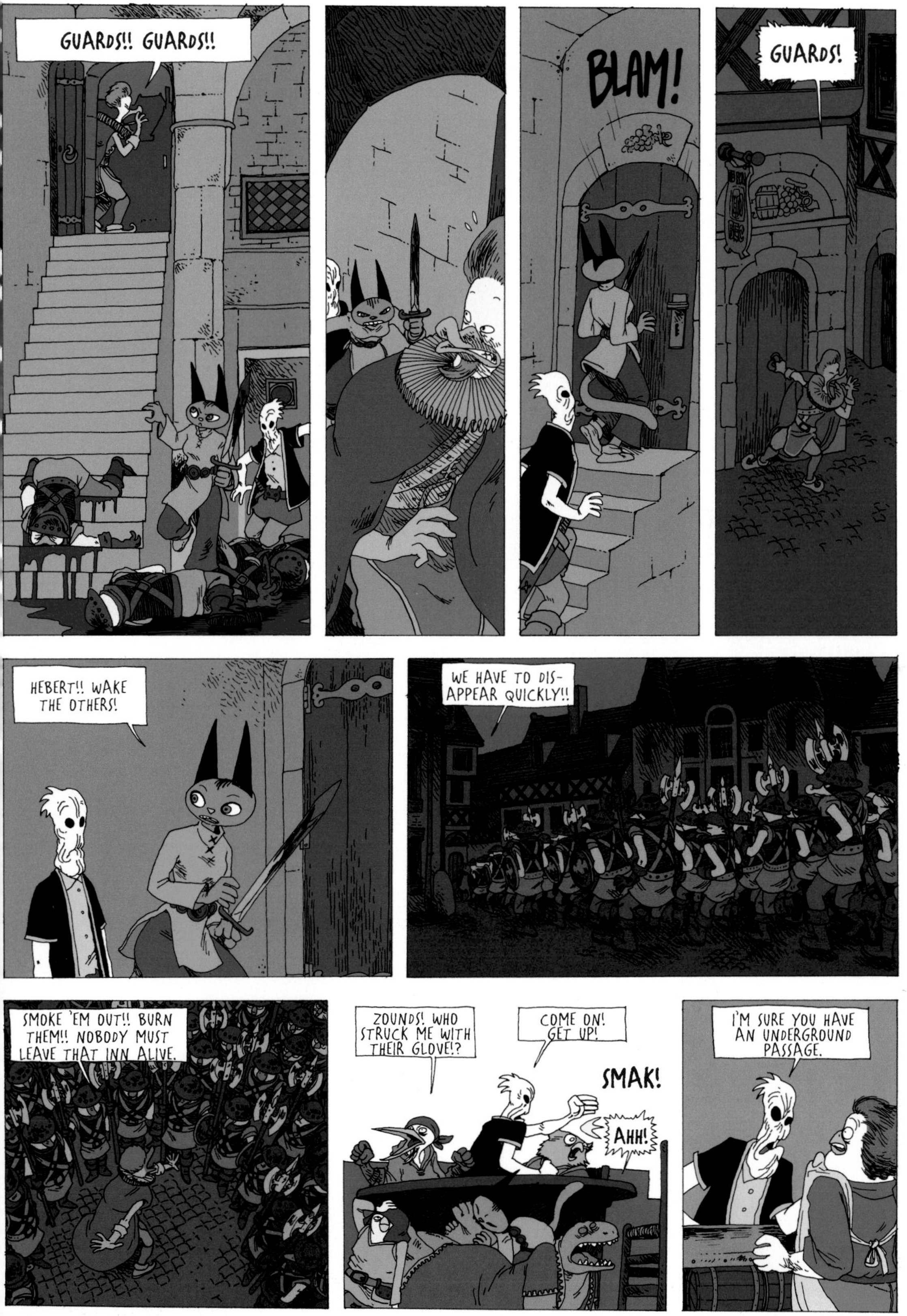
GUARDS!! GUARDS!!
BLAM!
GUARDS!
HEBERT!! WAKE THE OTHERS!
WE HAVE TO DIS-APPEAR QUICKLY!!
SMOKE 'EM OUT!! BURN THEM!! NOBODY MUST LEAVE THAT INN ALIVE.
ZOUNDS! WHO STRUCK ME WITH THEIR GLOVE!?
COME ON! GET UP!
SMAK!
AHH!
I'M SURE YOU HAVE AN UNDERGROUND PASSAGE.

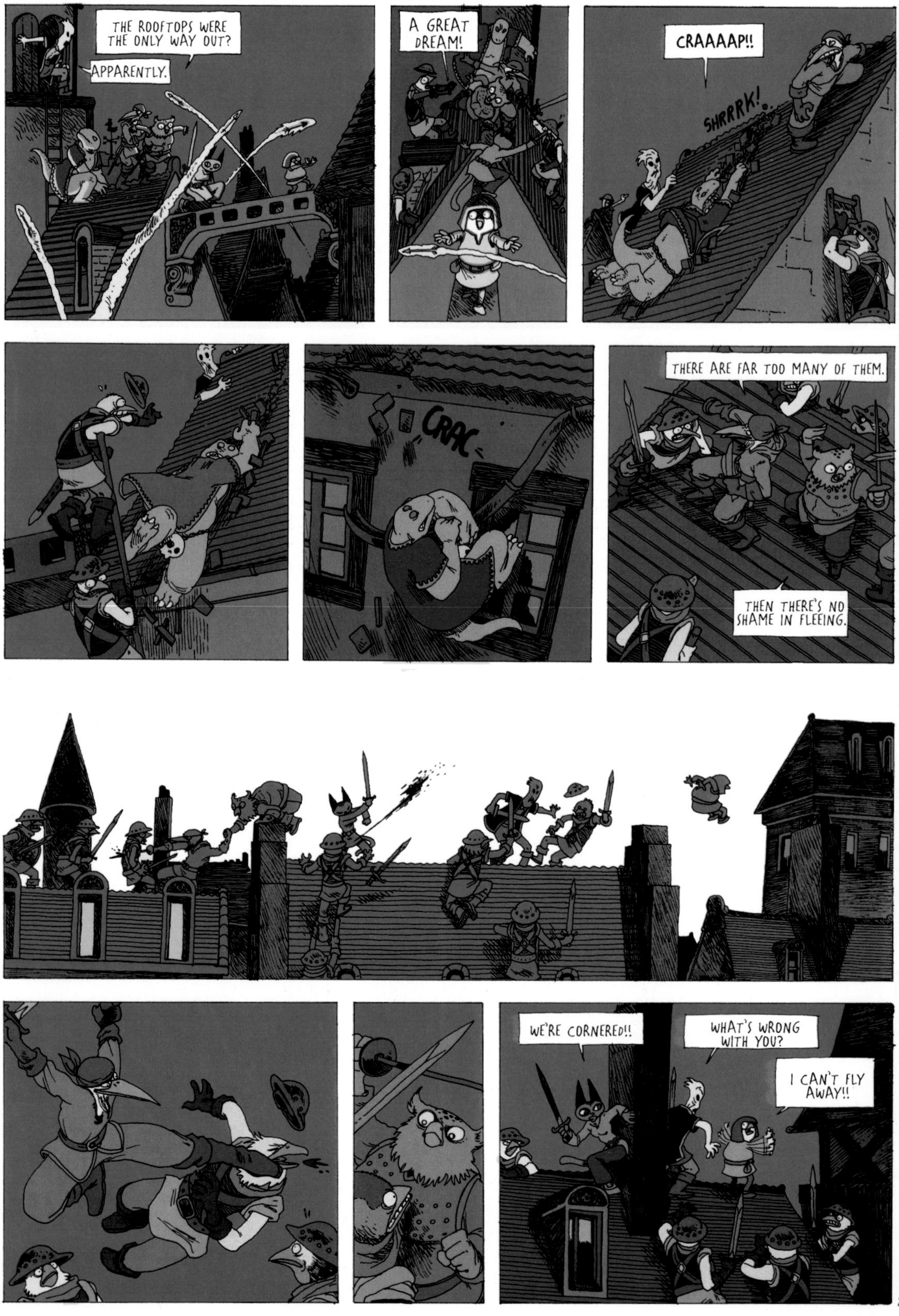
THE ROOFTOPS WERE THE ONLY WAY OUT?
APPARENTLY.
A GREAT DREAM!
CRAAAAP!!
SHRRRK!
CRAC
THERE ARE FAR TOO MANY OF THEM.
THEN THERE'S NO SHAME IN FLEEING.
WE'RE CORNERED!!
WHAT'S WRONG WITH YOU?
I CAN'T FLY AWAY!!

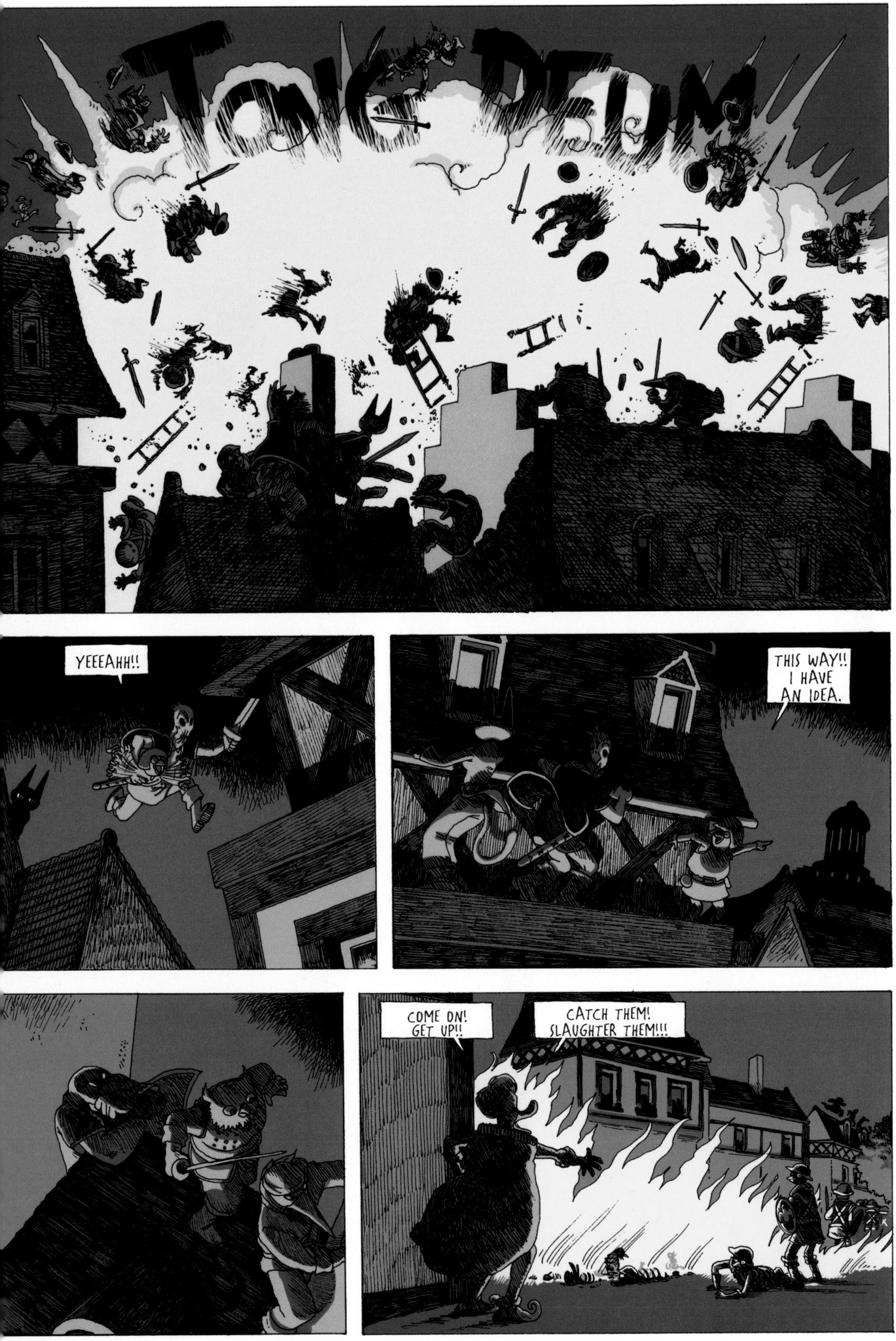
TONG DEUM
YEEEAHH!!
THIS WAY!! I HAVE AN IDEA.
COME ON! GET UP!!
CATCH THEM! SLAUGHTER THEM!!!

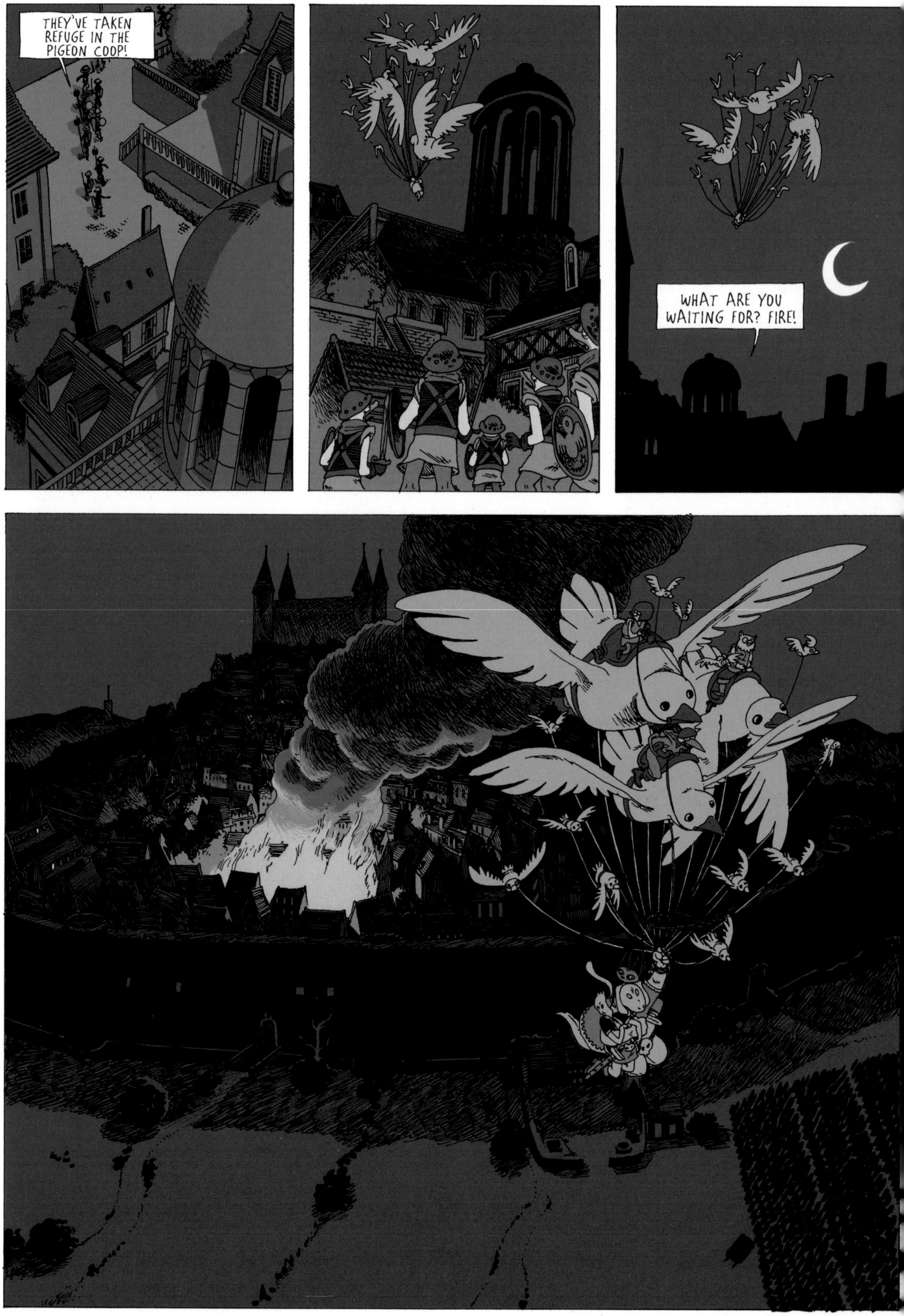
THEY'VE TAKEN REFUGE IN THE PIGEON COOP!
WHAT ARE YOU WAITING FOR? FIRE!

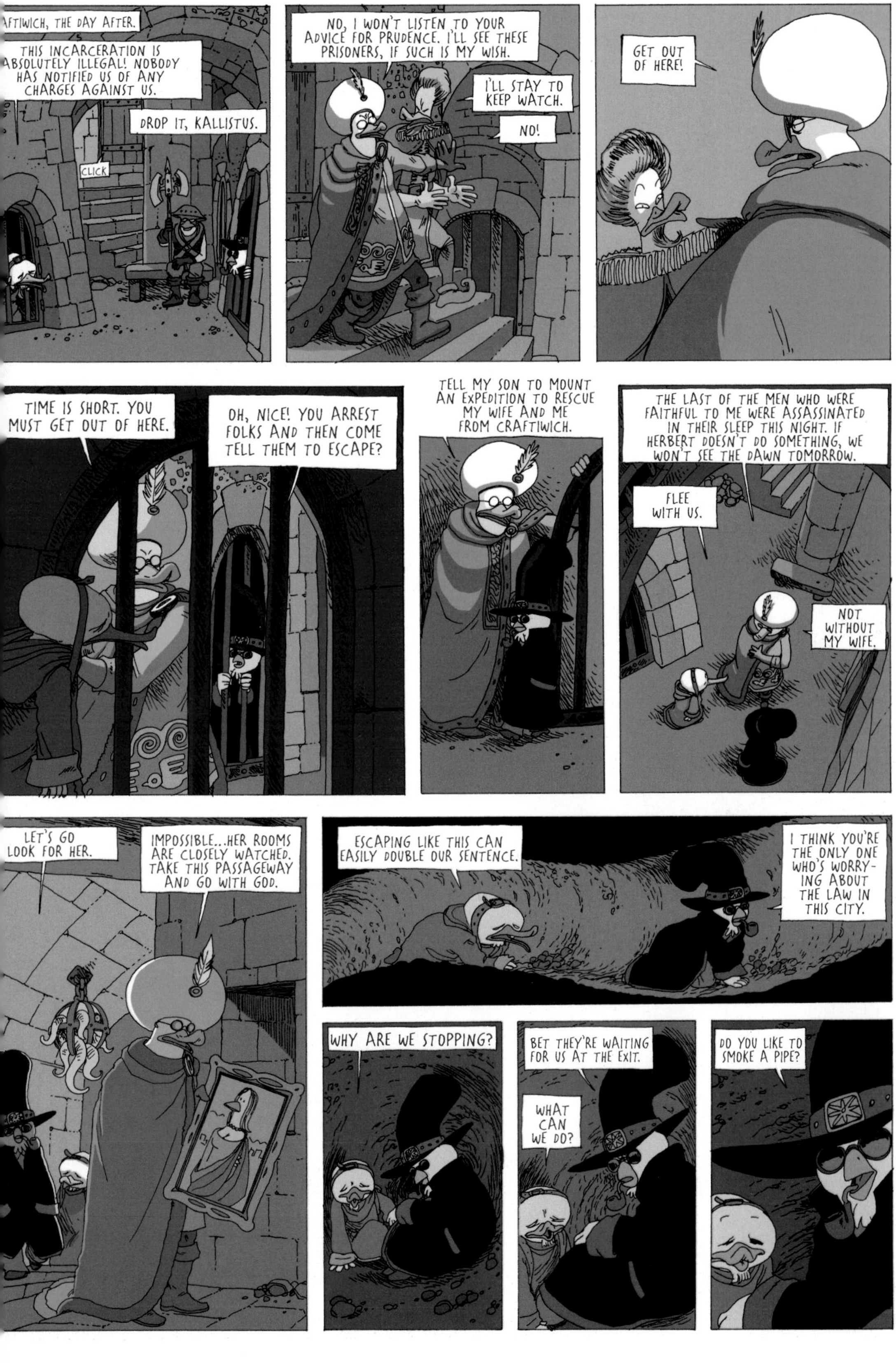
AFTIWICH, THE DAY AFTER.
THIS INCARCERATION IS ABSOLUTELY ILLEGAL! NOBODY HAS NOTIFIED US OF ANY CHARGES AGAINST US.
DROP IT, KALLISTUS.
CLICK
NO, I WON'T LISTEN TO YOUR ADVICE FOR PRUDENCE. I'LL SEE THESE PRISONERS, IF SUCH IS MY WISH.
I'LL STAY TO KEEP WATCH.
NO!
GET OUT OF HERE!
TIME IS SHORT. YOU MUST GET OUT OF HERE.
OH, NICE! YOU ARREST FOLKS AND THEN COME TELL THEM TO ESCAPE?
TELL MY SON TO MOUNT AN EXPEDITION TO RESCUE MY WIFE AND ME FROM CRAFTIWICH.
THE LAST OF THE MEN WHO WERE FAITHFUL TO ME WERE ASSASSINATED IN THEIR SLEEP THIS NIGHT. IF HERBERT DOESN'T DO SOMETHING, WE WON'T SEE THE DAWN TOMORROW.
FLEE WITH US.
NOT WITHOUT MY WIFE.
LET'S GO LOOK FOR HER.
IMPOSSIBLE...HER ROOMS ARE CLOSELY WATCHED. TAKE THIS PASSAGEWAY AND GO WITH GOD.
ESCAPING LIKE THIS CAN EASILY DOUBLE OUR SENTENCE.
I THINK YOU'RE THE ONLY ONE WHO'S WORRYING ABOUT THE LAW IN THIS CITY.
WHY ARE WE STOPPING?
BET THEY'RE WAITING FOR US AT THE EXIT.
WHAT CAN WE DO?
DO YOU LIKE TO SMOKE A PIPE?

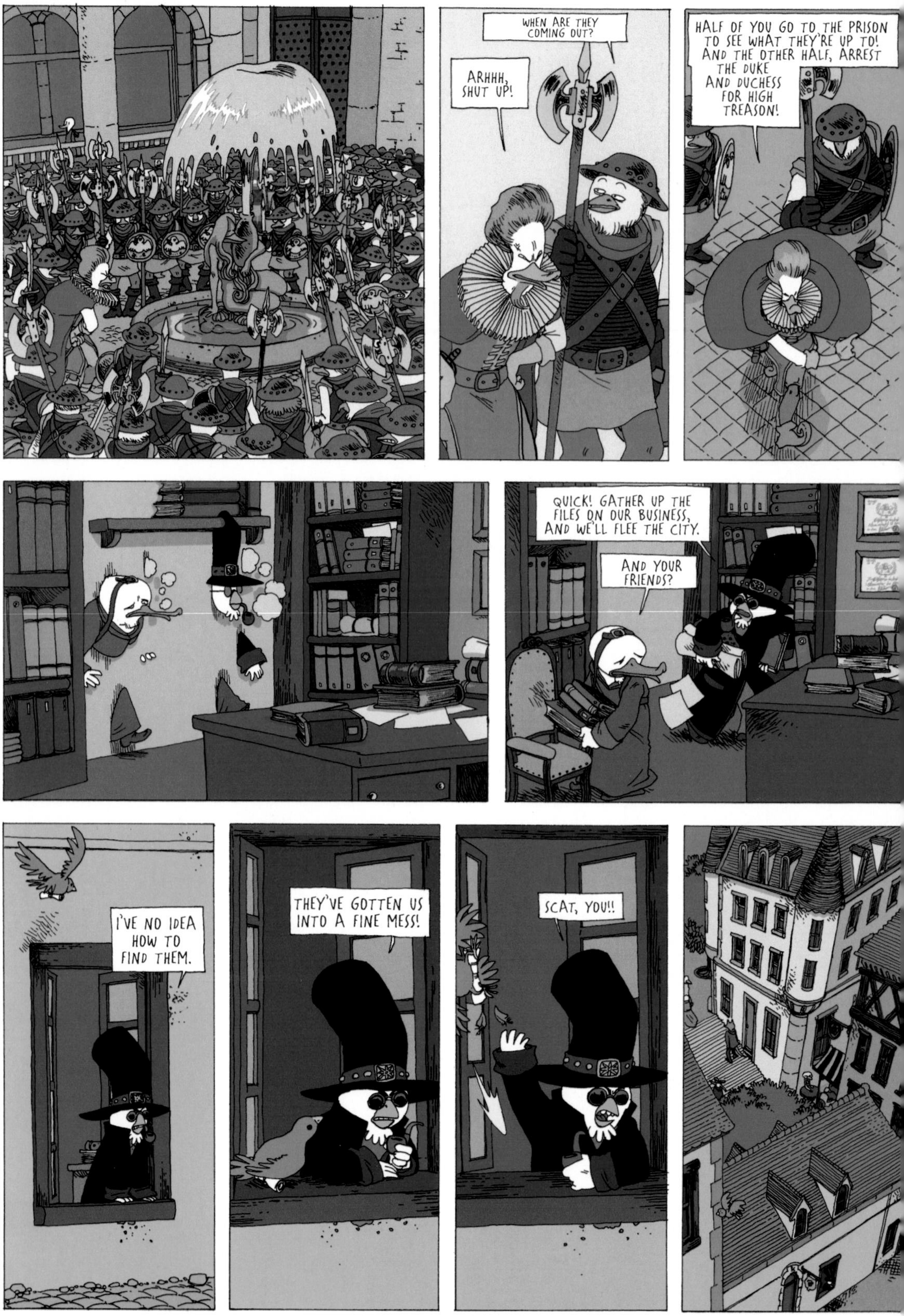
WHEN ARE THEY COMING OUT?
ARHHH, SHUT UP!
HALF OF YOU GO TO THE PRISON TO SEE WHAT THEY'RE UP TO! AND THE OTHER HALF, ARREST THE DUKE AND DUCHESS FOR HIGH TREASON!
QUICK! GATHER UP THE FILES ON OUR BUSINESS, AND WE'LL FLEE THE CITY.
AND YOUR FRIENDS?
I'VE NO IDEA HOW TO FIND THEM.
THEY'VE GOTTEN US INTO A FINE MESS!
SCAT, YOU!!

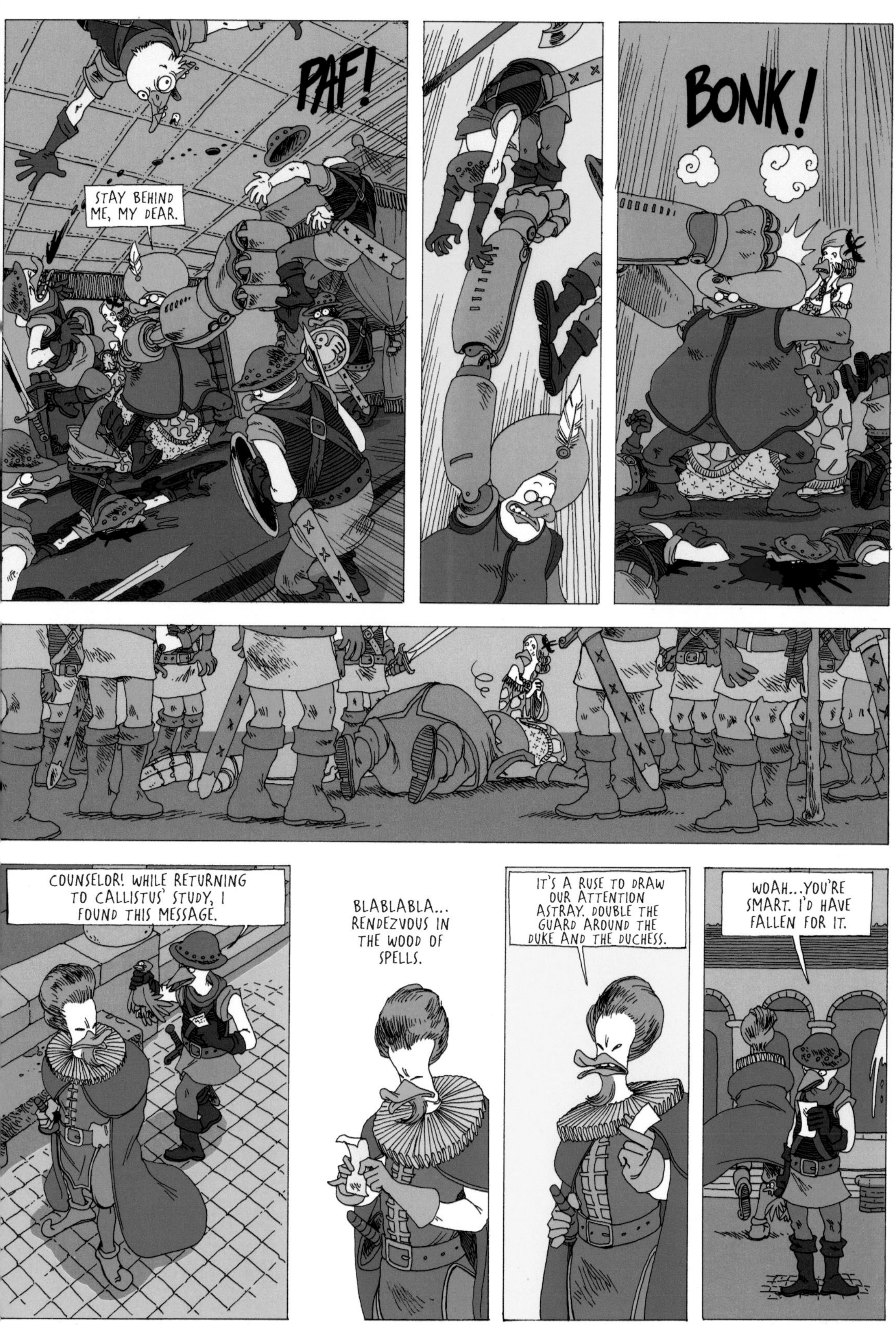
PAF!
STAY BEHIND ME, MY DEAR.
BONK!
COUNSELOR! WHILE RETURNING TO CALLISTUS' STUDY, I FOUND THIS MESSAGE.
BLABLABLA... RENDEZVOUS IN THE WOOD OF SPELLS.
IT'S A RUSE TO DRAW OUR ATTENTION ASTRAY. DOUBLE THE GUARD AROUND THE DUKE AND THE DUCHESS.
WOAH...YOU'RE SMART. I'D HAVE FALLEN FOR IT.

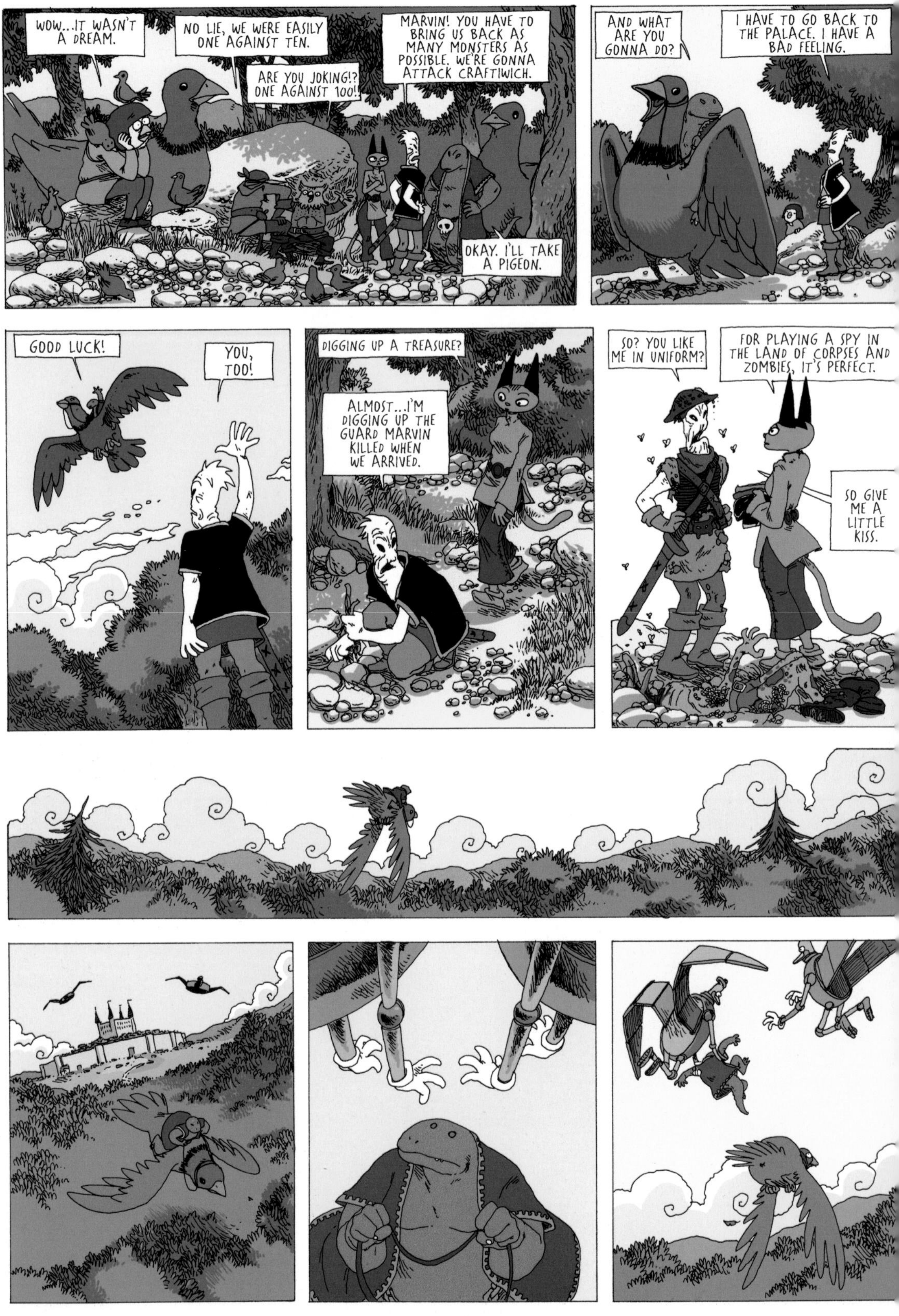
WOW...IT WASN'T A DREAM.
NO LIE, WE WERE EASILY ONE AGAINST TEN.
ARE YOU JOKING!? ONE AGAINST 100!!
MARVIN! YOU HAVE TO BRING US BACK AS MANY MONSTERS AS POSSIBLE. WE'RE GONNA ATTACK CRAFTIWICH.
OKAY. I'LL TAKE A PIGEON.
AND WHAT ARE YOU GONNA DO?
I HAVE TO GO BACK TO THE PALACE. I HAVE A BAD FEELING.
GOOD LUCK!
YOU, TOO!
DIGGING UP A TREASURE?
ALMOST...I'M DIGGING UP THE GUARD MARVIN KILLED WHEN WE ARRIVED.
SO? YOU LIKE ME IN UNIFORM?
FOR PLAYING A SPY IN THE LAND OF CORPSES AND ZOMBIES, IT'S PERFECT.
SO GIVE ME A LITTLE KISS.

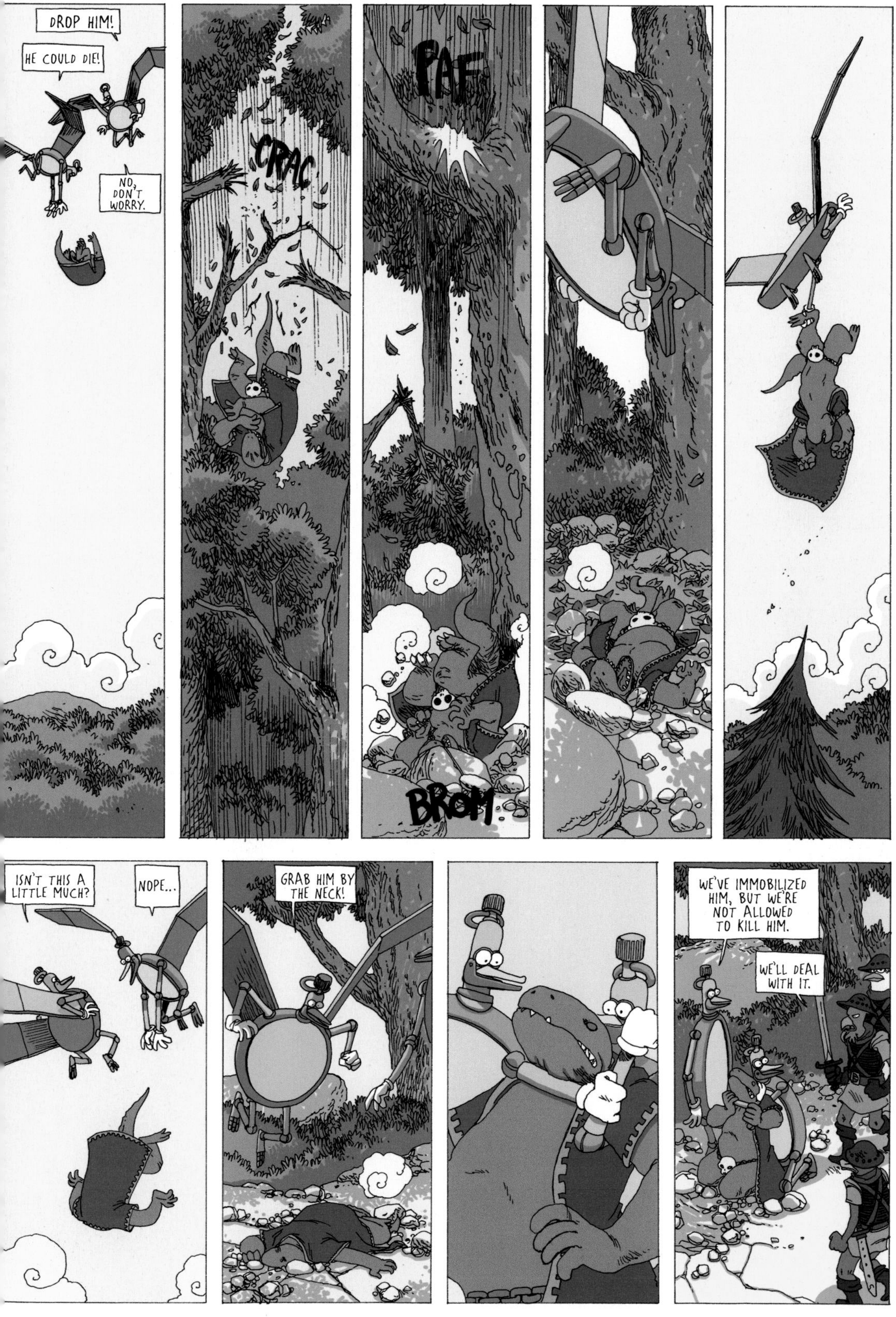
DROP HIM!
HE COULD DIE!
NO, DON'T WORRY.
CRAC
PAF
BROM
ISN'T THIS A LITTLE MUCH?
NOPE...
GRAB HIM BY THE NECK!
WE'VE IMMOBILIZED HIM, BUT WE'RE NOT ALLOWED TO KILL HIM.
WE'LL DEAL WITH IT.

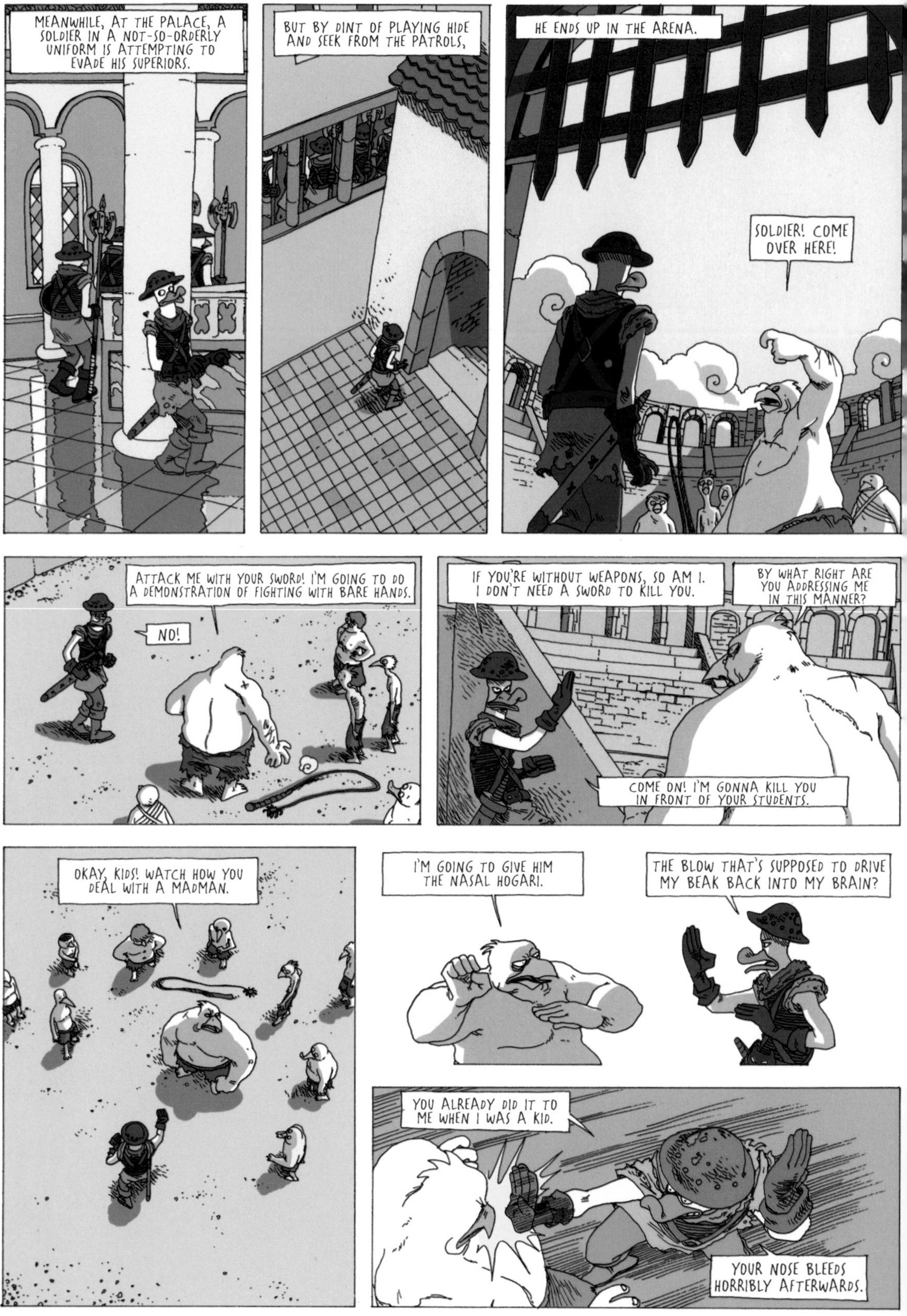

MEANWHILE, AT THE PALACE, A SOLDIER IN A NOT-SO-ORDERLY UNIFORM IS ATTEMPTING TO EVADE HIS SUPERIORS.
BUT BY DINT OF PLAYING HIDE AND SEEK FROM THE PATROLS,
HE ENDS UP IN THE ARENA.
SOLDIER! COME OVER HERE!
ATTACK ME WITH YOUR SWORD! I'M GOING TO DO A DEMONSTRATION OF FIGHTING WITH BARE HANDS.
NO!
IF YOU'RE WITHOUT WEAPONS, SO AM I. I DON'T NEED A SWORD TO KILL YOU.
BY WHAT RIGHT ARE YOU ADDRESSING ME IN THIS MANNER?
COME ON! I'M GONNA KILL YOU IN FRONT OF YOUR STUDENTS.
OKAY, KIDS! WATCH HOW YOU DEAL WITH A MADMAN.
I'M GOING TO GIVE HIM THE NASAL HOGARI.
THE BLOW THAT'S SUPPOSED TO DRIVE MY BEAK BACK INTO MY BRAIN?
YOU ALREADY DID IT TO ME WHEN I WAS A KID.
YOUR NOSE BLEEDS HORRIBLY AFTERWARDS.

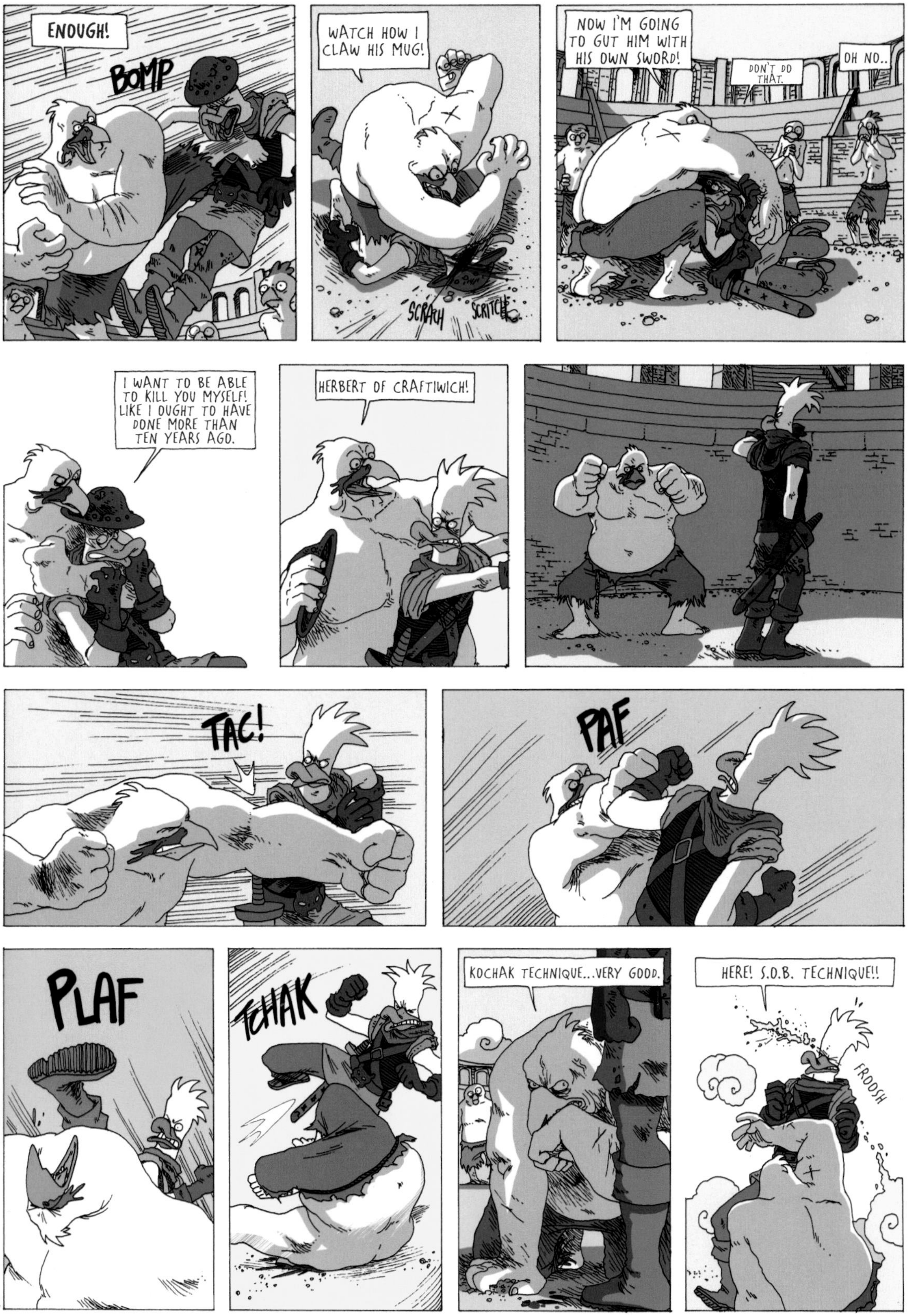
ENOUGH!
BOMP
WATCH HOW I CLAW HIS MUG!
SCRATCH
SCRITCH
NOW I'M GOING TO GUT HIM WITH HIS OWN SWORD!
DON'T DO THAT.
OH NO..
I WANT TO BE ABLE TO KILL YOU MYSELF! LIKE I OUGHT TO HAVE DONE MORE THAN TEN YEARS AGO.
HERBERT OF CRAFTIWICH!
TAC!
PAF
PLAF
TCHAK
KOCHAK TECHNIQUE...VERY GOOD.
HERE! S.O.B. TECHNIQUE!!
FROOSH

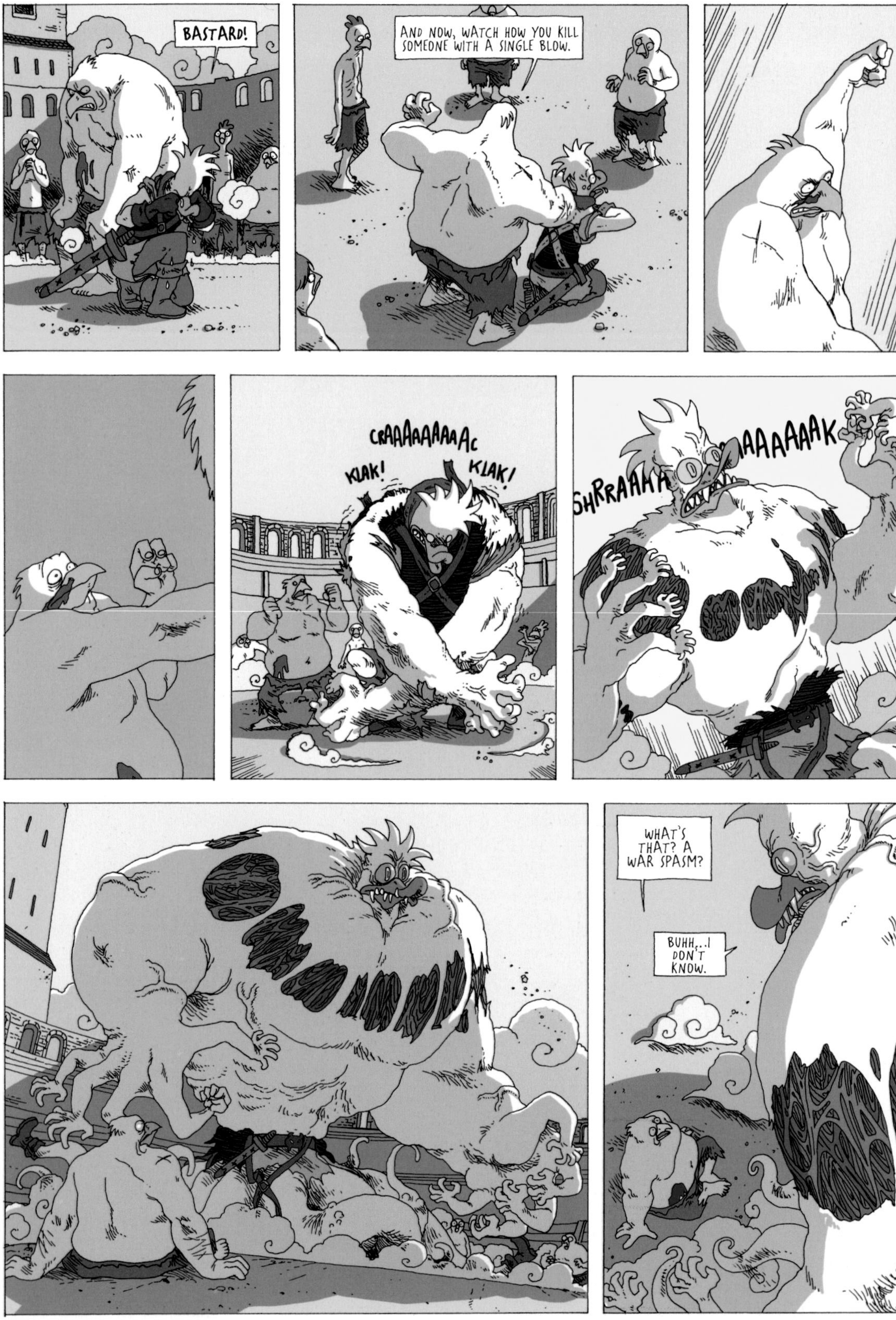

BASTARD!
AND NOW, WATCH HOW YOU KILL SOMEONE WITH A SINGLE BLOW.
CRAAAAAAAAAc
KLAK!
KLAK!
SHRRAAAA
AAAAAAK
WHAT'S THAT? A WAR SPASM?
BUHH,..I DON'T KNOW.

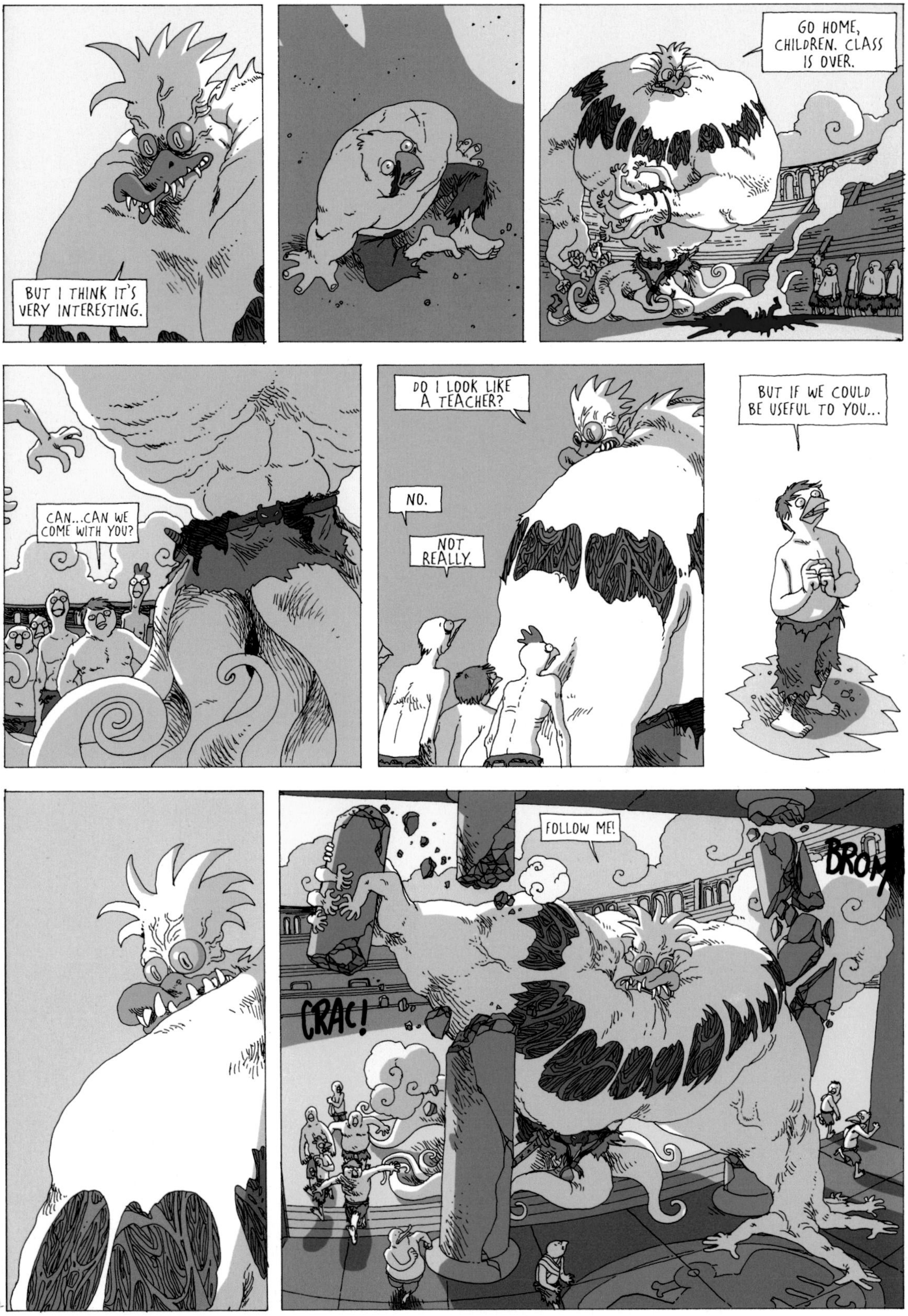
BUT I THINK IT'S VERY INTERESTING.
GO HOME, CHILDREN. CLASS IS OVER.
CAN...CAN WE COME WITH YOU?
DO I LOOK LIKE A TEACHER?
NO.
NOT REALLY.
BUT IF WE COULD BE USEFUL TO YOU...
FOLLOW ME!
BROM
CRAC!

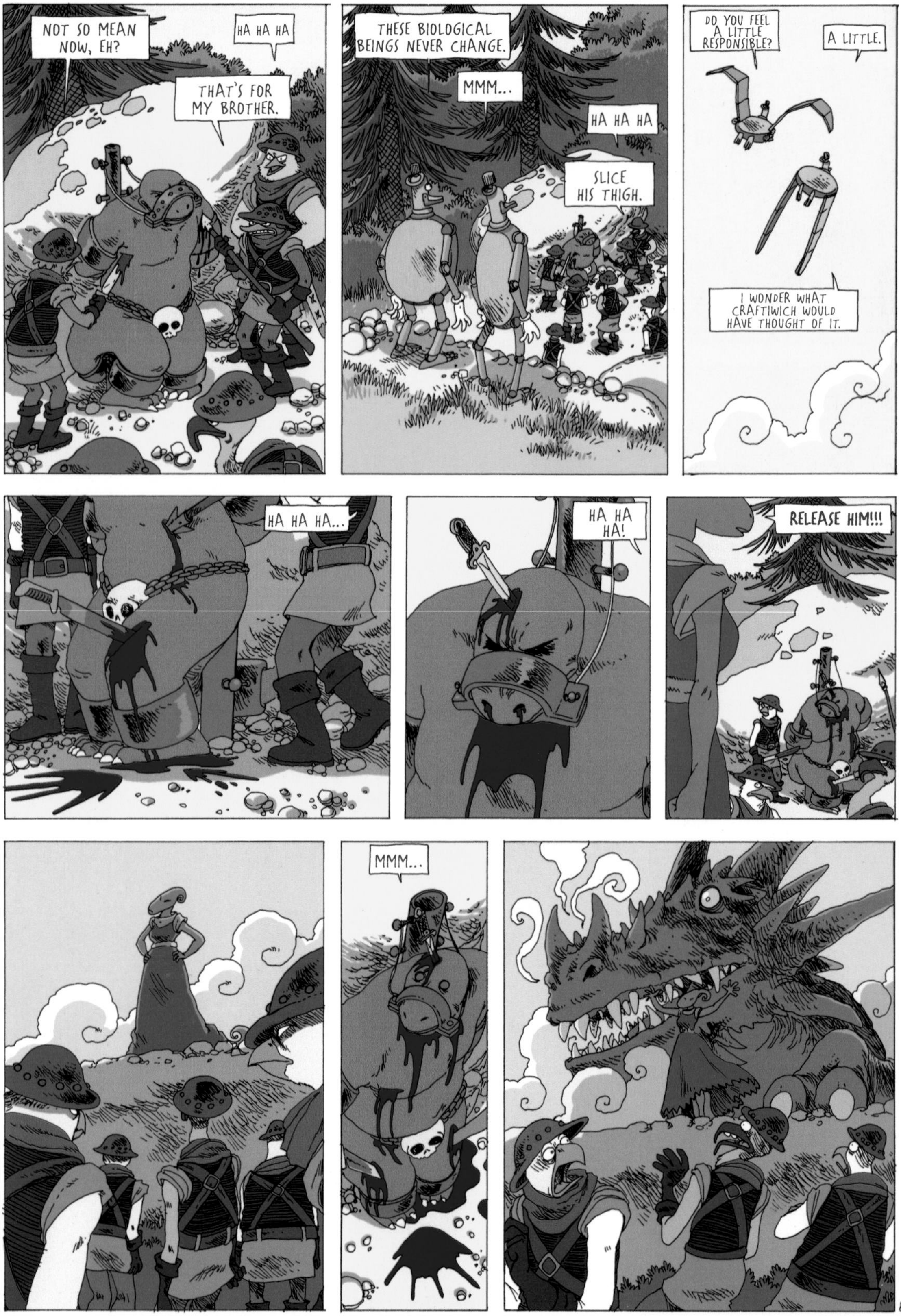
NOT SO MEAN NOW, EH?
HA HA HA
THAT'S FOR MY BROTHER.
THESE BIOLOGICAL BEINGS NEVER CHANGE.
MMM...
HA HA HA
SLICE HIS THIGH.
DO YOU FEEL A LITTLE RESPONSIBLE?
A LITTLE.
I WONDER WHAT CRAFTIWICH WOULD HAVE THOUGHT OF IT.
HA HA HA...
HA HA HA!
RELEASE HIM!!!
MMM...

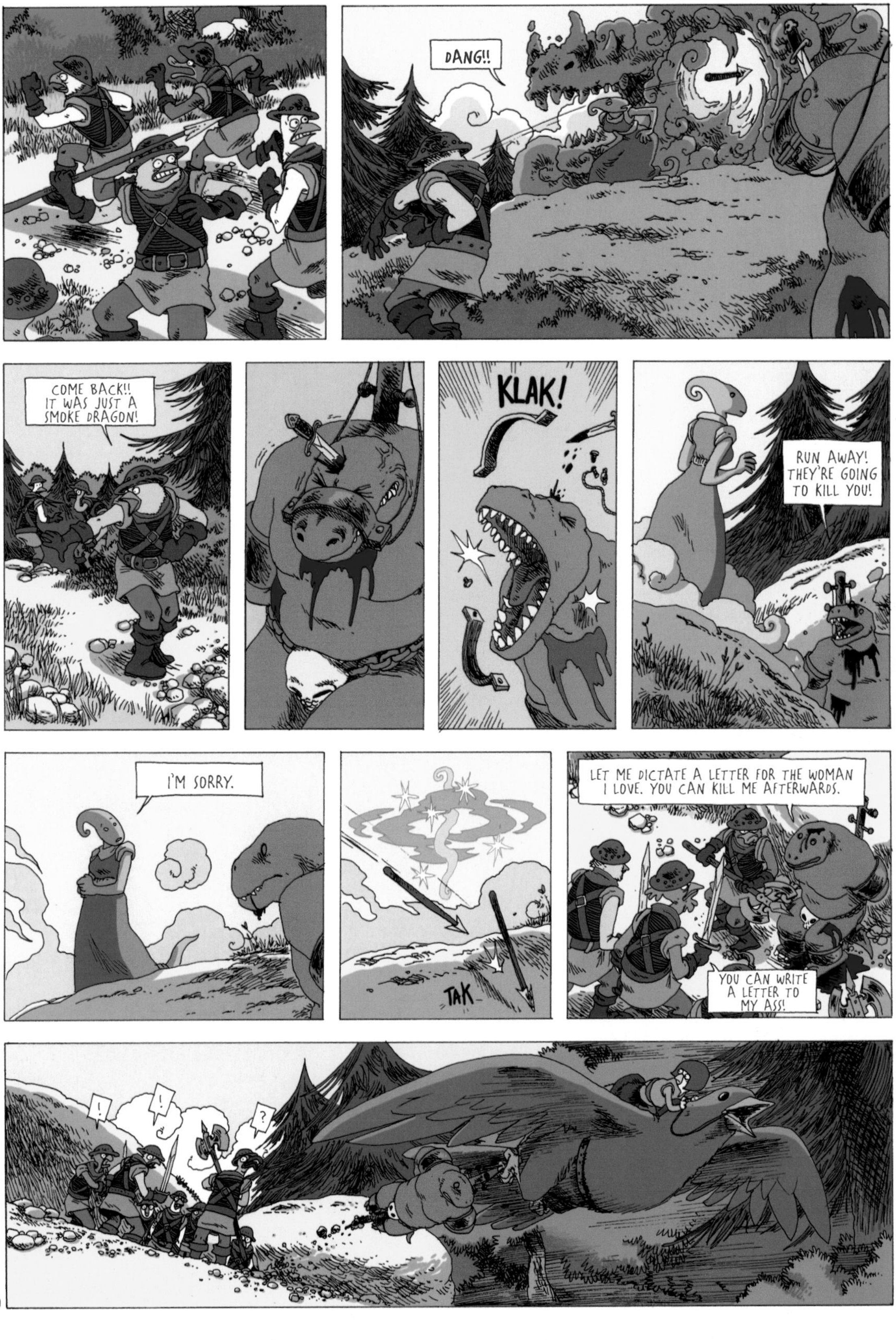
DANG!!
COME BACK!! IT WAS JUST A SMOKE DRAGON!
KLAK!
RUN AWAY! THEY'RE GOING TO KILL YOU!
I'M SORRY.
TAK
LET ME DICTATE A LETTER FOR THE WOMAN I LOVE. YOU CAN KILL ME AFTERWARDS.
YOU CAN WRITE A LETTER TO MY ASS!
!
!
?

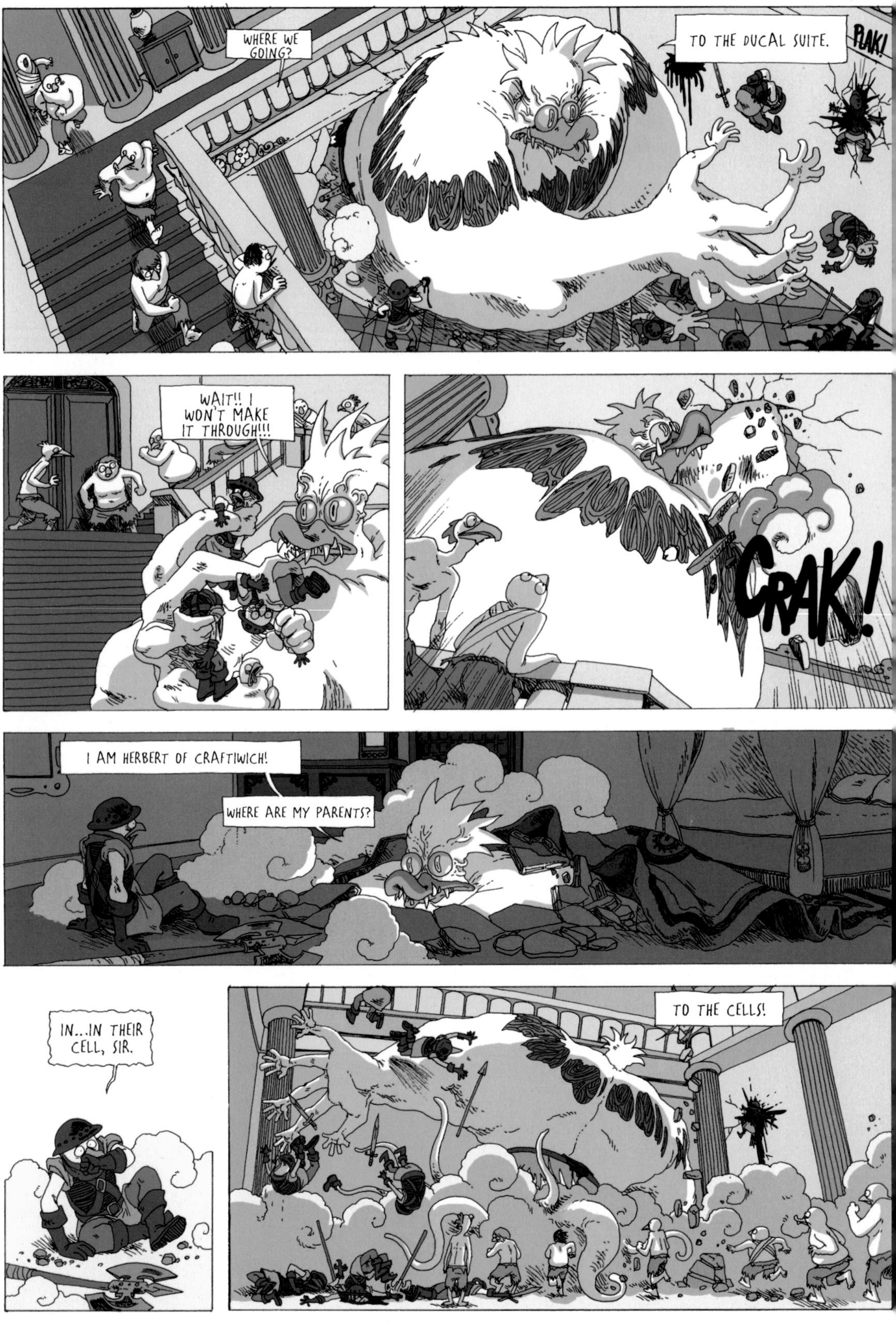
WHERE WE GOING?
TO THE DUCAL SUITE.
PLAK!
WAIT!! I WON'T MAKE IT THROUGH!!!
CRAK!
I AM HERBERT OF CRAFTIWICH!
WHERE ARE MY PARENTS?
IN...IN THEIR CELL, SIR.
TO THE CELLS!

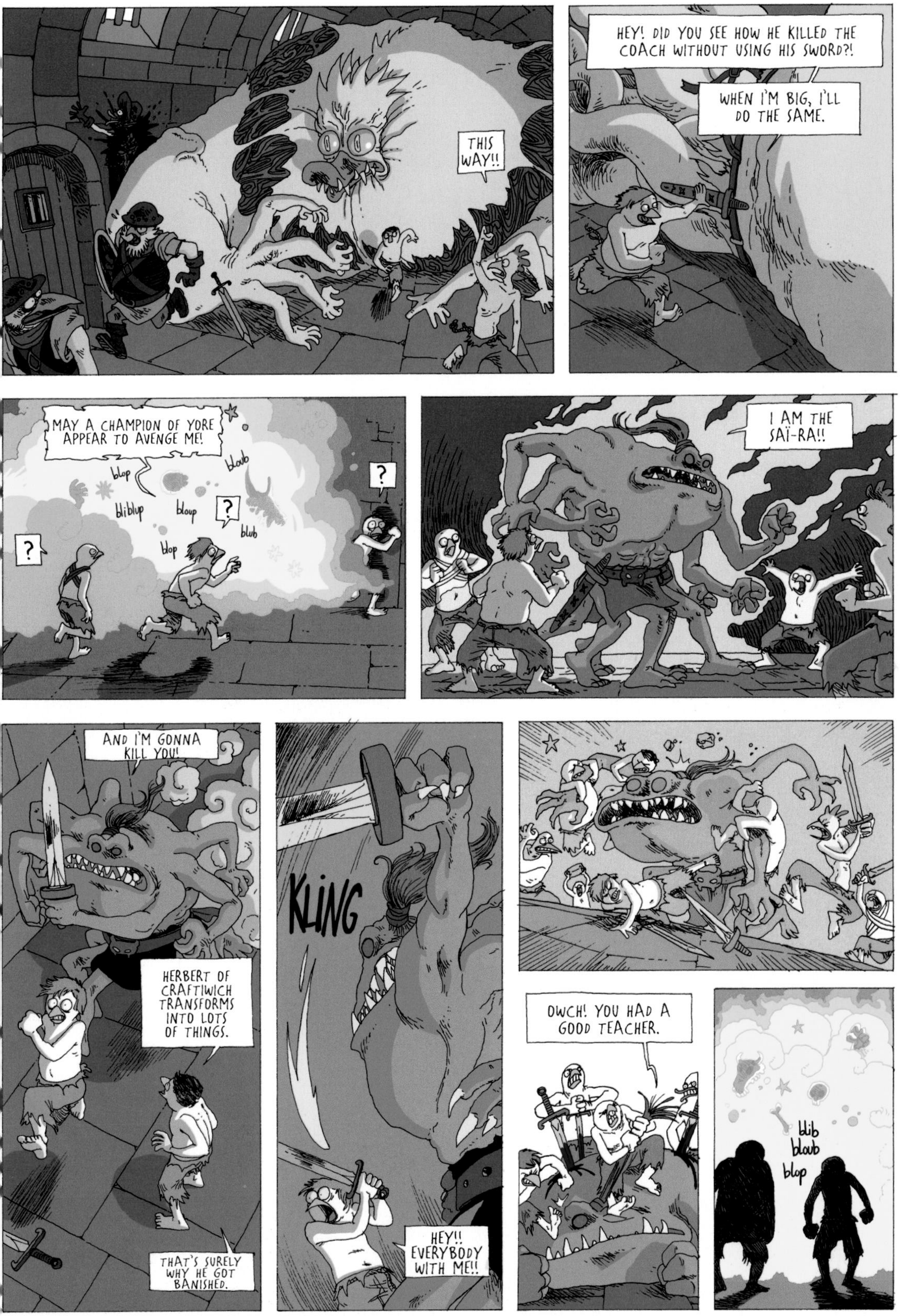
THIS WAY!!
HEY! DID YOU SEE HOW HE KILLED THE COACH WITHOUT USING HIS SWORD?!
WHEN I'M BIG, I'LL DO THE SAME.
MAY A CHAMPION OF YORE APPEAR TO AVENGE ME!
blop
bloub
bliblup
bloup
?
blub
blop
?
?
I AM THE SAÏ-RA!!
AND I'M GONNA KILL YOU!
HERBERT OF CRAFTIWICH TRANSFORMS INTO LOTS OF THINGS.
THAT'S SURELY WHY HE GOT BANISHED.
KLING
HEY!! EVERYBODY WITH ME!!
OWCH! YOU HAD A GOOD TEACHER.
blib
bloub
blop

SIR?

WHAT DO YOU WANT US TO DO?

GO RESCUE MY PARENTS AND ALL OF YOU QUIETLY LEAVE THE CITY.

COUNSELOR! THE DUKE'S SON TRANSFORMED INTO AN INVINCIBLE MONSTER AND HE MASSACRED ALL THE GUARDS.

BRING ME THE MONSTER-POCKET WATCHES.

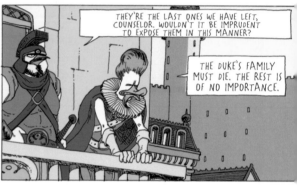

THEY'RE THE LAST ONES WE HAVE LEFT, COUNSELOR. WOULDN'T IT BE IMPRUDENT TO EXPOSE THEM IN THIS MANNER?

THE DUKE'S FAMILY MUST DIE. THE REST IS OF NO IMPORTANCE.

SWORDBELT! WHAT DID YOU COOK UP IN THE ARENA?

WHAT ARE YOU TALKING ABOUT?

THE BIT WITH THE GIANT MONSTER. I'M SURE THAT WAS YOU.

HA HA HA...NOT AT ALL! BUT I KNOW WHERE IT CAME FROM.

AND OF COURSE, YOU'RE NOT PLANNING TO REVEAL IT TO ME.

THAT WOULD BE TOO EASY.

SWORDBELT...

YES?

ONE DAY, I'LL FIND THE MEANS TO DESTROY YOU.

HEY! SOLDIER!

WE'RE LOOKING FOR THE INVINCIBLE MONSTER THAT WRECKED THE CASTLE, BUT NOBODY COULD LAY A HAND ON HIM.

YOU WOULDN'T HAVE SEEN HIM?

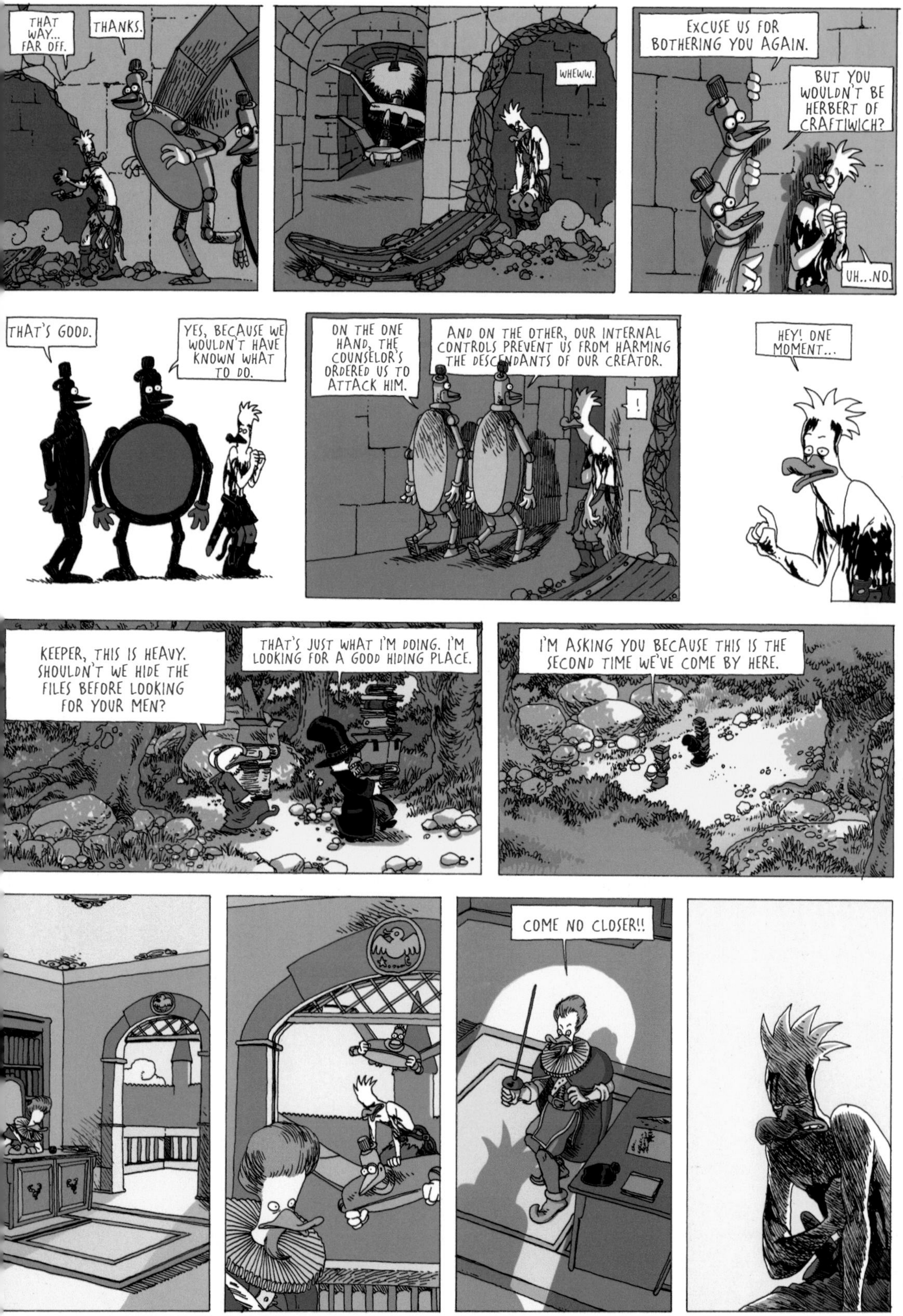
THAT WAY... FAR OFF.
THANKS.
WHEWW.
EXCUSE US FOR BOTHERING YOU AGAIN.
BUT YOU WOULDN'T BE HERBERT OF CRAFTIWICH?
UH...NO.
THAT'S GOOD.
YES, BECAUSE WE WOULDN'T HAVE KNOWN WHAT TO DO.
ON THE ONE HAND, THE COUNSELOR'S ORDERED US TO ATTACK HIM.
AND ON THE OTHER, OUR INTERNAL CONTROLS PREVENT US FROM HARMING THE DESCENDANTS OF OUR CREATOR.
!
HEY! ONE MOMENT...
KEEPER, THIS IS HEAVY. SHOULDN'T WE HIDE THE FILES BEFORE LOOKING FOR YOUR MEN?
THAT'S JUST WHAT I'M DOING. I'M LOOKING FOR A GOOD HIDING PLACE.
I'M ASKING YOU BECAUSE THIS IS THE SECOND TIME WE'VE COME BY HERE.
COME NO CLOSER!!

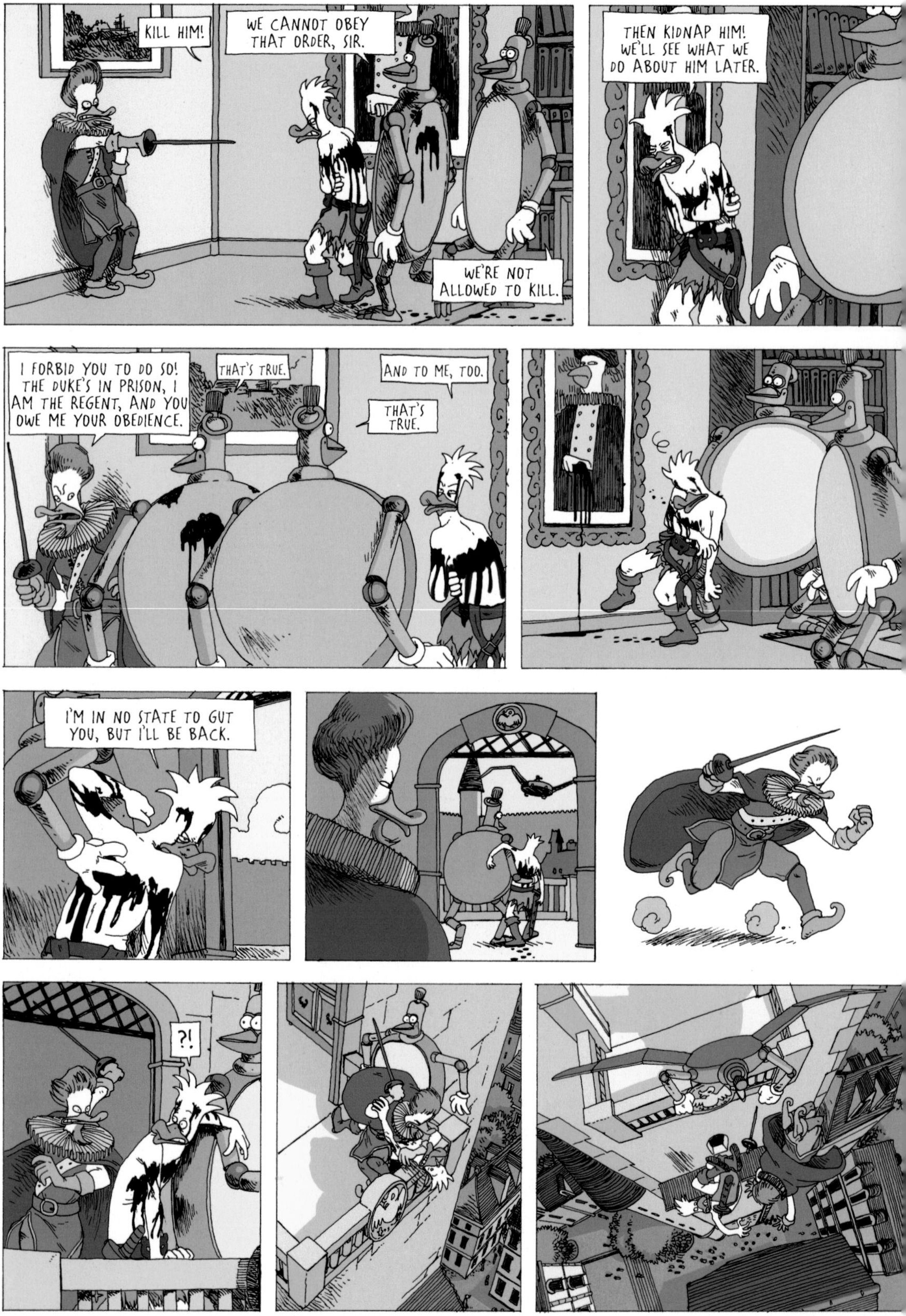
KILL HIM!
WE CANNOT OBEY THAT ORDER, SIR.
WE'RE NOT ALLOWED TO KILL.
THEN KIDNAP HIM! WE'LL SEE WHAT WE DO ABOUT HIM LATER.
I FORBID YOU TO DO SO! THE DUKE'S IN PRISON, I AM THE REGENT, AND YOU OWE ME YOUR OBEDIENCE.
THAT'S TRUE.
AND TO ME, TOO.
THAT'S TRUE.
I'M IN NO STATE TO GUT YOU, BUT I'LL BE BACK.
?!

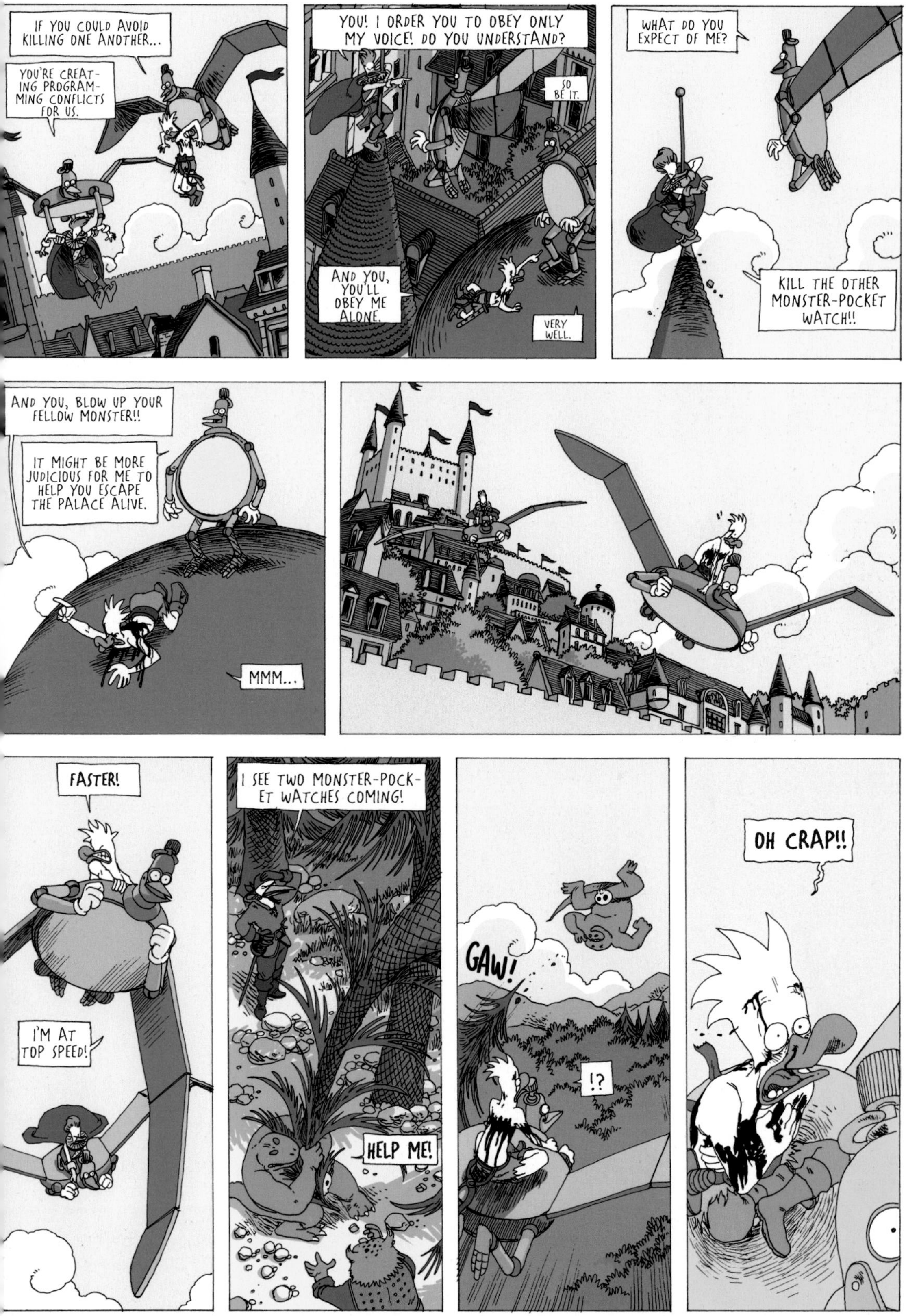
IF YOU COULD AVOID KILLING ONE ANOTHER...
YOU'RE CREATING PROGRAMMING CONFLICTS FOR US.
YOU! I ORDER YOU TO OBEY ONLY MY VOICE! DO YOU UNDERSTAND?
SO BE IT.
AND YOU, YOU'LL OBEY ME ALONE.
VERY WELL.
WHAT DO YOU EXPECT OF ME?
KILL THE OTHER MONSTER-POCKET WATCH!!
AND YOU, BLOW UP YOUR FELLOW MONSTER!!
IT MIGHT BE MORE JUDICIOUS FOR ME TO HELP YOU ESCAPE THE PALACE ALIVE.
MMM...
FASTER!
I'M AT TOP SPEED!
I SEE TWO MONSTER-POCKET WATCHES COMING!
HELP ME!
GAW!
!?
OH CRAP!!

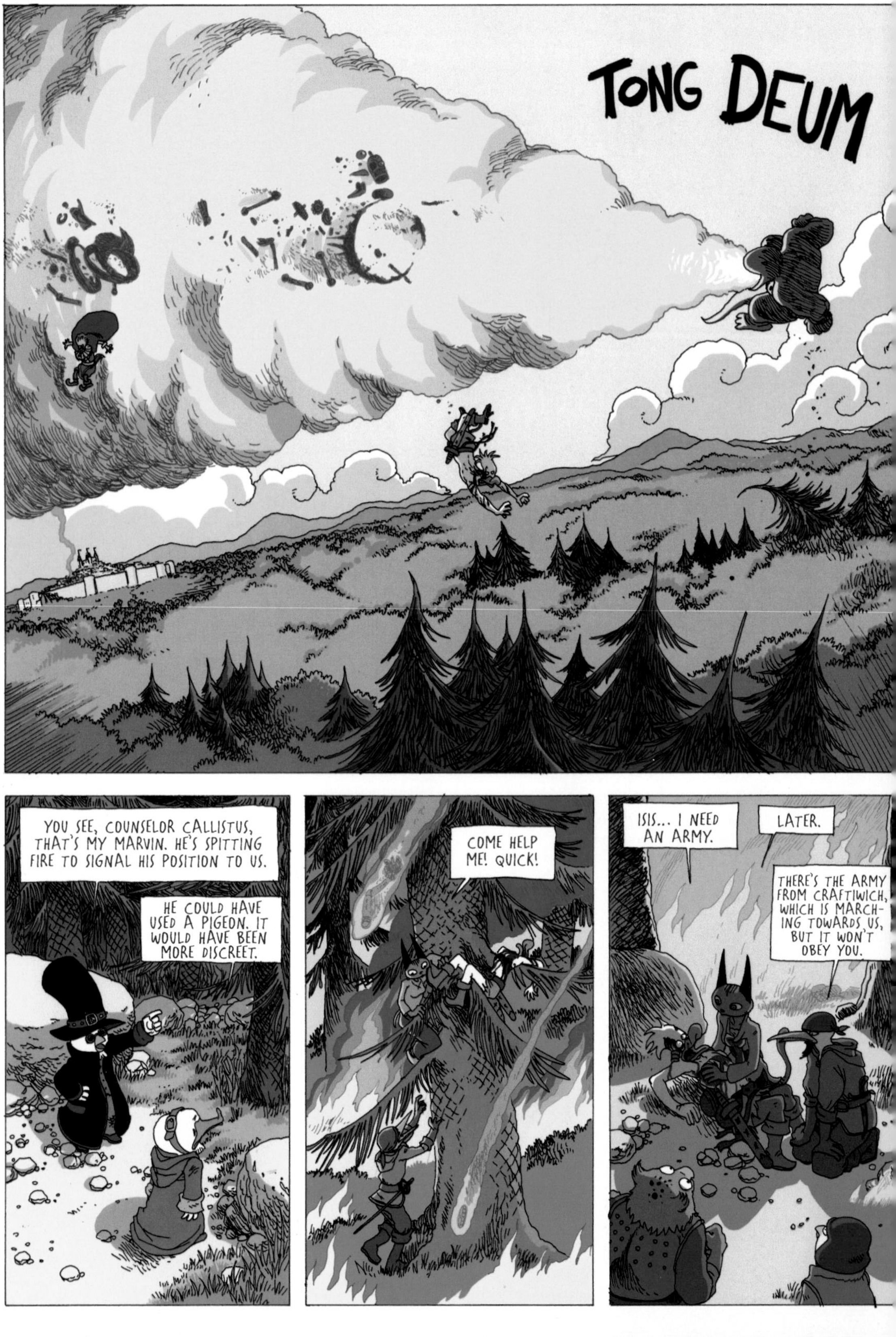
TONG DEUM
YOU SEE, COUNSELOR CALLISTUS, THAT'S MY MARVIN. HE'S SPITTING FIRE TO SIGNAL HIS POSITION TO US.
HE COULD HAVE USED A PIGEON. IT WOULD HAVE BEEN MORE DISCREET.
COME HELP ME! QUICK!
ISIS... I NEED AN ARMY.
LATER.
THERE'S THE ARMY FROM CRAFTIWICH, WHICH IS MARCHING TOWARDS US, BUT IT WON'T OBEY YOU.

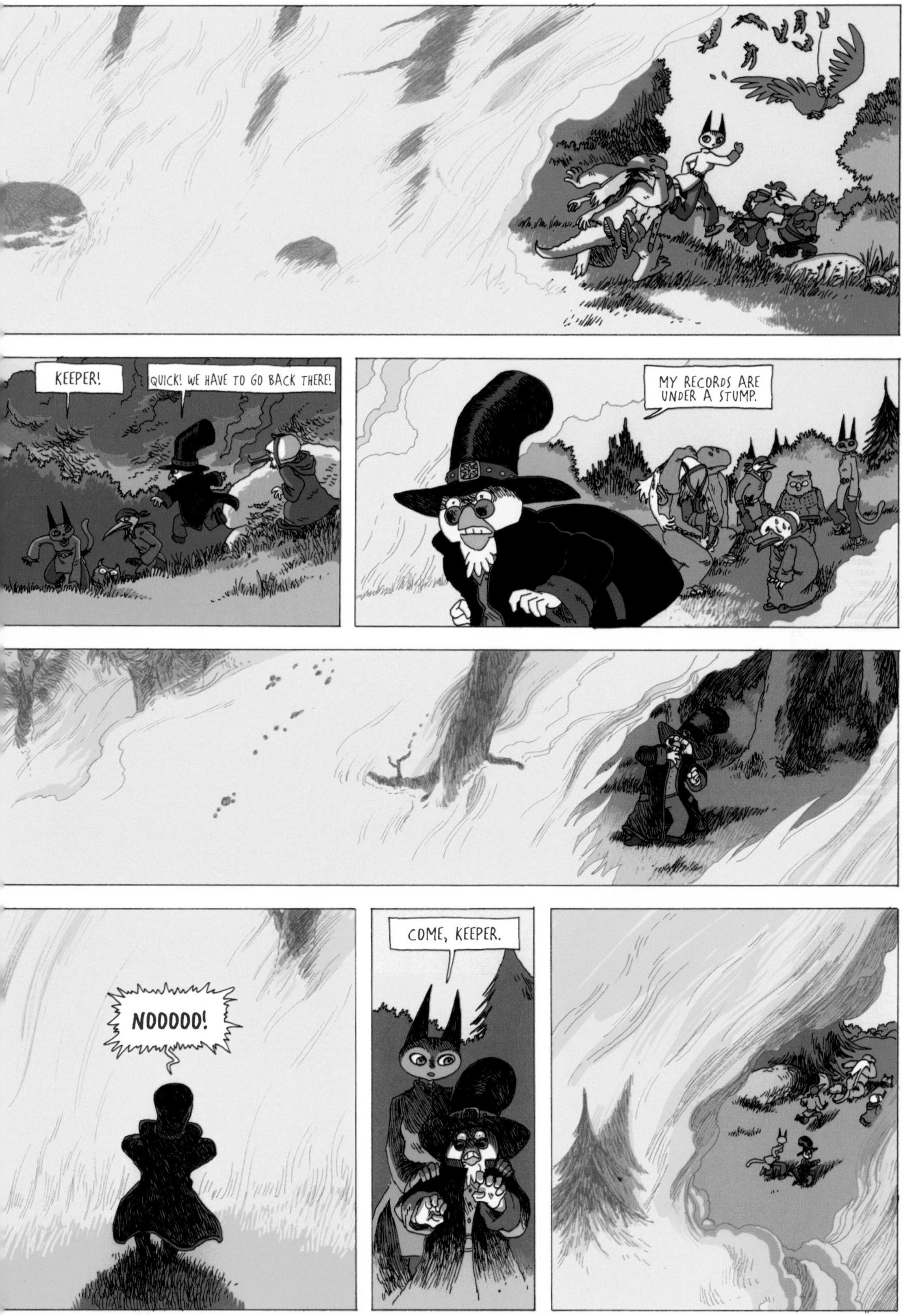
KEEPER!
QUICK! WE HAVE TO GO BACK THERE!
MY RECORDS ARE UNDER A STUMP.
NOOOOO!
COME, KEEPER.

NOW, NOW, MY DEAR. EVERYTHING WILL BE ALL RIGHT.

I HAVE A FEW TALENTS WITH MARIONETTES, AND WE CAN CERTAINLY GET BY ON THAT.

HERBERT WILL TEACH US HOW TO FIGHT, AND WE'LL CHASE AWAY THE COUNSELOR.

MMM...

IF WE FIND OUR SON AGAIN.

Joann Sfar & Lewis Trondheim -BOULET-